NETTLEWOOD

NETTLEWOOD

a novel by
MARY MELWOOD

A Clarion Book

THE SEABURY PRESS
NEW YORK

First American Edition 1975
Copyright © 1974 by Mary Melwood
Printed in the United States of America

Library of Congress Cataloging in Publication Data

Melwood, Mary.
  Nettlewood.

  SUMMARY: Circumstances beyond their control bring
proper Lacie Lindrick and outspoken Gertie Sprott
together in a decaying British country house filled
with past and present secrets that inevitably touch
both girls.

  I. Title.
PZ7.M5173Ne   [Fic]   74-19426
ISBN 0-8164-3142-6

This book is lovingly dedicated
To MORRIS
whose interest and belief in it helped me to write it

Acknowledgement

I should like to thank Mr F. A. Sleight, Divisional Engineer of the Trent River Authority, Northern Division, Gainsborough, for all his kind help in giving me information about the Aegir, and the tidal reaches of the Trent.

Contents

NETTLEWOOD

1

Trains and Telegrams

Lacie Lindrick was the only person to get out of the train when it stopped at Hawksop station.

After a few minutes she realized with a feeling of dismay that nobody was waiting to meet her. What about the telegram? Perhaps it had never arrived at School Cottage and the cousins did not know she was coming.

A man popped out of a door, took her ticket from her and popped back again, then with her baggage in one hand and a straw hat in the other, she walked slowly to the end of the deserted platform where there was an opening into the station yard. This too was empty of human life, though against the railings there were several bicycles propped up and some fowls in a crate were clucking and flapping.

There was a seat near by. She sat down on it and waited.

Everything had been done in such a hurry, the packing, the explanatory note sent to school, the checking of times and trains. There had hardly been time to think. The thinking had begun on the train journey to – this place, hawksop. But she was going to Owsterley, which hadn't a station, and was miles away from anywhere. She sat and considered.

It seemed a long time since she had got into the train that morning at King's Cross. Her mother had been concerned at leaving her alone, but of course Lacie would be all right. She was twelve, wasn't she? Not a child any more.

'The cousins must have had my telegram by now,' said her mother. 'They're sure to be waiting for you. Remember where you change trains . . . ask the guard if you are in doubt about anything.' Then, after a last hug and kiss she had torn herself away and gone to catch the boat train at Victoria, leaving Lacie to begin her long journey to the Midlands alone.

Now here she was on a seat in a deserted station at seven o'clock on a summer evening and the cousins whom she had never seen – and who were not her cousins but her father's – were not waiting for her.

There was only one thing to do. She would have to ask somebody the way to Owsterley and then go there.

But first, she had to find somebody to ask.

She was just about to go back into the station when a small red sports car roared into the yard and came to rest a feather's distance from the fowls, startling them so much that they all squawked and cackled and struggled to get out of the crate.

The driver of the car kept the engine running, tooted the horn and called out, 'You're Lacie Lindrick. I can tell by your face. Get in.' Then she added as Lacie picked up her bag, 'Chloë couldn't come. She's got a meeting of school managers or something. Oh – and I'm Nora.'

The engine was still running and the fowls were still squawking so she still had to shout.

'Throw your suitcase into the back. Don't touch that door. The handle comes off. Climb over, you've got long legs.'

The car moved off, and the fowls and the station and the little town were left behind.

'You're a quiet little thing,' remarked Nora after a time. 'Still, that's all to the good. These days, children have far too much to say for themselves. If there's one thing I can't stand it's – '

She broke off with an exclamation and glared at a man on a bicycle. At least he had been on a bicycle but now he was not.

'Did he get off or fall off?' she asked. 'It's Ebenezer Bonem. Riding a bicycle at his age! He's a menace to the community.'

The car was now going so fast that Lacie gripped the edge of her seat and pressed her feet to the foot-board as if she could work an invisible brake. She had taken off her hat and her hair was streaming behind her.

'This is the long way round,' shouted Nora. 'It's a better road. Chloë made me promise to bring you this way. The other's full of potholes and she thinks it's dangerous in the car.'

Lacie was looking at the view.

'I suppose you're thinking it's flat,' Nora still had to shout.

Lacie was thinking it.

The road was winding through level fields which were divided by water instead of hedges. At her left there was a ditch as wide as a canal and Lacie was keeping a nervous eye on it. Nora told her that it wasn't

13

called a ditch but a drain and that Dutch engineers, in the seventeenth century, had drained the land or it would still be fenland and swamp.

The fields were full of crops now with not a sign of a swamp.

'There's still the river, though,' said Nora, 'and it's a very floody river.'

Lacie had been looking for it and asked where it was. Nora pointed out a ridge which curved across the landscape.

'It's behind there,' she said. 'The banks are being raised to stop the flooding . . . but water still gets over sometimes. The other road to Owsterley follows that ridge. Yes, the road with the potholes in it.'

Presently the car whizzed past a boy on a bicycle. He wobbled, but regained his balance by a feat of dexterity which would have done credit to a tightrope walker.

'Cyclists !' muttered Nora. 'They want all the road. Oh, it's Bertie Bisset !'

Lacie looked behind her. The boy was now walking and pushing the bicycle.

'He must have got a puncture,' said Nora when Lacie expressed some concern about him. 'It's that old crock of a bicycle. Anyway, he hasn't far to walk. He lives just across there, at Celery Cottage. That one, not far from the church.'

The cottage she pointed out was at least three fields away from the road.

Lacie remarked on its name, and Nora explained, 'The Bissets are celery growers. At least Mrs Bisset is. There's only her and Bertie.'

She drove round the corner of a large red-brick house

that jutted out into the road. Some fowls ran in front of the car, and she was annoyed.

'People simply won't bother to keep their livestock fastened up,' she exclaimed, 'it's too much trouble, but, oh my goodness, the fuss if anything's run over.'

The car came to a halt so suddenly that Lacie was certain something had been run over, but Nora was only stopping to talk to somebody. It was Mrs Bisset who came up to the car and smiled at Lacie.

'We heard you were coming,' she said. 'Bertie and me both hope you'll have a happy time in Owst'ley. Of course' – she looked serious – 'we were sorry to hear of your bad news but' – she smiled again – 'I'm sure you'll soon be hearing something better . . .' She turned to Nora, 'I've just taken the eggs to School Cottage. There was nobody in so I left them on the back doorstep. I must be off now, or Bertie's tea won't be ready.'

'We've just seen Bertie,' said Nora. 'He seems to have a puncture or something, anyway he's walking home.'

This remark perturbed Mrs Bisset. She blamed Bertie's bicycle for being old, and herself for not being able to buy him a new one – then she hurried away.

Nora did not speak again until the car stopped in front of School Cottage and soon Lacie was making acquaintance with her new abode.

Next morning as she woke up she seemed to hear the train still going. It took her some time to realize that it wasn't a train. A clock was ticking – but she hadn't a clock in her bedroom at home. Then she remembered that this wasn't home, it was Owsterley.

'Owsterley begins with an o w,' Nora had told her, 'because it's so ugly it gives you a pain.'

There were sounds downstairs. Perhaps somebody was making breakfast. Yes. Lacie could smell it.

Sunshine was coming into the room. A breeze was blowing the curtains. Ducks were quacking somewhere, cows mooing, pleasant sounds Lacie only heard on holiday. Yet something was not like a holiday. What was it?

Memories began to come back.

Telegrams. Trains. First the telegram with the bad news in it, then the telegram sent to the cousins asking if Lacie could stay with them at Owsterley.

Lacie dug her face under the bedclothes.

'It isn't a holiday. I'm here because something's wrong . . . because Father's had an accident abroad and Mother's gone to him.'

She got out of bed, suddenly in a hurry to be moving. Just as she was beginning to dress her other cousin came in, a softer, rounder more smiling one, the one she had not yet seen.

Chloë.

'I'm sorry I was out when you came last night,' said Chloë. 'You were asleep when I got home.' She hesitated, then went on, 'We were dreadfully sorry to hear about the accident.'

Nora hadn't seemed dreadfully sorry. She hadn't even mentioned it.

'You must feel awful,' Chloë was continuing, 'so . . . so far away from home and everything . . . but you'll soon get to know us and feel happier.'

16

Lacie said nothing, but sat on the bed and stared at her feet. Chloë sat beside her.

'Let's look at it sensibly,' she said. 'That's what I always do. Everything's being done that can possibly be done. Doctors are so clever nowadays you know. Goodness only knows the things they can do.'

Lacie stared down at the floor. Chloë went on.

'Your father's always been so strong and healthy, that counts a lot. And your mother is with him. That counts too. So you see, what with one thing and another there's every reason to be hopeful. Don't you agree?'

Lacie looked up and nodded.

'Well, then.' Chloë looked as if she had proved something. She patted Lacie's hand. 'Everything's going to be all right.'

'Is it?'

'Of course it is.'

How did grown-ups know?

Chloë waited a moment.

'We've just got to look on the bright side,' she said, and she looked bright. Her eyes, her hair, her teeth all shone as Lacie looked at her.

'But he – they're – I'm so far away,' Lacie said.

'Nonsense!' replied Chloë. 'After all it's the 1920s. We've got express trains and motor cars and telephones and – and all sorts of modern things. You mark my words, Lacie Lindrick, it won't be long before you hear some good news.'

She was so convincing that Lacie began to cheer up.

'That's better,' said Chloë, standing up. 'I always look on the bright side if there is the slightest possible reason for it. It's by far the best way ... and it isn't fair to be a misery to everybody else. Remember that.'

Lacie smiled and said she would remember it.

'Good girl!' said Chloë. 'Will you be comfortable in this little room do you think?'

'I love it already,' Lacie replied. 'There are so many nice things in it.'

She was looking at a glass case with a stuffed owl in it. Chloë smiled.

'I'm glad that's caught your fancy. I was so fond of it once.'

'Was it really alive?' Lacie asked.

'Of course it was. Somebody gave it to me – oh long ago, for a pet. It came from Nettlewood, across the river.' Chloë had gone to the window to draw back the curtains. 'The woods there are full of owls. You'll hear them hooting at night.'

'I heard them,' said Lacie.

'*Hibou!*' said Chloë suddenly, then laughed. 'That's French for "owl".'

'I know it is,' said Lacie.

At breakfast there was an egg which was larger and browner than the others. It was specially for Lacie with her name and the words *A present from Celery Cottage* written on it.

A wisp of smoke came in from the scullery and Nora followed it with a plate of charred bread.

'They say it makes your hair curl,' she said, putting the plate on the table and sitting behind the teapot.

'Lacie and I don't need to eat it then.' Chloë scraped charcoal on to the side of her plate, and Nora took up the teapot.

'The best cure for a troubled mind,' she said,

looking at Lacie, 'or so everybody has been telling me, is hard work. Do you know anything about making yourself useful?' Lacie immediately felt that she ought to begin some very hard work at once. But what?

Chloë had a suggestion. Her only teacher was away with measles. Would Lacie like to go into school and help with the infants? Not this morning, though, the afternoon would be better.

Lacie was excited and said what fun it would be.

'It'll be fun all right,' said Nora, 'especially if Gertie Sprott's there, but that's not likely, I suppose.'

'Gertie Sprott shouldn't be with the infants at all,' Chloë remarked. 'She's much too old. She missed such a lot of school you see. When her father was in the war she went to live at Celery Cottage. She hadn't a mother, so Mrs Bisset took care of her. Poor Mrs Bisset. She's a widow,' she added.

Nora had gone into the scullery. Lacie whispered, 'Is she a war-widow like Cousin Nora?'

'No,' Chloë whispered back, 'only an ordinary widow. Her husband died when Bertie was small. Nora's husband – ' But Nora came in. 'So you see,' Chloë went on in a louder voice, 'what with it being such a long way for her to walk and her being so young and – and one thing and another, poor little Gertie seemed to miss quite a lot of school while the war was on.'

'A habit which she has managed to hang on to as long as possible,' said Nora, 'poor little Gertie!'

'I've had a serious talk with Fred Sprott about her,' Chloë said, 'and he's promised to see that she attends regularly.'

'Huh !' said Nora.

'She's keen to go up into the Big School at the beginning of next term,' said Chloë. 'I don't think she'll play truant any more.'

She stopped. There was a clanking sound outside as if tins were being knocked over.

The sisters jumped to their feet.

'The milk !' cried Chloë.

'Gertie Sprott !' screamed Nora and dashed to the back door.

Full of curiosity Lacie followed.

On the step, a milk can dangling from each hand, stood a sturdy child whose smile was surrounded by a milky moustache.

'You've been drinking the milk,' cried Nora. 'I can see it all round your mouth, so don't tell stories.' She looked into the milk cans. 'Just look !' she said to Chloë. 'Look how much has gone !'

'There was a great big cat at the front door,' said Gertie. 'I bet it was that cat what drinked your milk.'

'Rubbish,' said Nora. 'I feel like throwing it down the sink,' and she marched off with the milk cans.

Gertie looked at Lacie then said, 'I'm the biggest infant in the school.'

'You're the oldest infant in the school,' said Nora bouncing in again, 'and the rudest.'

'What if I am ?' Gertie answered the first part of the remark and ignored the rest of it. 'It wasn't my fault if I was kept back. All the rest on 'em went up, all 'cept me an' they all laffed at me.'

'If you came to school regularly like everybody else –' Chloë was beginning.

'I've got to help medad,' Gertie said quickly.

'He's only got me. Somebody's got to mind t'boats when he's not there.'

'Sprotts!' muttered Nora . . . 'Boats!' and she went away again.

Gertie pulled a face behind her back. Lacie couldn't help smiling so Gertie did it again.

'That's enough of that,' Chloë said. 'You wouldn't like your face to stop like that, would you?' Then she put on her school coat, an old woolly one with pockets full of chalk. Outside there was the ever-rising sound of children.

'Time for school,' said Chloë, and taking Gertie firmly by the hand, walked down the garden path.

Together, they disappeared through a door in the wall.

2

Springles

LACIE was left to herself. The breakfast table had
already been cleared at lightning speed by Nora who
was now rattling pots in the back kitchen. When Lacie
inquired if she could give any help the answer was
no so she went upstairs to finish unpacking and tidy
her room.

It didn't take very long, not long enough, and when
she came downstairs again Nora looked surprised as if
she had forgotten that anybody else existed. When Lacie
remarked that she was looking for something to do
Nora told her that there was never anything to do in
Owsterley, never had been, never would be, then she
disappeared.

Lacie stepped outside.

The back of School Cottage looked south. Outside
the kitchen door was a paved yard with a pump in it,
then a lawn surrounded by flower beds, then a vegetable
patch. At the other side of the hedge was a field where
a slow stream wound its way to join the river. 'And
that's behind there,' thought Lacie, looking at a high
green ridge which curved its way into the distance. She
intended to go and explore but stopped to pick up some

little green pears which had fallen from a giant pear tree. Suddenly, from the Little School, which bounded the east side of the garden, there came sounds of strife. There was the babble of voices, then Chloë's voice sounded above everything as if she were telling somebody off. There was a crash of something broken . . . glass . . . a yell of protest, a scuffle of boots on wooden floorboards, footsteps, then the slam of a door.

'Gertie Sprott,' thought Lacie, and waited to hear more, but peace seemed to have been restored. Nothing else happened. Disappointed, she left the garden and went to the front of the house.

The main street of Owsterley straggled away to her right. Opposite, was the Big School. To her left the street ended at a brick wall. She was just about to go and look over it when a loud voice said, 'Hey', and she saw Gertie Sprott hanging over the railings of the Little School playground.

'I got wet through wi' a jam-jar full o' water,' she reported as Lacie went up to her. 'An' I've been sent out to get dry. A lad did it a purpose, but I kicked him for it.'

(That was the yell, thought Lacie.)

'Anyhow — it's better out here than being in wi' that lot in there, so I don't mind,' and Gertie gave her unique Sprott smile.

That lot inside began to chant multiplication tables and she remarked how much she disliked sums and spelling and reading and anything to do with school.

'What do you like, then?' asked Lacie.

'T'river . . .' said Gertie. 'I wish I was on it now.'

At this point a diversion occurred.

'A motor car!' shouted Gertie poking her head so

far through the railings that Lacie wondered if it would ever get back again.

It was not a car but a motor bicycle and side-car. It back-fired twice, then stopped at the Big School gate.

'It's old Springles,' said Gertie, 'new headmaster, well nearly new. He's late for school but nobody'll cane him for it.'

She drew in her head and looked disapprovingly across the road.

In the Little School everybody must have stood up because the windows were full of faces, including Chloë's.

Mr Springles, with his motoring goggles pushed up into his hair, did not go into the Big School but came across the road and opened the gate into the Little School yard. He noticed the two girls and said, 'Well you two, been sent out have you?' and went into school before either of them could reply.

'He got wounded in t'war,' said Gertie, 'from standing too near summat that got blowed up. He should a run away a bit faster, the silly fool.'

'Run away!' cried Lacie. 'Soldiers aren't supposed to run away!'

'He's got a bit of iron inside him,' said Gertie, 'and nobody durst take it out.' She paused. 'Medad was a soldier, but he never got hurt. He never got a scratch till he came home and fell down our steps and busted his nose. I'm going in now.' And she ran into school.

There was the sound of feet scraping the floor as the infants stood up and chanted, 'Good morning, sir'. Then Gertie reappeared looking annoyed. Apparently her presence was still not desired in class.

Soon the other children came out into the playground. Gertie glared at them contemptuously, saying that they were only kids and she was sick to death of them and would soon be in the Big School – 'when I'm ten.'

'When I'm ten,' was Gertie's constant theme.

'It's two numbers, a one an' a nought. That's better than one. An' I'll be nearer to leaving school, then I can help medad. I'm sick o' being the biggest infant in the school,' she said.

'You won't be the biggest when you're across there,' Lacie replied, looking across at the Big School yard which was filling up with young giants. 'And you won't be able to boss them about,' she added.

'They'd better not try bossing me,' retorted Gertie, thrusting out her bottom jaw.

A Big School teacher came out and strolled to the fence.

Gertie groaned and turned her back. 'That's old Piff'ny Throssel,' she said. 'Is she looking at me?'

'I can't tell who she's looking at,' replied Lacie. 'She's looking over here though.'

Gertie groaned again. 'I dread bein' in her class. I wish she'd leave. She'll pay me out for sure 'cos I've called old Wiff'ny Piff'ny after her. What's wrong wi' that? Piff'ny's her name...' Lacie was looking incredulous. 'Her sister's at the post office and her name's Jessima.'

Lacie had never heard of such names but Gertie assured her that Piff'ny and Jessima were real names out of the prayer-book and Lacie didn't know the prayer-book well enough to argue.

The sound of a whistle came from across the way.

The seniors formed lines and went into school. Still the infants went on playing.

Gertie became bored.

'If I wasn't so scared about not going up I wouldn't 'ave come to school today. I'd be on t'river in *Wobbler*; that's medad's boat. He's got two. One's *Wavey* an' one's *Wobbler*.'

Lacie thought what strange names she was hearing this morning, but she only said that she hadn't yet seen the river.

'Not seen t'river!' Gertie was astounded. 'It's over there. See that wall across t'street? It's behind that. Come on! Let's go and look at it.'

Lacie refused, saying, 'You're not allowed to leave the school premises.'

Gertie replied with a word that startled Lacie.

'And you're not allowed to say that.'

'Medad says it,' said Gertie. 'Let's go.'

But Lacie closed the gate. Some infants were staring at them. Gertie shoved the nearest one away, then gazed out into freedom again from between the railings.

'See that house at end o' t'road? That's ours. Me and medad live there.'

Further up the road on the same side as the Big School was a tall narrow house with unusually shaped windows.

'It's nearly on t'top of t'river,' said Gertie with gloomy pride. 'Folks say it's a wonder it don't fall in,' and she went on to describe how water often came into the cellars and sometimes rushed through the house like a 'cat'ract'.

'Medad can remember it coming right through

26

t'kitchen and half-way upstairs when there was a big Aegir.'

Gertie's pronunciation of ordinary English had sounded strange enough to Lacie that morning. Now when Gertie said AEGIR Lacie thought that she meant OGRE and imagined some sort of a watery monster that came out of the river and went into the Sprott house.

This she dismissed as a tall story of Gertie's.

'A big Aegir,' Gertie was going on, 'as big as – that!' and she pointed to the top of the school. 'It comes up-river like – like – ' Words failed her and she had to blow out her breath and wave her arms violently to indicate the size and ferocity of the apparition.

'When does it come?' asked Lacie.

Gertie replied – 'It all depends on what t'river's like an' the weather an – oh, lots o' things. Sometimes it comes. Sometimes it don't. It pleases itself.'

Lacie was sceptical. Had Gertie seen it?

''Course I've seen it,' said Gertie – then added, 'but I've never met it.'

If she hadn't met it how could she have seen it? So it *was* a tall story!

Gertie was going on, 'An' I kept missing it 'cos I lived at Celery Cottage for such a long time an' that's right away from t'river.' A far-away look came into her eyes. 'I'll see it soon, though ... now I live at home I can't miss it when it does come ... an' I'll meet it, one day. I'll take a boat on t'river an' I'll meet it all by meself.'

The discussion ended as some children came up with a skipping rope and begged for somebody to turn it for them, but Gertie bustled them away.

'I might see medad if I stop here.' She still hung on to the railings. 'He goes into t'pub most dinnertimes.'

The King of the River was opposite to the Sprott house. Very convenient it must have been for Mr Sprott.

'When folks got drunk,' said Gertie, 'they used to walk straight out o' t'pub an' tumble into t'river. They can't now that wall's been built.'

She sounded disappointed.

'Some of 'em got drowned,' she said, ''specially if tide was up . . . else they only got covered wi' mud.'

She was quiet for a time, then she said with a sigh, 'I wish I could hurry and be grown up. I'm sick o' being a kid. I'll be done wi' school an' I'll help medad on t'ferry an' – an' I'll take a boat and go down river to meet old Aegir all by meself – or p'raps I'll go wi' medad.'

It was nearly midday when Mr Springles and Chloë emerged from the Little School.

Mr Springles hurried across the road to the Big School and Chloë sent the infants home – all except Gertie who unwrapped some bread and jam and began to eat it and play hopscotch at the same time, saying that her dad had told her to stop in school till teatime because he'd gone to Nettlewood.

'Oh, has he?' said Chloë. 'Well, don't get into mischief.'

'No, Miss – Scampion.'

'Don't go near my inkwells. Don't go near *anything* – and remember – I can see *everything*, even when I'm not looking.'

'Yes, Miss – Scampion.'

'And my name's not Scampion. I keep telling you,' said Chloë.

'No, Miss Sc . . . C-Campion.'

And Gertie kicked a stone and grinned a jammy grin as Chloë and Lacie went back to School Cottage.

3

- and Sprotts

THERE was no sign of a meal. Nora had forgotten to get one ready. She didn't apologize, just went upstairs looking exasperated. Chloë made excuses as she cut bread and butter. Nora's nerves weren't strong just now because of her experiences in the war in France. She'd been nursing in the thick of danger and death.

Nora heard the last bit as she came downstairs again and said that the danger in Owsterley was in being bored to death.

'You'll soon be in London,' Chloë answered, 'so you can put up with being bored for a bit.'

'No I can't,' said Nora. 'I *can't*.'

Lacie looked from one to the other and felt that it would be better if she were not there. Chloë must have thought so too for she said, 'Why not run and have a look at the river. We'll call you when lunch is ready.'

Soon Lacie was outside the garden and running up a grassy bank, and there it was.

The river!

It was wide, much wider than she had expected it to be, and urgently flowing. There were patterns on the surface of the water, smooth dark places and brighter rippley ones and places where the current seemed to swirl around and go the other way. There were reeds and osiers where water birds were bustling about.

The river scent came up warm and strong.

Looking north with the flow of the water she could see tables on the terrace of the King of the River where men were drinking and talking. Further on, a bit of the Sprott house jutted out. She could see the stone steps that descended from it to the water. Two boats were moored there. What were their names? The *Wavey* and the *Wobbler*.

'Well, they are waving and wobbling,' she thought as they bobbed up and down in the current.

Across the river, a water-meadow's distance away from it and on higher ground, was a large house, partly hidden by a wood. Above the water level on the opposite bank was a wooden landing stage with some steps leading up from it, and some down into the water.

After a time she heard Chloë calling her and went back to School Cottage.

'We're picnicking,' said Chloë. 'Help to carry these things into the garden.'

The picnic was spread under the pear tree.

'There are always too many pears for us,' said Chloë, 'so they are taken into the schools and given to the children on a special day. We call it Pear Day. It's a tradition in Owsterley now. You'll see for yourself if you're still here.'

This remark somehow reminded Lacie of why she was here at all and her face clouded. Chloë noticed, and mentioned the river.

Lacie's face brightened again. It was a marvellous river!

'Not so marvellous when it's in the kitchen,' said Nora, who was eating bread and butter, 'and running down the street so that you can't get out.'

'They're talking about better flood defences now,' said Chloë, then went on to say that Owsterley was mentioned in the Domesday Book, and it was a ferry even then. 'It won't be one much longer, though,' she said, 'now there's a new bridge at Bridgeover. Hawksop bridge used to be the only one for miles so the ferry here was important. It's not so busy now. Fred Sprott has hardly any ferrying to do.'

Nora laughed. 'That'll suit him,' she said.

'I saw the boats,' Lacie said, 'the *Wavey* and the *Wobbler*.'

Chloë smiled. The *Wobbler* was the *River Warbler* when Fred Sprott first got it, but Owsterley folks weren't going to have a fancy name like that, so first it became t'*Warbler*, then t' *Wobbler* . . . The *Wavey* is usually called t'other 'un.'

Lacie mentioned the river-ogre as big as the school.

'You mean the Aegir,' said Chloë.

'Is it true?' Lacie asked in surprise.

'Certainly it's true,' replied Chloë. 'It's a wave which comes up river with the tide.'

'Can I see it – today?' cried Lacie ready to dash out and wait for the next one.

'Oh, no! It doesn't come with every tide . . . only at special times. Conditions have to be just right before it forms – the weather, the state of the river – and – and so on.'

'Just what Gertie said,' remarked Lacie.

'If she knows anything it is about the river,' said Chloë. 'Although she lived away from it for so long, now she's back she's taken to it like a duck to water.'

'A Sprott to water,' said Nora.

'You must ask Mr Springles about the Aegir,' Chloë was going on, 'he'll tell you all about it scientifically, about it being a standing wave on the toe of the tide and – and everything. I only know what I've seen of it . . . and the stories people tell of how they've met it and how sometimes boats have gone down in it –' and she went on to tell how 'in the old days', before the banks were built up, a man used to walk up and down the riverside, ringing a bell and shouting 'Ware Aegir, 'Ware Aegir, to warn people when the wave was coming.

Lacie wanted to know about the name Aegir. Chloë spelt it for her and said that as far as she knew it had come from the Danes who had sailed up the river years and years ago, and settled in this part of the country. They had seen the great wave leaping up from the estuary and had thought it was a sign of anger from Aegir, a sea-god.

'He wasn't a very nice god, by the sound of him,' said Chloë. 'Or perhaps I've got him mixed up with another one. I'm rather weak on gods, but Mr Springles will tell you if you ask him.'

'He'll tell you if you don't ask him,' said Nora.

There was a silence. Lacie thought it rather uncomfortable and broke it by mentioning two other strange names she had heard from Gertie.

'They're out of the prayer-book. Piff-piff'ny and Jess-something.'

'She means the Throssels,' said Nora. 'Epiphany and Septuagesima.'

Lacie knew that Epiphany came just after Christmas but wasn't sure about Septuagesima.

'Third Sunday before Lent,' Chloë said. 'I suppose they were born on those days. Piffany is the teacher and Jessima looks after the post office.' She broke off and then – 'Gertie Sprott!' she exclaimed. 'How many times have I told you not to leave the school premises?'

'Ever so many,' said Gertie.

She had little bits of the hedge sticking to her, which was not surprising as she had just crawled through it. Lacie had seen her but had not liked to tell tales.

'What are you doing here?' asked Chloë.

Gertie looked virtuous.

'I've finished me dinner – an' I've just seen medad. He's been to school and gived me a message.'

'Well?' asked Chloë. 'What is it?'

Gertie looked at Nora, then away again.

'It's for her,' she said, 'that one.'

'Are you sure?' Nora was puzzled.

'Course I'm sure – an' he's outside t'front gate . . . he wants to speak to you.'

'What a blithering cheek!' exclaimed Nora.

'Tell him – ask him,' Chloë spoke, 'ask him nicely if he will kindly come here,' Gertie was already speeding away, 'and don't you be unnecessarily rude to him,' Chloë added to Nora.

'The impertinence,' said Nora, 'sending me messages!'

'It may be something interesting,' said Chloë, 'I wonder what he wants . . .' She stopped as Gertie appeared with Fred Sprott.

He was wearing a red knitted cap which Nora called his Bolshie cap. It was tilted over one eye and

34

Lacie thought it gave him a wicked look. He nodded to the two sisters and noticed Lacie with a slight relaxation around his lips which was his way of showing that he was feeling friendly. She edged away from the scene.

There wasn't a chair for him to sit on so without invitation he dropped on to the grass. Nora, who had been lolling on some cushions, immediately got up. Gertie sat as near to him as possible. He put out a long, dark brown arm and rumpled her hair all over her face, then he picked a stem of grass and began to chew it. His attitude was one of sociability between equals and Lacie felt offended by it. He was behaving almost as if he and Chloë and Nora were friends, not at all as if . . . as if . . . While Lacie's mind struggled to fix Fred Sprott in his proper place Nora by her manner promptly began to put him where *she* considered it was.

'I'm told you have a message for me,' she said.

'Aye, that's right. I have.'

'From the post office? Did Jessima Throssel give it to you?'

'No, she didn't.'

He chewed the stalk of grass.

'Want to go on guessing?' he asked, 'or shall I tell you straight off? If you're going to t'bottom of t'garden,' he raised his voice, 'I can shout.'

Nora came back.

It was perfectly obvious that she detested him, but what his feelings were about Nora Lacie couldn't tell. He just looked amused as if he were playing at something. His dark eyes glittered, he had white teeth which he showed a lot when he smiled. He didn't seem at all upset by Nora's brusqueness.

35

Lacie's thoughts were in confusion. He shouldn't have sat down without being asked. He shouldn't make himself so much at ease in her cousins' garden. He shouldn't chew a piece of grass between those strong white teeth. He's rough and he has black whiskers and . . .

'So Little Miss Disdain is staying with you for a bit, is she?' he said, looking at Lacie.

She moved her eyes away quickly. She had just discovered the place where his nose had been 'busted' when he fell down those steps.

'Just say what you've got to say — if there is anything,' said Nora, and as good as added by the tone of her voice, 'and get out of our garden.'

'Hear! Hear!' thought Lacie.

'I've been across the river this morning,' Fred Sprott said, chewing the piece of grass between his words.

Nora looked uninterested, but Chloë said, 'How are things at Nettlewood?' as if trying to put an amiable note into the conversation.

'Not so good.' He looked at her as if he were pleased she had spoken. 'The old lady's in a bad way.'

'Granny Betts?' asked Chloë.

'No, me granny's all right. It'll take a lot to upset her . . . the other one.'

'Mrs Mountsorrel?'

'Aye. Nothing agrees with her in the place.'

'She should have stopped in Italy, then,' said Nora. 'It was ridiculous to come back at all, after being away all that time. People have no common sense.'

'Perhaps it was Nettlewood that pulled her back,' said Chloë, 'and she had to come and see it again for the last time . . . I know I'd have to come back if I ever left Owsterley.'

'Oh, you!' said Nora.

Fred Sprott's look hardened.

'You wouldn't understand that,' he said to her. He turned to Chloë. 'Me granny Betts says it was conscience that dragged her back. Well, whatever it was, the old girl is here . . . and it looks as if she'll stop here . . . The doctor from Hawksop says she's got to have somebody with her, all the time.'

'There's Granny Betts.'

'Oh, Granny's getting past it . . . and she's not a trained nurse . . . though she's always claimed she's better — and I will say her medicines have worked wonders — plenty of times.' He stopped.

'Well then, let her work some more wonders,' Nora said. 'I don't know why you're looking at me.'

'You're a trained nurse. And you're here, on the spot.'

'I've got a post. I'm going to London.'

'Not till September,' said Fred Sprott. 'And you'd be free before then, by the way things are looking. It wouldn't be a long job.'

'I don't want a job at all. Any job . . . until I go to London. And what's it got to do with you, anyway?' She was beginning to get agitated. 'I certainly don't want you getting me jobs, thank you very much.'

'I thought you might not be above doing a good turn for once,' said Fred Sprott.

'I like your impudence,' Nora glared at him.

'I'm glad you like it,' he said, 'because now I'm going to tell you something else. I told the doctor that you might come over and take it on for a bit.'

37

Nora was speechless.

'Don't let's lose our tempers,' said Chloë.

Fred Sprott took a letter from his pocket.

'Shall I take this back then, and tell Mrs Mountsorrel you wouldn't read it?'

'Couldn't you have given it to me in the first place,' asked Nora, 'instead of spouting and preaching?'

'Aye, I could,' he answered, 'but I enjoyed the conversation. I wouldn't have missed it.'

Nora took the letter.

'There's no need for you to wait,' she said.

Fred Sprott shrugged and smiled at Chloë.

'I don't seem very popular around here.' To Nora he said, 'I thought, if you want to go across the river this afternoon . . .'

But Nora turned her back on him and began to walk back to the house. She stopped and said that if she decided to see Mrs Mountsorrel she was quite capable of getting to Nettlewood by herself.

'Going to swim?' asked Fred Sprott.

'By road,' said Nora. 'I shall go through Hawksop.'

'It's a long walk for a hot day.'

'I shall drive.'

'Oh. I forgot you was a motorist. Well, please yourself. I've done my part.'

'Thanks,' said Nora. 'Sorry you've been troubled.'

'No trouble,' replied Fred Sprott straightening his long legs. 'I never give myself any trouble if I can help it.' Then he called after her as she walked away, 'If you change your mind and want a boat, just send our Gertie.'

'Ooh! yes, can I go?' Gertie came to life suddenly.

He pulled her hair.

'Our Gert won't mind nipping out of school for a few minutes if you want her to fetch me.' He gave Gertie a push at the side of the head which was his equivalent of a paternal caress. She recognized it as one and reciprocated it with an affectionate thump. He shook her off his arm and after a nod to Nora and a smile to Chloë — Lacie had been so quiet in the background that he had forgotten she was there — he lounged out of the garden, Gertie hanging on to his heels like a puppy.

''Op it,' they heard him say. 'Go on. Go back to school.'

When she was sure he had gone Nora opened the letter.

'I think I'll go,' she said. 'It'll be something to do this afternoon.'

'Well!' said Chloë.

'Don't think I'm stupid enough to get tied up in anything,' said Nora, 'because I'm not.'

'It'll be interesting to see Nettlewood again, anyway,' replied Chloë. 'I wonder how Mrs Mountsorrel is looking. It must be twenty years since she went away. Let me think . . .' but her thinking had to stop. The noise in the school yard was deafening.

'Goodness! Look at the time!' She gave a shriek and fled.

Lacie felt that she had been forgotten. No school for her this afternoon!

Suddenly Nora looked at her.

'Want to come with me to Nettlewood?' she asked. 'There's only a field road from Hawksop. You can save me getting out of the car to open the gates.'

4

Across the River

'I CAN see why they call it Nettlewood,' said Lacie.
'Soon there'll be more nettles than trees.'

The name had nothing to do with nettles. Carthusian
monks had built a monastery long years ago –
Methelwude – the house in the middle of the wood.
The site had appealed to them because it was so lonely
and inaccessible, surrounded by floods and fens. The
monastery had eventually fallen into ruins and later a
manor house had been built over them – and the name
became Nettlewood.

'Appropriately, by the look of it,' said Nora.

She was being pleasant and talkative this afternoon.
Perhaps the slightly adventurous flavour of the expedition was appealing to her as it was to Lacie.

It had been an interesting drive from Owsterley.
First they had gone along the bridle road to Hawksop.
It was full of holes and there was a hump-backed
bridge where two drains met that Lacie would remember for a long time. She had nearly flown out of the
car.

After crossing Hawksop bridge they had left the
main road and by following another lane, a mere

cart-track, they had found their way into the drive of Nettlewood.

'It's always seemed a gloomy sort of place,' said Nora. 'Even though people were living in it when we were children we were a bit afraid of it –' she broke off.

Lacie had caught her breath. 'I thought I saw somebody amongst the trees,' she said, and Nora laughed, saying that she didn't suppose it was the Nettlewood monster because it never came out in daylight. Seeing Lacie's startled look she added that it was just a silly story.

'The place is riddled with underground cells and tunnels – all that's left of the old monastery. People have to invent *something* about them – you know what people are.'

She negotiated another pot-hole.

'Wh – what sort of a monster is it – was it – supposed to be?' asked Lacie.

'As nobody ever saw it,' Nora was driving more carefully now, 'nobody ever found out. We imagined our own I suppose. My particular monster was ...' but she broke off with an exclamation as she drove over a big stone and Lacie never found out what Nora's idea of a monster was. When the subject was mentioned again all Nora said was, 'Don't talk nonsense'.

They came into the open and, she stopped the car.

In front of them a rickety wooden bridge spanned a wide ditch.

'I'm not driving across that,' said Nora.

They sat for a few moments and looked around.

The only sounds were from the wood where thrushes and blackbirds called and wood doves cooed.

Nora got out of the car. Lacie followed her.

They stood and looked at the house. Windows which still had glass in them were glinting in the sunlight.

'Talk about ruins!' said Nora.

The house faced south – but –

'It must be gloomy as hell at the back,' she said.

An unexpected current of cool air flowed from somewhere and made them both shiver.

They walked to the bridge.

Lacie stopped and looked down. A house with a moat! – though it was a dried-up one.

Nora said that once upon a time water must have flowed into it from the river, or out of it into the river, or in and out of it, or something. Anyway there was still an old dried-up channel going across the watermeadow – not exactly dried-up, the grass was all swampy sometimes.

'I lost my shoes in it once,' she remembered, then said impatiently, 'Come on! Let's go.'

Lacie was still fascinated by the moat, and remarked that if water was in it the house would be on an island.

Nora said that as it had been built on the only bit of ground that was above flood level it often had been on an island and would be again.

'Why?' asked Lacie.

'Floods,' said Nora. 'They haven't stopped happening yet. I'll have to leave you now.' She told Lacie that she could look about a bit, if she liked, but to keep near the house.

Lacie said only half-jokingly, 'In case – in case I see the monster?'

But Nora looked impatient again.

'I mean, don't wander far away. I don't want to spend time looking for you. Sit in the car if you like.'

She had to go through long grass to get to the house. Perhaps she felt she had been too abrupt for she turned back and smiled.

'If you do see the monster of Nettlewood,' she called, 'just toot the horn and I'll dash out to meet him.'

Then she ran up the steps of the terrace and went through the front door.

Lacie was alone.

Everything was extraordinarily still. The birds seemed to have stopped singing. Not a breath flicked the tops of the trees. A bee suddenly buzzed over her head. It sounded like an aeroplane. A wood pigeon made a velvety call from the wood. When it stopped the silence seemed deeper than ever.

Lacie thought, 'If I screamed what would happen? Would people come running out? Would all this disappear? Would I wake up?'

After a time she realized that she was holding her breath as if listening. Listening for what?

What did she expect to hear?

'Nonsense!' she said aloud.

Her voice jarred against the silence as if she shouldn't have spoken.

If only a dog would bark! Even a fierce dog!

But there were no dogs. Nothing moved.

Her hand began to hurt.

She looked down at it and saw that she had been gripping the handrail of the ramshackle bridge so hard that she had pressed a splinter of wood into her palm.

The sun was beating down strongly. The sharp pain in her hand made her feel dizzy.

Near the bridge was an alder tree. It hung over the dried up moat as if still remembering that water had once flowed around its roots. Lacie moved so that she could sit in its shade which reached right across the ditch on to what had once been a lawn.

She looked about her.

Between the moat and the house, and climbing up to the terrace in a steep bank, lay an expanse of long grass – lawn which had turned into meadow.

Apparently it was never mown for it was knee-high and full of clover, moon-pennies, sorrel and butter-cups. Much nicer than an ordinary lawn.

She began to swish through it to the back of the house. It was shady there and if there were any life in the place that was where it would be.

The back windows looked into a courtyard. By an open door there was a turned-up pail and a mop with its head in the air.

Somebody existed here. Somebody mopped floors. Lacie felt relief at this sign of humdrum life.

Delapidated outbuildings formed the other three sides of the courtyard. They must be barns, stables – yes – and fowl-houses, for behind them she heard a stir of sound, a commotion of cluckings and scatterings and somebody's voice.

She soon discovered that shut in between the buildings and a high stone wall there was an unpaved yard.

It was crowded with hens.

In the middle of them stood a youth with a scoop full of corn.

He saw her but went on calling the hens, 'Chuck! chuck! chucketty! chuck! chuck!' Then he threw a handful of corn in her direction.

He threw another handful of corn, then another, at her feet until the hens rushed towards her clucking and pushing each other, while showers of grain fell all about her. All about her? All over her.

She put up her hands, laughing, 'Wait a minute, please. Not so much all at once! Just a minute, please.'

It was a joke of course. It was fun. All these feathery greedy creatures were amusing, but they were pressing so close and pecking so fiercely.

'Hey! That's my leg,' she cried. 'Go away, shoo!' Then of all unexpected things a flight of pigeons wheeled out of the sky from nowhere and swooped down amongst the hens.

'No!' cried Lacie. 'No, no! Go away, please.' For one bird had actually perched on her head.

She put up her arms to protect her face. She seemed to be looking through a maze of swirling wings.

'Go away, all of you,' she cried. 'Shoo! Shoo!' Then in response to no sign that she could see or hear all the hens left her as suddenly as they had rushed upon her and went mildly back to the youth. The pigeons flew away and floated about in the sky as calmly as a summer breeze.

He emptied the scoop then, putting it on his head, rat-tatted it with his fingers.

'Nice hat,' he said and went away so quickly that he could almost be said to have vanished.

'I certainly didn't see where he went,' Lacie said to herself, feeling rather dazed.

The hens were peacefully pecking up the last of the grains and took no more notice of her.

Whew! She scooped up the hair from the back of her neck and shook it out. She was so hot.

She could see the tops of fruit trees showing over the stone wall.

45

The kitchen garden, certainly. It was too early in the year for apples but there must be something eatable inside. She was so thirsty even a bit of rhubarb or a few sour gooseberries would be better than nothing.

She found a door but it was closed. She couldn't move it — then she noticed an over-hanging branch of an apple tree. If she could only climb up far enough, she would be able to pull herself to the top of the wall and see into the garden.

'Then I shall know if it's worth the trouble of getting in,' she thought.

There were not many footholds in the wall and it wasn't easy to climb. She had to cling to the stone with her toes and fingers and her toes and fingers were not used to clinging to stone.

She set her teeth. Her arms ached. They were almost breaking. She was nearly at the top of the wall, almost within reach of the branch. She would, would, would reach it — then —

'Well, I never! What next! Before me very eyes. Peepin' an' pryin'.'

Lacie tumbled down in a cloud of dust and sat on the ground with a grazed knee and torn frock.

A voice went on above her head.

'Torn thy frock and broke thy knee. That's what comes of being a nosey parker.'

Lacie looked up and saw an old woman in a pink sunbonnet. She was holding a rhubarb leaf with some raspberries on it.

'After the rasps, eh?' The old woman glared down at Lacie, 'Well, there's none left, 'cos I've got 'em all.'

'I don't want the raspberries.' Lacie struggled to her feet as she spoke. Her knee was smarting, and so were her hands. 'I never even thought of raspberries,' she said quite truthfully, for she had only thought of gooseberries and rhubarb.

'Well, what art thou after, then, ferretin' about o'er folks's walls? Apples aren't ripe. They're as green as goose-gogs.'

'I don't want anything,' said Lacie.

'That's likely!' retorted the old woman. 'Climbing walls for nothing.'

'I wouldn't have climbed the wall if I could have got in through the door,' said Lacie.

'Oh, indeed.'

'I just wanted to see . . . to see what was on the other side.'

'I'll tell thee what's on t'other side,' said the old woman. 'There's cabbiges, an' onions, an' 'taters, an' sparrergrass, an' rhubarb all gone to seed. Better be off now I've told thee an' get thi frock mended.'

'I'm sorry if I've offended you,' said Lacie.

'*I'm* not offended.' The old woman rammed her sunbonnet further down on her head, the rhubarb leaf trembling in her hand. 'It's not my business that's been poked into.'

There didn't seem to be anything else to do so Lacie smoothed her dusty dress and began to hobble away.

From across the river there came the sound of children just let out of school.

'Stop a bit!' called the old woman.

Lacie stopped.

'Thou's not from round here. I can tell by thy talk,' the old woman said. 'Running away eh? Is that it? Who's with thee?'

Lacie stared at her then said. 'I'm not running away — and there isn't anybody with me except — '

'Ah! I thowt as much,' cried the old woman. 'Come on! Speak up. Where are they?'

'There isn't any "they". There's — there's only my cousin, Nora. She's in the house on — on a visit.'

'Oh! Her!' said the old woman, her chin moving up and down, then she turned her back and began to walk away.

Lacie was shaking the dust from her clothes when she heard her again.

'Hey!'

The old woman was holding out the hand with the rhubarb leaf in it.

'Go on! Tek 'em. They're red-ripe and sweet as sugar.'

'No thank you,' said Lacie.

'Please thi sen.' And the old woman went off muttering to herself.

Lacie sighed with relief — though she would have appreciated a mouthful of raspberries — and limped away in the opposite direction, trying not to look round.

When she gave in to temptation and did look it was to see the old woman staring back at her.

They both looked away again quickly.

The next time Lacie looked back the old woman had gone.

'I never see where people go to in this place,' Lacie muttered to herself.

She walked away from the kitchen garden, ran down a slope, crossed the moat into the water meadow, then turned towards the river.

Yes, there was an old channel. It wandered in the

direction of the bank where it disappeared into a mass of rich grasses and reeds and willow striplings.

It was swampy there. Too late Lacie remembered about shoes. SQUELCH ! In bare feet she climbed to the top of the river bank and set about drying her socks and scraping away mud from her sandals.

She was thankful for a cooling breeze and the calm sound of water lapping.

A blob of red caught her eye.

A boat was bobbing about on the river, one of the Sprott boats, and it had a Sprott in it wearing a red cap.

But it was not on Mr Sprott, it was on Gertie.

She made no sign that she had seen Lacie but dipped an oar into the water and spun the boat around.

'Showing off,' muttered Lacie.

Gertie certainly knew some tricks. She manipulated the boat into midstream and proceeded to give a dazzling display of her skill.

'She must have seen me,' thought Lacie, 'or she wouldn't be doing all that. She must think somebody's watching.'

A string of barges came up on their journey from the seaport. Gertie politely nipped out of their way and they saluted her. She grinned, then rested her oars and let the boat go with the current, while she enjoyed a few moments of gazing about. She was perfectly at ease in her true element, a water-sprott.

'No wonder she doesn't like school,' Lacie thought, 'when there's all this to do, just outside.' And, suddenly, rowing a boat seemed more desirable than all the reading and writing in all the world.

'I wonder if she'd teach me, some day?' Lacie thought, and longed to be in a boat.

Gertie was alert again and rowing vigorously in the wake of the barges, when there was a loud bellow from the top of the Sprott steps. Her father had appeared and was making peremptory gestures which she at once obeyed by putting to shore.

When she disembarked he gave her a push at the side of her face then grabbed the red cap and put it on his head. Gertie tried to grab it back and, pushing each other, they went up the steps and out of sight.

There was something in the sight of Gertie larking about with her dad that jogged the sad feelings which Lacie had been trying to suppress. She sat and stared across the river but the view became blurred and disappeared as her feelings surged up beyond control and spilled over.

She was so far away from all she knew best, everything here seemed so strange . . .

Sitting still was no good.

Suddenly she remembered Nora.

'She'll be furious if she's waiting for me.'

The thought did much to restore Lacie to a more practical state of mind.

She jumped up quickly, put on her muddy socks and sandals, and ran to the front of the house.

5

Nettlestings

NOBODY was there.

The air shimmered above the long grass and insects shimmered in the air.

Lacie hesitated, then walked up the steps to the terrace and crossed to the front door.

At one side of it was a statue of a boy. He stood in a downcast attitude with his own broken-off head at his feet.

She took one step over the threshold and waited.

There was no sound. So many windows had been filled in that the only light, a golden beam of it in which myriad specks of dust were dancing, came through the open door.

A wide staircase lifted itself into shadows where there was the vague outline of a balcony.

A door creaked.

Still nobody came. She stood in the middle of the hall ready for flight.

Darkened windows, closed doors. The house was sealed off from life.

Suddenly she turned and ran outside. She had already been accused that day of peeping and prying.

She crossed the long-grass lawn, went over the bridge and stood by the car. Its leather seats were hot to the touch. Suppose she pressed the horn. Would its sound bring the place to life? It would certainly bring Nora running out, and she wouldn't be pleased. She would think something had happened, an emergency, the monster.

Lacie smiled rather a shaky smile. Her sad feelings hadn't been quite dismissed.

On an impulse she turned away from the car and walked into the wood.

'This is the owls' wood.' She thought of the stuffed owl in the glass case at School Cottage.

All the owls in this wood were asleep however, though wood doves cooed deep amongst the trees.

Wincing at the touch of nettles, she went on until she came to a hillock shaped like a Christmas pudding and covered with ivy. There was a door at the side, locked of course. The most interesting doors were always locked. She tried to look through the keyhole but it was filled up with rust and decay.

The place was too small for a monster to live in. She could smile at the thought of that monster now.

People would imagine such things!

The hillock was only as high as a farm gate and in two good giant strides she was on top of it, looking around her. Then, amongst the rustlings and whisperings of the wood she heard another sound, a very welcome one for she was hot and thirsty and her knee suddenly reminded her that it was extremely sore. Somewhere underneath the tangle of nettles and undergrowth, was water. But where? She searched but could not find it.

Deeper and deeper into the wood she went, not caring for nettles that stung nor thorns that pricked, until at last, thirstier than ever and hot, tired and sore she flung herself down to rest. The tops of the trees whirled together and she closed her eyes.

The next sound she heard was a toot-toot from the car.

She looked up to find that she was at the very edge of the wood within sight of the little red car and Nora.

Another car, a bigger and shinier one, was slowly moving away down the drive.

As Lacie went up to her Nora said, 'That was one of the doctors from Hawksop – he kept me talking . . .' She broke off, staring as if she couldn't believe her eyes.

'It can't be true,' she said, 'you can't have got into such a mess!'

'I got lost in the forest.' Lacie was rubbing her eyes.

'Forest?' said Nora. 'There's only a few trees and some nettles . . . I could see you chasing about. I thought you'd been stung by a gad-fly.'

'No, nettles,' replied Lacie looking at her arms and coming back to full consciousness.

She was smarting all over.

'You must have been rolling in nettles,' said Nora. 'I wanted to call and have tea with some people in Hawksop, but now you're not fit to go anywhere.'

Lacie began to smooth her dress and straighten her hair.

'That's useless,' said Nora. 'We'll just have to go home at once. Serves me right for being such an idiot as to bring you . . .' She broke off. 'Get in,' she said, 'while I start it up.'

She began to crank the car.

She cranked until she was red in the face. At the sight of her Lacie felt guiltier than ever.

'Damn the thing,' said Nora.

Her head disappeared under the bonnet and a string of words came out, words which Lacie thought of as being 'Sprott' words, rather unfairly, because up to now she had only heard one Sprott say one of them.

'Just my rotten luck,' said Nora at last. 'That's what I get for trying to do somebody a good turn, I ought to have more sense by now.'

She was twiddling various knobs and screws and under her breath she was saying the names of parts. 'That's the carburettor – seems all right. Those are the sparking plugs.' And so on. It sounded like an incantation but there was no magic in it. Nothing happened. The motor stayed dead.

Finally with oil on her fingers and a black smear across the front of her white dress she sat on the running-board and said, 'The blithering thing won't go.'

The afternoon slept on. No help was at hand. The only change in the scene was the lengthening of the shadows from trees.

'Look at it,' said Nora, staring about her. 'Absolutely deserted! We may as well be on the moon.'

'There's an old woman,' began Lacie.

'I know there's an old woman,' said Nora. 'I've just spent all afternoon talking to her – or about her. That's why I'm in this mess!'

'There's another one,' Lacie said and told of her encounter with the pink sunbonnet.

'Oh, Granny Betts. She lives round the back somewhere with her grandson.' Nora seemed to have given up her struggle with the car and was trying to clean the oil from her fingers with a handkerchief.

'I've seen him too,' said Lacie. 'At least . . . there was somebody feeding the fowls. Somebody not quite – '

'He's simple,' Nora said. 'Poor Tom, he calls himself. Granny Betts was a servant here years ago. She's been in charge all the time Mrs Mountsorrel's been abroad.'

She threw the handkerchief away and stared at her fingers.

'They've had the place to themselves for so long that they don't like it coming to life again . . . Some life ! Anyway Granny B made it plain she doesn't like the idea of me being around. She came in with one of the concoctions she's been dosing Mrs Mountsorrel with and I threw it away.' She got up. 'Well, it's no good waiting for a miracle. We'll have to do something. We'll have to shout for the ferry !'

They left the car and began to walk to the river, Nora grumbling about the blithering nuisance of having to get that wretched Sprott.

When they reached the waterside the wretched Sprott was not to be seen. The Sprott steps were deserted. The tide was on the ebb.

'The fleet's in,' said Nora, 'all two of 'em. We'd better shout.'

They shouted. They shouted until they were hoarse.

'He's doing this on purpose,' said Nora, 'he'll be shut up inside that horrible house laughing at us.'

At last somebody came out into the yard of the King of the River.

'What's he doing in there at this time of day?' said Nora. 'It's only five o'clock. If he's drinking already they deserve to lose their licence.'

All the time she was talking she was imperiously waving her arm to the figure across the water. If Fred Sprott noticed her he made no sign but crossed the street to his own domain and disappeared.

'Well!' said Nora sitting down on the bank. 'Well!'

'If only we could see Gertie,' Lacie said. 'She was on the river, earlier on. She made the boat spin round and round.'

'She would,' said Nora. 'They're good at showing off, those Sprotts, but they're not so good at being where they're needed – ' She broke off. Mr Sprott had come out of the house. She stood up and waved frantically. 'He's seen us,' she cried, 'so he needn't pretend he hasn't.'

Mr Sprott descended the steps, then put on his red cap.

'His badge of office,' said Nora.

Just as he was untying one of the boats Gertie rushed out of the house and hurled herself down the steps. There appeared to be an argument. Gertie made a grab for the red cap, her father, laughing, shoved her away and pushed off from the bank without her. Thereupon Gertie rushed up the steps and disappeared.

'Which boat is it?' asked Lacie. 'The *Wavey* or the *Wobbler?*'

'How should I know?' said Nora. 'And I'm sure I don't care!' She sat down, her face showing a mixture of relief and exasperation.

The boat came smoothly towards them across the water.

Suddenly Mr Sprott began to sing.

'Oh Lord!' said Nora.

His deep voice came pleasantly through the evening air.

> *The wind sighs over the water,*
> *The dragon fly fades in the air.*

He was using a single oar over the stern of the boat and he wasn't in a hurry.

> *I'll row once more.*
> *To the opposite shore*
> *But she won't be waiting there.*

'I don't blame her,' muttered Nora.

As he drew nearer he called out, 'Sorry if I was a long time getting started. I was busy.'

'Busy!' said Nora.

The sunlight was falling softly over them all and Lacie's heart was eased. She was touched by the pathetic note in Mr Sprott's song and almost began to like him.

Nora said he was a damn fool.

'You've certainly taken your time,' she greeted him.

'I had a bit of an argy-bargy with our Gert,' he replied as smoothly as his boat was skimming the water. 'The trouble is she thinks she owns the river.'

'She's not the only one,' muttered Nora.

The boat came alongside. He jumped on to the landing stage.

'Well, girls! What's up?' he said.

Nora gave him a freezing look but he didn't seem to notice it.

'Thought you'd got a car,' he said to her.

There was an awkward silence during which Nora had to swallow her pride.

'It won't start,' she admitted.

'Won't start?' He gave a bellow of laughter. 'Well, if a hoss won't start all you have to do is give it a kick.'

Nora looked as if she would like to kick him.

'Where is it then?' he asked. 'Let's have a squint at it.'

Nora stared at him.

'What good would that do? What do you know about cars?'

But he was already up the bank and swishing through the grass. Nora almost had to run to catch up with him. Lacie followed her.

'I know more than you do, let's hope,' Mr Sprott said over his shoulder. 'I'll have it right in ten seconds.'

Nora was already seething. There was something about him that seemed fatal to her good humour. He got to the car before she did. When he lifted up the bonnet and began to look at the motor it was more than she could bear. She grabbed hold of the bonnet and slammed it down again. He only just got his hand out of the way in time.

'Don't touch it!' she cried. 'It's none of your business. I'll get a mechanic from Hawksop. I won't have ignorant ... ignorant ...' She couldn't find a word and just gasped ... 'messing about with my car. Let go ... keep away from it.'

'Please yourself!' he said, and added something under his breath.

'And remember,' she cried, 'there's a child present.'
He was already striding back to the boat.

'You can get a mechanic from Hawksop,' he said, 'and you can walk back to Hawksop on your knees and elbows for all I care.'

If it had been almost a race to the car it was a race away from it and back to the boat.

Both Lacie and Nora had to run to keep up with him. Lacie was sure that he would reach the river first and go back without them. Nora seemed to have the same thought for she ran as fast as she could and caught up with him just as he was getting into the boat.

'I've a right to order the ferry,' she was struggling to get her breath, 'and I've ordered it. You've no right – no right to refuse . . . get in, Lacie.'

Lacie got into the boat, then Nora got in, catching the heel of her shoe somewhere and nearly tumbling in head first. She gritted her teeth.

Mr Sprott made no offer to help her nor did he laugh at her misfortune. He looked into the distance. His bottom jaw was sticking out just like Gertie's.

Nobody spoke. Lacie trailed her fingers in the water, puzzled by the angry feelings seething around her. She looked from one face to the other and tried to think of something pleasant to say.

She opened her mouth.

'You'll catch flies if you sit with your mouth open,' snapped Nora, so Lacie closed it again without saying anything.

The boat glided on. The wind sighed over the water.

After a time Nora said, 'I'm surprised you haven't

asked me about what happened over there this afternoon.'

'I shall know if I want to,' Mr Sprott replied,
'without asking you.'

What a strange discomforting man he was. Just
when she had decided to be friendly!

When they reached the bank Gertie was standing on
top of the steps, her nose in the air. Evidently she was
still feeling annoyed with her father.

He shouted to her,

'Here, Gert! Tie her up. And take that daft look
off thy face.'

He went up the steps leaving Nora and Lacie to
scramble out of the boat by themselves.

'You've forgotten something,' Nora called after him.
He turned round and she waved her purse.

'Give our Gertie a penny if you like,' he said and
went into the house.

Gertie came up to Nora and held out her hand.
'That'll be tuppence,' she said.

'Nonsense! Your father said a penny and that's all
you'll get.'

Gertie sniffed. 'It should be tuppence, ne'er mind
what he says, and threepence on Sat'dys.' She took the
penny and put it in her pocket.

Lacie had found the name on the boat.

'It's the *Warbler*,' she said and thought of Mr
Sprott singing and said it was a good name for his
boat. Nora didn't think there was anything good about
him or his boats.

'Sprotts!' she said as she and Lacie walked away
from the river. 'Damn Sprotts!'

6
Firelight

As THEY reached the gate of School Cottage they could hear sounds of activity in the Little School. Nora called through the window and Chloë looked out. When she saw Lacie she gasped.

'Nettlewood's lived up to its name,' she said. 'What awful nettlestings.' Then she wanted to know about Mrs Mountsorrel and whether Nora had decided to take the nursing job.

Nora frowned in the direction of some nearby infants who were hanging about.

'Little pigs have big ears,' she said, unfortunately catching Lacie's eye at the same time.

'I hope she didn't mean me,' thought Lacie. She felt indignant and went away to School Cottage.

The sun had slid into the west, poised over Nettlewood. An air of evening was settling down over everything. It was the time when if one is feeling sad one can't help feeling sadder.

There had been times in the day when Lacie had felt cheerful and interested, when she had almost forgotten the being-so-far-from-home feeling, yet it was that which had been at the bottom of everything all day ... and it was coming up again now. For two pins she'd run upstairs and fling herself and all her smartings and achings on the bed. It would be a relief to go up there and howl about home.

It was good to cry sometimes. She wiped the tears away but not as quickly as they came.

The fire was out. There was a kettle, a black iron one, in its usual place on the hob at the side of the fireplace. If you put a kettle on in Owsterley you had to light a fire underneath it. Lacie looked about for sticks and found some in an old oven in the back-kitchen. There was a coal-house in the yard. Matches? On the chimney-shelf of course.

Soon she had a fire going and had only used two matches. Only two matches. She was pleased about that. The kettle, filled at the pump in the yard, was sitting on the flames. Soon it would begin to sing.

Her cousins would surely be pleased to find she had made a fire and boiled a kettle. She was longing to please somebody. If only one, or both, would say, 'How nice it is to have Lacie here!'

She sat on the hearth and looked into the flames. Visions went through her mind – the old woman in the sunbonnet, the wings and beaks of the feeding hens, the young man who was called Poor Tom. She thought again of the wood and her search for the hidden stream, of the river she had crossed in the boat with Fred Sprott and Nora. She thought of their quarrel ... her head began to nod ... then Chloë and Nora came in.

'She's lighted a fire,' cried Chloë, 'and got the kettle boiling. How nice it is to have Lacie here!'

Later in the evening after a bath in the back kitchen – there was no bathroom in School Cottage – Lacie was colouring pictures for the Little School when Mr Springles called to take Chloë for a ride. Nora was out, telephoning about the car.

'That car!' exclaimed Chloë. 'It's more trouble than it's worth, but one can't tell her that. It belonged to him, you know.'

Lacie would have liked to have heard more. 'Him' referred to Nora's husband, she supposed. Chloë looked as if she were going to say something else, then Nora came in, fuming. Nobody could do anything. Only fools lived in Owsterley.

'Get Fred Sprott,' Mr Springles advised. 'He's got a flair for mechanics, picked it all up in the war, you know. Cars, wireless sets, nothing sets him fast.'

Lacie looked at Nora. There was no explosion. Perhaps she had no energy left.

Presently Chloë went upstairs to get a coat and Mr Springles went outside to start the motor bike.

Nora stood looking down at the fire. She put out her foot and turned over a log.

She had been married and her husband was already dead. He had been young like her; had driven that little red car. Now he was dead.

Lacie sat quietly.

Chloë came downstairs, winding a long scarf around her hair. She waited a second then said to Nora, 'Have you decided anything about going to Nettlewood?'

'Not really.' Nora was still looking into the fire – then she laughed. 'Do you want to get rid of me or something?'

Mr Springles sounded the horn on the motor bicycle.

'I must go!' cried Chloë, and ran out of the house. Lacie noticed that she had left Nora's question unanswered.

When Lacie got up next morning there was nobody in the house.

Breakfast was laid for her and the kettle was singing. Evidently she had been allowed to sleep late to restore herself from her exertions of the day before.

She ate her meal, cleared the table then sauntered out into the street.

No one was about. Should she go into the Little School? The infants were singing.

She stopped to consider, then turned the other way and walked to the river wall. It was easy to climb and soon she was dangling her legs and looking down into the water.

At her left the King of the River seemed deserted. So was the Sprott house at her right. The boats were tied up at the bottom of the steps. The *Wobbler* was dingier than the *Wavey*. Both needed a coat of paint.

Through the owls' wood across the river there was a glimpse of the turrets and chimneys of Nettlewood.

She was thinking over the events of the day before when something brought her out of her thoughts. She turned her head. Gertie was coming out of the Sprott house. She was wearing her dad's red cap.

'Hullo.'

'Sssh!' Gertie gave a wary look towards the school, put a hand to the side of her face and looked doleful.

'What's the matter? Toothache?'

Gertie nodded and gave a groan. She came to sit on the wall beside Lacie and they began to throw bits of stone into the water.

'I saw you yest'dy,' Gertie remarked.

'Why didn't you wave?' asked Lacie.

Gertie shrugged her shoulders and went on throwing bits into the water.

'Could I learn to row?' Lacie asked her.

'You could if you'd got a boat.'

That finished it then.

'What was me granny chinning at you about?' Gertie went on.

'Is she your granny? I thought – '

'She's medad's – but I call her Granny. Cross old thing. She don't like kids. They shout after our Tom and pester him.'

'I saw him,' said Lacie.

'I haven't got to jabber about him,' Gertie said, 'or medad'll knock my head off.'

'I only said I saw him,' said Lacie. 'I don't call that jabbering.'

'Medad says I've got to keep me mouth shut about them over there,' and Gertie did shut her mouth with a snap like the snap of a mousetrap.

But she quickly opened it again.

'Look, there's a motor car,' she cried. 'An' it's better than the one your cousin's got.'

It was the car Lucie had seen leaving Nettlewood yesterday. Now it drew up outside School Cottage.

'Doctors from Hossup! Both of 'em, young 'un and old 'un.' Gertie turned to Lacie. 'It must be important. Who's badly?'

'Nobody's ill,' replied Lacie.

'What's doctors come for then?'

Lacie decided that she wasn't going to jabber about her relations in School Cottage and said nothing.

'Well, they must a come for summat,' said Gertie, 'an' I can soon find out.'

She got down from the wall and looked as if she were ready to go and investigate.

'Be careful somebody doesn't see you,' Lacie reminded her, 'and ask about your toothache.'

Gertie was brought to a halt.

'Folks are always trying to stop me gettin' to know things.' She was annoyed. 'But H-Hi — ' she emphasized the 'I' with a double 'h'. 'H-Hi always find out.'

Lacie was by now taking it for granted that whenever it was possible for Gertie to drop an 'h' she dropped one and would then make up for it by putting one where it didn't belong.

Children were coming out to play in the school yards.

'H'I'm off,' said Gertie and faded away through the dark doorway of the Sprott house.

At midday Nora was moody and hardly ate anything. She pushed her plate away and lit a cigarette.

'Smoking!' exclaimed Chloë.

'Oh damn!' said Nora, and flounced out into the garden where she sat on a log and smoked furiously.

'I hope nobody sees her!' said Chloë. 'I don't know what's happening to the world these days.' She looked into the garden at the column of rising smoke, then frowned and went on, 'Did she — has she mentioned anything to you about going to Nettlewood to nurse Mrs Mountsorrel? I didn't have a chance to talk to her this morning. The doctors have been here, I know. I suppose they came to discuss things.'

'I wasn't with Cousin Nora this morning,' Lacie said. 'I've been by myself – except for Gertie Sprott.'

'Gertie Sprott? She wasn't at school.'

'I know. She's got toothache.'

'H'm!' said Chloë. After a pause she went on. 'Perhaps you'd better come into school this afternoon and keep out of the way. We'd better leave Nora to herself while she makes up her mind about Nettlewood. I don't want her saying I've pushed her into it. I don't know why people can't make up their minds. It's simple enough. You either say yes or you say no.'

That evening Chloë had to go to a parish meeting. Mr Springles had to go too, and came into School Cottage for tea so that he and Chloë could go together.

'I think Cousin Nora has gone for a walk,' Lacie told Chloë.

'She's tramping the fields somewhere,' said Chloë, 'thinking and smoking. Really, it's very difficult sometimes – '

She broke off and poured tea for Mr Springles.

'I'll have to leave you by yourself till she comes back,' she said to Lacie. 'I don't suppose she'll be long. Anyway, it isn't as if it's dark.'

Lacie said she didn't mind being by herself, and looked at the large bookcase.

When Chloë and Mr Springles had gone Lacie set a place for Nora at the table, then did the washing-up.

She chose some books but the evening was so fine and warm she changed her mind about reading and decided to work on a small bed of lettuces and radishes which had been made her responsibility.

It was a soothing job. The scent of the soil and leaves was pleasant. She liked putting her fingers in the earth and soon became absorbed in what she was doing.

After a time she became aware of a presence near by and looked up to see Mr Sprott watching her from the other side of the hedge.

Her heart jumped. He had appeared so silently.

'Where's your a'ntie?' he asked.

She was tired of explaining that Chloë and Nora were cousins — second cousins — and did not correct him.

She merely replied, 'Which one?'

'Never mind.' His eyes were looking over her head. 'There she is.'

Nora was standing at the back door.

Mr Sprott leapt over the hedge.

'Wait a minute,' he called to Nora. 'I've got something for you.'

Nora waited for a moment on the doorstep then moved forward to meet him. She looked puzzled as he took a small paper bag from his pocket.

'What is it?' she asked, impatient yet curious, and held out her hand. He turned the bag upside down and let the contents trickle over her fingers.

'It's corn,' she cried, drawing back her hand, 'why are you giving it to me?'

'Because it's yours.'

'Mine? Is this your idea of a joke?'

'I got it out of the petrol tank. Your car will start now.'

Nora took a deep breath and Lacie waited for her outburst.

It didn't come.

'I was over at Nettlewood this morning,' Mr Sprott was going on in a mellow voice, 'and I just took a look. No harm in that, was there?' He sounded as if he had never been bad-tempered in his life. 'Well — that's all that was wrong,' and he threw a few grains of corn to a sparrow. 'I've cleaned out the tank and filled it with petrol. If you'd like to nip over the river . . .' Lacie noticed his white teeth gleaming — 'you could drive back.'

'I haven't had a cup of tea yet.' Nora's manner was as mild as his.

She began to walk back to the house and after a second's hesitation he followed her.

The atmosphere seemed peaceful up to now and Lacie returned to her lettuce patch. The next time she looked up there was nobody to be seen but she heard the rattle of tea-things in the house.

She went on working in the garden until she realized she had become quite cold. Everything was quiet. She put her gardening things away and went into the house.

There was nobody there.

Two cups and saucers were on the table, and there were two plates with crumbs on. Lacie decided that Mr Sprott must have been invited to have tea, in gratitude for the car, she supposed. She had thought it more likely that his reward would be a row.

It certainly was difficult to predict the actions of grown-ups.

The back part of School Cottage lost the sun in the

evenings as it slid over to the west behind the woods of Nettlewood. Now, after the still-bright garden, the living-room seemed sombre, yet it was too early to light the lamp.

Lacie took a jacket and went outside again. Shadows were lengthening. The scent of flowers was strong.

A thrush called from the top of the pear tree.

A small voice inside her grew louder and insisted on being heard.

It wasn't fair. Nora should not have disappeared. She was grown-up and in Lacie's world at home grown-ups were always where they were supposed to be. Now when they were not, things fell out of place.

Lacie felt herself to be of no importance here. People forgot her. Everybody had gone. Everybody had things to do.

She wandered out of the garden into the field where some children were shouting and having a good time. When she went up to them they drifted away and she felt more lonely than ever.

Now that she was away from home she was amazed to find how much time was always waiting to be filled up.

She went to the lazy stream at the bottom of the field where some fun was going on. Some of Chloë's infants were paddling and splashing. They crowded about Lacie who took off her shoes and socks and soon was as wet as they were.

The mud at the bottom of the stream squelched between her toes. Some of the infants began to pick up handfuls of it — it was like soft dark chocolate — and throw it about.

'Stop that, you kids!' said a voice.

Lacie looked up.

'What are you playing wi' them for?' Gertie Sprott, red cap askew, was standing scornfully on the bank.

'Get off home, you kids,' she commanded. 'Go on, look sharp, or you won't half catch it.'

They were all so used to being bossed about by her that they obeyed immediately, collected their damp belongings, and ran off.

Lacie was sorry to see them go.

'That's got rid o' them,' said Gertie.

Lacie dried her feet as well as she could and put her socks and shoes on. She wished Gertie would mind her own business but was glad of somebody to talk to.

'Why are you all by yourself?' asked Gertie.

Lacie did not reply, but Gertie had the answer. She had seen Chloë go off with Mr Springles and she had seen Nora.

'She's gone wi' medad to Nettlewood. They've gone in *Wobbler*. Let's go an' look for 'em coming back.'

Once more they were on the river wall swinging their legs.

Wobbler was still tied up at the other side of the river.

'They're still there,' said Gertie, 'I wonder what's going on? P'raps the old woman is dead.' Her voice grew low. 'I wouldn't like to be there – not now it's dark – except with medad.'

The sun had dropped away. The river was the colour of green ink. Owls were hooting in Nettlewood.

Lacie shivered. She spoke in a low voice. 'Do you think . . . do you believe there – *is* a monster?' She gave an uncertain little laugh to show that her question was – almost – a joke.

''Course not,' said Gertie. ''Cos medad says it's daft – but . . .'

They looked at the outline of trees and chimneys and their voices dropped to whispering.

'Some folks say,' Gertie came closer to Lacie's ear, 'that there's things buried underneath.'

'What sort of things?' asked Lacie. 'Do you mean treasures and . . . and – jewels and things . . . or – or – what?'

Gertie was not sure.

'There's secret places,' she said. 'Tunnels and rooms that nobody ever goes into now . . . except our Tom . . . he knows everything about t'place. I should think he knows more than anybody. Why, our Tom ought to have been – '

She looked confused and stopped. She must have reminded herself that she was 'jabbering'. She jumped off the wall and ran into the Sprott house.

Left by herself and looking across the river Lacie could have believed in monsters. She could have believed in anything.

The silence was shattered by an outburst of music if such tinny scratchy sounds as were now coming out of the house could be called music.

Soon Gertie reappeared with two thick slices of bread and dripping.

'Hi mungry,' she said.

'So am I,' said Lacie and after the slightest hesitation – for the thought of the dark Sprott house and the sight of Gertie's hands did give her a qualm – she accepted a slice.

'That's medad's new gram'phone,' Gertie said, obviously enjoying the sound of it as much as she was enjoying the bread and dripping. 'It's a new old 'un really 'cos he made it out of one somebody chucked away.'

She ate some of her bread and dripping, then added, 'That's his fav'rit song.'

In the depths of the Sprott house a thread of a voice unwound itself.

'It's called, *Lay my head on your shoulder, Daddy*,' said Gertie, 'it nearly makes me cry sometimes.'

The song ended and she dashed away to take off the record.

'The boat's coming over,' Lacie called, and Gertie dashed out again.

'Good job I turned it off,' she said in relief. 'I haven't got to touch that gram'phone.'

It was almost too dark to see the boat but they could hear the oars splashing. Soon Mr Sprott's voice bellowed out instructions to his daughter. She hurried down the steps.

Nora was not in the boat.

Mr Sprott glanced at Lacie. He seemed surprised to see her, then told her that her an'tie was on the road to Hossup, and that she'd be half-way home by now.

'In the car?' asked Lacie.

'She's not walking it. Get inside, our Gert, and get yourself off to bed. Respectable folk's kids are all in bed by now.'

In spite of Gertie's protests — in her philosophy it was never the right time for bed — she was shoved into the house by her father and once again Lacie was left on her own.

She threw the last piece of bread into the water. The ducks would get it tomorrow.

The lights of the King of the River shone out. Inside people were laughing and talking.

She wished somebody would call her name, and say 'Come home, Lacie!' Even Nora's voice would be a welcome sound.

A big patch of light shone out of the King as a door was opened. A song rushed out into the night. Somebody came out and looked in her direction. Instinctively Lacie shrank into the shadows.

A light showed in School Cottage.

Somebody was home.

With relief she went in.

'I wondered what had happened!' exclaimed Chloë as soon as Lacie opened the door. 'Where's Nora?'

Lacie told as much as she knew. Chloë frowned and wanted to know what she had been doing since teatime. Lacie told her that and added, 'When Gertie went home I sat on the wall and listened to the singing in The King of the River.'

Chloë was horrified.

'Sitting outside a pub at night! What on earth would your parents think?' She stopped as she noticed Lacie's downcast face. 'Well, never mind.'

'I was listening for the motor bike,' said Lacie.

Chloë had walked home with Miss Throssel. George – Mr Springles – was still at the meeting.

'I'll make you some hot cocoa,' said Chloë, 'then you must go to bed. You look worn out. Really, Nora is the limit and when she comes in I shall tell her so.'

Lacie was in bed when the car stopped.

It wasn't pleasant to lie upstairs and hear the sound of quarrelling below and Lacie knew by the tone of the raised voices that quarrelling it was. In some way she felt herself to be a part of it which made her feel even worse.

Her bedroom was over the parlour at the front of the house, and the voices came from the living-room at the back, so she couldn't hear anything that was said, but the sound was disturbing. She pressed her face into the pillow and longed to be at home.

A door was closed sharply, not exactly slammed but closed in the sort of way that if you had closed it – and if you were a child – you would have been hauled back to close it properly.

Whoever had closed the door ran upstairs. There was another bang. Nora's door.

After a time Chloë came upstairs.

The house grew quiet. There were only the small sounds of the middle of the night. A sudden creak, a scratching in the roof. Birds. A scrabbling in the walls. Mice. A curtain's flap and flutter that startled the heart for a moment.

The owls in Nettlewood called and called – then the rest of the night was gone, it was time to get up and everything felt different.

7

The Silver Queen

IN A few days' time Nora packed her things and drove off to Nettlewood.

Looking at Lacie she said, 'Whenever you want some more nettlestings you know where to come to, don't you?' Then she got into her car and was gone.

The dust settled down in the street and peace flowed through School Cottage.

'Only one more week to the holidays!' Chloë stretched her arms above her head and screwed up her eyes against the sun. 'A week today we shall have finished school for a whole month.'

She and Lacie were sitting in the garden after a midday picnic.

'I feel as if it's the holidays already,' Chloë went on in a lazy voice, and yawned.

'Well, it's Saturday tomorrow,' Lacie replied, 'and it *is* a holiday.'

'So it is.' Chloë came to life again.

She thought for a moment then said, 'Tell you what. You must go with me into Hawksop. I've got to go on a – a bit of business. We'll go on the Silver Queen. It'll be a little celebration.'

Lacie wondered what there was to celebrate but only asked, 'What's the Silver Queen?'

The Silver Queen was a bus, a big double-decker open-top motor bus painted silver. On its way from Bridgeover twice a week, on Wednesdays and Saturdays at two o'clock in the afternoon, it passed the bottom end of Owsterley's main street, then went on a round about route through the villages to Hawksop.

'It's a lovely ride for sixpence,' said Chloë, 'especially if it's a fine day and we sit on the top deck.'

Modern times had arrived in Owsterley with the Silver Queen.

'Up to now,' said Chloë, 'we've had to walk to Hawksop, or go on a bicycle or get a lift in a carrier's cart. Of course, now I can go with Mr Springles in the side-car – but tomorrow . . .' she hesitated, 'yes, tomorrow we'll go a bit earlier and you can come with me. We'll have a bus ride.'

Lacie was delighted at the prospect. Bus rides in the country must be different from bus rides in a city.

'I've got things to do in Hawksop . . . as I said,' Chloë was going on, 'some shopping and – and one or two other things. There's a nice little café that's famous for cream buns.'

Then she went off to school, grumbling in a pleasant way that she was much too lazy to work, it all felt so much like a holiday already.

Lacie had been promoted to housekeeper. She tidied away the remains of the picnic and felt important, and the rest of that pleasant Friday slipped away. The house was at peace. No doors banged. Nobody broke any pots, nobody burned anything. Nobody had to look out for sudden squalls.

And on Saturday morning –

'Lacie! A letter for you!'

The words brought Lacie hurtling downstairs almost before the postman had got through the front gate.

Chloë was smiling.

'I've got one too, from your mother. It's good news. I told you it would be. Didn't I tell you everything would be all right?'

How could she possibly have known? But she had.

'He's passed the crisis.' Chloë was reading a page of her letter – 'Sitting up and joking, and talking about seeing his – ' she turned a page – 'his dear little Lacie again. Well, it'll soon be goodbye to poor old Owsterley for you.'

Lacie took her letter away and read it again, then again, and yet again as if she hadn't been able to take in everything it said . . . then suddenly she had taken in everything and it was all right.

'Tomorrow you must write a nice long letter in reply,' said Chloë, 'there's always plenty of time on Sundays.'

And Lacie put the letter safely away in the top drawer of the dressing-table amongst her clean underwear.

From now on the day burst into extraordinary delight. Even doing ordinary things became exquisitely pleasurable. Breakfast smelt better, tasted like a feast. The washing up almost did itself.

The sun shone. The garden shone. The house shone. Light glittered from every pane of glass.

'My shoes have never had such a polish,' Chloë said, when Lacie had finished with them. 'Come upstairs and help me to decide which dress to wear.'

'The white one is the prettiest,' said Lacie and it was her opinion which counted. Chloë wore the white dress.

There were two crystal bottles on her dressing-table, with cut-glass stoppers in them. She opened first one, then the other and gave each one to Lacie's eager nose.

'One is Jockey Club, and one is Grekis,' she said. 'I don't know which to use today.'

'This,' said Lacie firmly and gave her the Jockey Club.

Chloë sprinkled the scent on a delicate handkerchief, and dabbed herself behind each ear.

'Now the bottle's empty,' she said, 'you can have it to put amongst your handkerchiefs.'

Lacie accepted it and went at once to put it away. She put it on top of the letter in the dressing-table drawer. When she went back Chloë was just burying her face in a swansdown powder puff. Her nose came out with a cloud of white on it. She looked rather guilty and brushed off the surplus powder with a handkerchief.

'Lots of people do it nowadays,' she said, 'it's becoming quite the thing.'

Lacie wore a blue dress, not her favourite but she didn't mind. It was Chloë's choice.

'And your hat,' said Chloë, finding it in a cupboard where Lacie had hidden it.

Lacie pulled a face, then pulled it back again as Chloë looked reproachful.

'It's just that I don't like it,' said Lacie banging the hat on her head, 'with all these stupid daisies and blue ribbons on.'

She had snatched it up in a hurry as she had left home

and had actually felt like throwing it through the train window when she realized she had got it on her head.

'But it's so pretty,' cried Chloë, looking into the mirror at her own hat. 'People will think we're going to Buckingham Palace.'

Lacie was looking through the window, and said, 'There's Mr Sprott.'

'Come away,' said Chloë. 'It isn't nice to be seen peeping out of windows at people. What is he doing?'

'Gertie's with him. They look as if they've got their best clothes on. Anyway, they look different.' Lacie still peeped.

Chloë went to the window. She stood well back and stretched her neck.

'H'mm! They're certainly spruced up for something. Fred Sprott's had a shave. He's quite respectable. I wonder where they're going.'

A slight presentiment ruffled Lacie's peace of mind. It passed over however in the final preparations.

Chloë glanced at her watch. It was time to go.

The gate clicked. They heard Gertie speaking to her father. She was shouting, 'Goodbye!'

Chloë stood in the middle of the room.

'Did you tell Gertie Sprott about us going to Hawksop?' she asked.

Lacie looked troubled.

'I think I did.'

They heard footsteps down the passage. Gertie appeared in the open doorway.

They all looked at each other.

'Well,' said Chloë at last, 'you're looking very smart today, Gertie. Are you going out with your father?'

'No, I'm not,' said Gertie. ''Cos he won't have me.

He's told me to clear off by myself. He won't go on the Silver Queen. He says he can walk it for nothing when he wants to go to Hossup.'

Chloë said, 'He's going to Hawksop, is he?'

'No, he's not,' said Gertie. 'He won't tell me where he's going. But it's somewhere special. I know it's special 'cos he's had a shave.' Then she added, 'I'm goin' on t'Silver Queen. Medad gave me sixpence so nobody can stop me.'

'Oh?' said Chloë.

By this time Chloë and Lacie had exchanged glances; evidently there was to be a third person on the excursion.

'Look sharp.' Gertie began to bustle them about. 'Bus won't wait for us if we're not there. I don't want to miss it if you do,' and she rushed them out of the house.

As they were hurrying through the village she grinned her famous grin, looked up at Chloë and said, 'Medad said you wouldn't let me come with you, but I knowed you would. He said I'd got a damn cheek for asking.'

'So you have,' Chloë replied, forgetting to admonish her for the damn. 'So you jolly well have.'

They waited at the end of the street where it joined the road from Bridgeover to Hawksop. Nobody else from Owsterley was there.

'There it is!' shrieked Gertie jumping about in excitement. 'Bus is coming. We're only just in time.'

'Now, Gertie,' Chloë looked serious, 'I want a word with you before we get on the bus.'

'Yes, Miss?'

'If you are coming with us you must behave nicely.'

81

'Yes, Miss.'

'Like a little lady.'

Gertie's smile modified itself.

'Yes, Miss.'

'Like Lacie,' Chloë added.

Gertie looked at Lacie – and said nothing.

The stately, silver-coloured bus stopped in front of them and Gertie shot up the stairs to the top deck. When Chloë and Lacie arrived there she was rushing up and down quite unable to settle herself. There were plenty of vacant seats and she looked as if she were going to try them all. Several passengers began tut-tutting to each other.

'Gertie!' hissed Chloë. 'Everybody is looking at her already,' she whispered to Lacie. 'Gertie!'

Gertie sat down then promptly got up again. Chloë stifled a groan, then, as if hoping to dissociate herself from her, looked steadily at the view.

It was wonderfully exciting to feel the swift motion and the way the wind came flowing from the fields.

'Whoops!' Lacie caught her hat before it flew away, and put it beside her on the seat with her purse in it to weigh it down. Chloë took a hat-pin from her bag and fixed her own hat more securely.

'Or it'll soon be hanging from the top of a tree,' she said. Gertie went into fits of laughter just behind them. She had moved yet again to be near Chloë and Lacie who had the front seat and a splendid view of where they were going.

At the head of the staircase there was a large notice which said:

Passengers are advised to Duck their heads when passing under TREES or BRIDGES.

Gertie gave Lacie a jab in the back and whispered – 'What's it say about ducks?'

Several passengers heard her and smiled.

Lacie resisted the temptation to say, 'Why don't you learn to read better?' and told her.

'Ssh! Don't talk so loudly,' said Chloë. 'And remember to do as it says when we come to the Biggills.'

'I can't see any hills,' Lacie remarked. The landscape was stretched out beneath them like a map spread out on a table.

'We call a molehill a mountain round here,' replied Chloë – 'or so Nora says. The Biggills isn't very high but it's a hill to us.'

The bus was going at a stately pace. Empty seats were being filled up.

The sunshine, the breeze, the hum of the engine, the swift yet steady motion, the blue sky with white clouds floating and the comforting memory of the morning's letter, all combined to give Lacie a sense of delicious happiness. She began to hum with the hum of the engine, a sound of contentment which escaped from her inward satisfaction. Chloë looked at her and smiled. Even Gertie had now given herself up to the soothing rhythm and was quiet. She leaned her chin on the arm rail and seemed to enjoy the jolts that went through her jaw.

Chloë warned her about it and said she'd break her teeth, and Gertie said she wouldn't, then laid her arms along the rail and her face on top of her arms.

Chloë looked at the view again and smiled. She was doing a lot of smiling this afternoon, in a vague, dreamy way.

As it was a Saturday afternoon there were not many

people in the fields. Bystanders waved as the bus went on, so did some children in a farm cart. A horse pulling a gig containing a farmer and his wife shied all over the road. The farmer got red in the face, and his wife shook an umbrella at the people who were laughing in the bus.

'There's Celery Cottage.' Chloë pointed over the fields. To Gertie's disappointment there was no sign of Mrs Bisset or Bertie.

'They'll be at market,' Chloë said, and got no rest until she had promised Gertie to visit them there.

A covey of bicyclists narrowly escaped being knocked into the ditch at the side of the road. They bawled insulting remarks about the driver and shook their fists. Gertie hung over the side of the bus shrieking with laughter and shouting back at them.

Chloë was dreadfully embarrassed. Lacie was sorry for her.

Suddenly there was a sound like a very loud bee. An aeroplane was flying towards them.

All the upstairs passengers except Chloë stood up and shouted. The pilot leaned out and put his hand up. Everybody waved. An old man shook his walking stick, a young man sprang on to his seat and saluted, a schoolboy threw up his straw hat and just managed to catch it again, a woman took off her scarf and let it fly in the breeze, and a youth waved a white apron he had seized from the top of a basket of eggs.

'Hey up!' said a woman. 'Mind them eggs – and that's my apron,' and she grabbed it from him and waved it herself.

All this inspired Gertie who had nothing to wave but her hands, to pick up Lacie's straw hat and wave that.

She crushed the brim and knocked the purse off the seat so that all Lacie's money was scattered over the floor.

It was Lacie who had to bend down and pick up what she could find of it.

Fortunately most of the money she had brought with her from home – a five-pound note – had been deposited with Chloë for safe keeping. Lacie was very glad about that as she scrabbled about under the seat. When she came up again Chloë was looking crossly at Gertie, who was taking no notice of her at all, but was squealing with excitement.

The pilot had brought down the aeroplane very low – so low that several women were giving shrill screams – and was circling about over the bus.

A man yelled out, 'I reckon he's lost,' then stood on his seat and shouted at the top of his voice –

'THIS IS OWST'LY. OW-W-W-ST-LY,' with a long-drawn out ow as if somebody had trodden on his toe.

'Sit down, you fool,' said his wife pulling at his coat. 'Stop bawling and don't be so daft.'

'You'll fall out, love,' an anxious woman called upwards, 'Get inside, think o' thy poor mam.'

But the schoolboy bawled, 'Oh go on, jump,' and kept dancing up and down and yelling, 'Jump! Jump!' until somebody pushed him on to his seat and told him to shut up.

The pilot flew lower, then up and over.

'He's looping the loop,' yelled the passengers. Delirious with joy they clapped and cheered.

Finally the pilot leaned out of the aeroplane, saluted and flew away.

Everybody sat down again – even Chloë had been

standing up — and watched the plane disappear into the distance.

There was a feeling of peaceful satisfaction tinged with regret that the performance was over.

The passengers laughed and chatted to each other. A bag of sweets was brought out and passed around. Lacie was sorry for the generous owner of it who only got an empty bag back.

After a time everybody settled down again.

Chloë looked at the view and smiled across the fields.

Lacie hummed her little tune and Gertie rested her chin on her arms and her arms on the rail.

Before long there was a slight stirring amongst the passengers. A word went round.

'Biggills.'

'Mind your 'eads,' shouted the conductor popping his head upstairs.

Lacie had not been expecting to see a mountain but it was amusing to find what they all called a hill — a Biggill.

She had seen the dark patch on the landscape for some time as the bus wound round and round and nearer and nearer.

'You'll have to be careful of the trees,' Chloë reminded her. 'They hang very low. Where's Gertie?'

Gertie had quietened down and was sitting peacefully by herself on the back seat.

There was now the pleasant anticipation of something slightly dangerous to spice the enjoyment of the ride.

The Silver Queen changed gear and began a mild ascent. The road had been cut through a ridge of higher ground and entered a tunnel of shade from low-hanging trees. Branches swished against the sides of the bus. Lacie could have put out her hand and picked ferns which were growing on the side of the road nearest to her.

The passengers laughed as they ducked their heads beneath the trees. Some of the women again gave little screams.

Nobody was thinking of Gertie. All were too busy dodging the trees.

A very low branch swung right across the road. This was to be the test for them all.

Everybody ducked in time.

Everybody except Gertie. Either she had left it too late or temptation was too much for her adventurous spirit but *she* did not duck. Instead, her arms shot up, she gave a jump and a swing – and the Silver Queen went on without her, leaving her aloft.

At her screech everybody looked behind and beheld her dangling from a tree over the middle of the road.

'Stop! Stop!'

'Stop t'bus.'

'Whoa! Whoa!'

People stamped on the floor and shouted.

'Stop t'engine!'

'Where's conductor?'

'Ring t'alarm bell!'

'Help!' shrieked Chloë. 'There's a child overboard!'

Noise and confusion. The conductor rushed upstairs to find out the cause of the pandemonium. A thicket of arms pointed to the dangling figure left behind.

'What the – ?' said the conductor. 'I must be dreamin'.'

The bus stopped. The driver shouted, 'What's up?'

'A kid's up,' the conductor shouted back, 'up a tree.'

'Don't be so daft,' bawled the driver.

'Get out and see for thiself then,' said the conductor and rushed downstairs.

Gertie swung frantic legs.

'Oh, Gertie, Gertie!' moaned Chloë.

Everybody was shouting advice to the driver. Some people got out of the bus.

'Back up! Back up!' yelled the conductor dancing about on the road.

'What d'y mean, back up?' The driver stuck out his head. 'If I go up hill kid stays up the tree.'

'Back down, then,' said the conductor, 'and look sharp about it.'

'All reight! All reight!' replied the driver. 'Keep thi hair on!'

At last the driver and the conductor seemed to be in agreement to reverse the bus, and as the passengers chorused advice and encouragement, it was slowly jerked back to Gertie and settled beneath her.

'Stop! stop! That's it! No, come on a bit.'

'No, back a bit!'

'STOP!'

Many willing hands would have reclaimed Gertie as the bus stopped beneath her but the conductor wanted his rights.

'Mind out, you lot,' he cried, 'I'll get 'er.'

'I can get down meself,' Gertie muttered, her feet swinging circles in the air to find the seat.

'You stay where y'are till I say different,' replied the conductor. 'Right. Now let go. Drop, you little devil.

Drop.' And exclaiming a Sprott word with which she was familiar he plucked her from the branch.

'Ah-h-h!' breathed the passengers.

The conductor looked for a moment, as a woman passenger pointed out a little later, as if he were going to 'give her one'.

Then uproar burst forth.

'I'd gi'e it 'er when I got 'er 'ome.'

'Whose bairn is she?'

'Is anybody with this child?'

'My word, I'd warm 'er jacket if she was mine.'

'You daft little monkey,' cried the dishevelled conductor to the dishevelled Gertie – both had twigs and bits of dead wood and leaves all over them – 'I've a good mind to break y'neck.'

Gertie said nothing at all.

Chloë, swallowing mortification, had to claim her.

'She's not my child . . . but she's in my charge.'

'It's teacher from Owst'ley baby school,' somebody whispered.

'My word, Miss, I'd keep her in a corner o' Monday,' said a woman.

'I've a good mind to put 'er off t'bus and let 'er walk it.' The conductor scowled.

Nobody objected.

'There y'are,' he said to the chastened Gertie. 'Nobody'd blame me if I did. You'll get this bus a bad name, you will.'

'Come and sit down, Gertie. At once!' Suddenly Chloë used her head-mistressy voice. It had an effect immediately. Gertie crept to Chloë's side and sat down like a mouse, the passengers settled in their seats and

89

the conductor said, 'I've never seen nowt like it in all me life.' But his voice was calmer.

The driver stood on the stairs and said, 'Is this bus ever goin' to get started?'

'Yes, that's right,' said the passengers, or, 'No, it's not right – stopping folks from getting where they're supposed to be goin'.'

Those people who had got out of the bus to see the goings on, got in again.

The engine started up and the Silver Queen went on its way.

'That's enough for one day,' said a plump woman with a sigh. 'What a to-do it's been, to be sure!'

Everybody was replete with excitement.

After a time Chloë said, 'Gertie.'

'Yes, Miss?'

'Never do that again.'

'No, Miss.'

And Gertie said not another word until they reached Hawksop.

Lacie whispered to Chloë, 'I don't suppose she's used to travelling. That's the trouble.'

'The trouble is,' replied Chloë, 'that I was a blithering idiot to bring her at all. I might have known she'd get up to something . . . but even I didn't think she'd get up a tree!'

8

Market Day

SATURDAY in Hawksop was market day.

The streets were already crowded as the Silver Queen crawled through a maze of horse-drawn drays and carts, bicycles, motor cars, vans, lorries, bullocks, sheep, pedestrians and a column of boys playing in a brass band.

Chloë seemed concerned about the time and kept glancing at her watch. 'We mustn't be too late,' she kept saying.

Lacie was trying to make out what tune the band was playing – it sounded familiar yet different – and did not ask what it was Chloë didn't want to be too late for. Not tea surely? It wasn't even three o'clock. There was plenty of time to find the tea-shop where the famous cream-buns were to be eaten.

In the High Street Chloë stepped out at a good pace, pressing through the crowd on the pavement. Gertie was just as eager to be off, somewhere, anywhere, as long as she could be first in the race which seemed to be going on between her and Chloë.

'Stop jumping on and off the pavement, Gertie,' said Chloë, a stern note still in her voice. 'You'll be run over, then you won't be able to spend your sixpence.'

Gertie, who had not had to pay her own half bus fare and was therefore threepence to the good, announced that she was going to buy 'medad' a present with it.

'All right,' replied Chloë, 'but you needn't shout and tell all Hawksop. Here's the Penny Bazaar – just the sort of place where you'll find something suitable. You two can go inside and look around while I pop into the draper's. I'll meet you here in ten minutes. If I'm not here, WAIT. You're not to move from this spot.' And she tapped her foot on the pavement. They all agreed it was impossible to make a mistake about the spot. Gertie even bent down and put her finger on it.

'Silly child !' said Chloë.

Inside the shop the goods were set out on stalls.

'How much money have you got?' Gertie asked, holding up her sixpence and looking at it with one eye.

'I haven't counted it,' Lacie replied, 'since you knocked it all over the bus.'

Gertie changed the subject and said, 'I'm goin' to get something for medad.'

'So am I,' replied Lacie.

'Are you?' Gertie was pleased, though surprised. 'For medad?'

'Of course not,' said Lacie, 'for *my* dad.'

'That's daft,' said Gertie.

'Why?'

''Cos your dad's not here. My dad is – ' and Gertie dashed away to another stall leaving Lacie rather less happy than she had been. She wandered around a counter full of jewellery and after some careful comparisons bought a tie-pin for sixpence.

Soon Gertie swooped down on her and Lacie showed what she had bought. Gertie was unimpressed. She had no intention of buying *her* dad a tie-pin. *Her* dad rarely wore a tie.

They went on looking around the store. Although it had seemed an Aladdin's Cave of treasures to Gertie when she first went in she was the one who could not find anything to buy. There was nothing in the shop good enough for Mr Sprott. He wouldn't like this. He wouldn't like that – and he wouldn't have THAT if you gave it to him. She picked and chose and changed her mind so often that Lacie soon didn't care two hoots whether he got a present or not.

She was looking at some hair-ribbons when Gertie came to her elbow, and dragged her away to a tray of clay pipes.

'Only a penny each,' cried Gertie. 'I can buy one for him and one for me as well.'

'I didn't know you smoked,' said Lacie. 'What do you want one for?'

'For blowing soap bubbles, of course.' Gertie was excited at the thought already.

On the same stall as the clay pipes were other smoking accessories. Lacie was much attracted by a neat leather tobacco-pouch, and decided that she could afford it. Gertie was most indignant. Her dad was only going to receive one present. Why should Lacie's dad have more?

Lacie took no notice of her and put the little parcel into her pocket with the tiepin.

'What's the good of it?' cried Gertie. 'You won't be able to give it him.'

'Yes, I shall. I'll give it to him when he comes home.'

'What if he don't?' said Gertie.

Lacie said slowly, 'What do you mean?'

'I mean, what if he don't come home?' Gertie was impatient. 'What if he dies?'

Lacie stared at her. The crowds pushed and jostled around them. The chatter, the movement, everybody, everything, receded from her leaving her in the middle of an island. She heard Gertie's voice from a long way off.

'Then you'll have wasted your money,' she was saying.

But Lacie had turned on her heel and was walking away. She heard Gertie call after her, but took no notice and plunged through the crowded shop into the street, not waiting, not even looking for Chloë.

Everything was in a blur and she walked away from the shop without realizing where she was going or what she was doing. Her feet went their own way until she came to the river, a quiet part of it well away from the bridge, where a few rowing boats were for hire and people sat under the trees.

She walked upstream away from the town and into the fields.

After a time the peaceful flow of the water and the amiable behaviour of some ducks seeped into her consciousness. She felt tired and sat down on the bank, her mind a prey to doubts.

Nobody had said that about her father – until Gertie had said it straight out – *Perhaps he'll die*.

Lacie shuddered. How would people tell her if he died? And then she remembered the letter.

Of course. The letter this morning. Two letters, in fact, one to her, one to Chloë, both saying the same thing, both full of cheerful news and the promise of better.

Lacie sighed out a long breath and with it her doubt left her.

But she hated Gertie Sprott!

She hated Owsterley.

She hated this place.

A breeze lifted up her straw hat so that she had to grab it to stop it from being blown off. A sudden rage filled her. She hated this hat.

She took it off and threw it in the river.

The ducks quacked and made a dash for it. She looked around guiltily to see if anybody had been watching.

The river was almost deserted. Further up one or two anglers were hunched up in their own thoughts and had not noticed her. On the opposite bank a young man and a girl were sitting but they were looking at each other.

Only one little boy, all by himself and looking rather forlorn, brightened up a bit as he came nearer to her and said, 'What did you do that for?'

She ignored him, hoping that he would go away, but he came closer and stood looking at the hat floating downstream.

'Why did you chuck it in? Didn't you like it? What will your mam say?' he asked nearly all at once.

'Go away!' said Lacie as he stopped for breath. 'Mind your own business or you may get your ears boxed.'

She walked away from him and soon felt sorry that she had snapped at him.

Her hat was in midstream now. She walked down-stream in the same direction as it was floating, and watched it.

Would it sail past Owsterley, past The King of the River, past the Sprott house and Nettlewood? Would it soon be pulled apart by water-birds or would it go floating on to the sea? Would it meet the river monster, the Aegir, and be dashed to pieces by the tides?

She felt rather sorry now, and helpless, as she saw it floating to its doom, its bit of blue ribbon trailing in the water.

Then she felt happier. Throwing it away had done her good, never mind what anybody would say about it. Chloë would probably tell her off but . . .

Chloë!

In a panic Lacie remembered her promise to meet Chloë on that spot outside the Penny Bazaar.

And what about Gertie? After all she was the younger. She was only an infant – even though a Top Infant – and she had been left alone, abandoned in the middle of a busy town. Suppose Gertie had come look-ing for her? There would be a lost child. There would probably have to be a town crier going round, a man ringing a bell, and wearing a notice board back and front.

'OYEZ! OYEZ! OYEZ! LOST! LOST! An infant girl called Gertie Sprott!'

Lacie had once seen a town crier in a town far away.

Common sense came to her rescue and stopped her panicstricken thoughts. If Gertie were lost Gertie would jolly soon find herself. If the worst came to the worst she could find her way back to Owsterley.

'I'll be as quick as I can,' thought Lacie, 'perhaps

they haven't been waiting so very long, after all.' But she had lost all idea of the time and soon found out that she had not much idea of the way back to the shops. In her headlong flight she had failed to notice a single landmark.

She turned first one corner then another. There was nobody to ask, for she was in a very quiet part of the town where the houses had their blinds drawn and stood in deserted gardens.

On a wall a sleepy cat sat and blinked. Lacie went up to it and stroked it. It didn't bother to purr or even to wave its tail. An impassive cat, it showed neither pleasure nor displeasure, nor any sign that it was aware of her existence.

'Not like a dog,' she thought, still stroking it from head to tail, 'a dog would have tried to say "Hullo". A dog would wag its tail or jump up at me. Even if it didn't like me a dog would do something.'

The cat did something, suddenly. It put out its claws and scratched her hand, then it arched its back, gave a resounding shriek, rushed into some bushes, and sat muttering to itself.

Instantly a nearby window opened and a voice cried, 'What are you doing to that cat?'

Lacie looked up and saw an angry face stuck out between the two halves of a window.

'Leave that cat alone!' cried the face. 'Just wait till I come down. I'll teach you to tease dumb animals.'

The 'dumb' animal, growling and spitting, was giving every sign of being able to look after its own interests.

The face disappeared. Lacie had no intention of waiting for it to come down and teach her a lesson so she ran down the street and was relieved when she turned the corner.

She was beginning to feel deceived by the world in general. So much had gone wrong this afternoon, people, cats, hats, everything.

'As if I look the sort of person who pulls cats' tails!' she thought.

After a time she saw a street piano propped up at the side of the road. A man was coming out of a gate by the side of a house. He was counting some coins in his cap and did not notice her. He put the coins in his pocket, the cap on his head, took up the shafts of the piano and began to wheel it up the street.

Lacie's deduction was that if he were trying to earn his living by playing the piano he would be going to the streets where the crowds were — which was where the shops were, which was where she wanted to be.

She decided to follow him.

The neighbourhood gradually became less grand, with shabbier houses and smaller gardens. The sun did not shine here, everywhere looked dismal. She wished the street piano would play one of its tunes to cheer things up a bit.

She had once seen a street organ with a monkey sitting on it. It had been rather amusing at first, but then sad, to see the small creature in its suit of red velveteen. It had held out a little cap to her. Her father had taken a snapshot of her giving it some coins.

The piano gave a sudden jangle of notes and she jumped back to the present with a shock. She had just opened her mouth in a smile to ask the man if he would mind telling her the way to the High Street when he planted down his feet, turned to look at her and said,

'Hey, kid, what are y' follerin' me for? 'Op it. Go an foller somebody else – ' and he wheeled the piano up a narrow passage between two narrow houses in such an aggravated manner that the notes jangled all the way.

The street led into another, and that into another. A small, red car slowly passed the end of the road ahead of her. The driver wore a red band around her head.

Nora.

Lacie began to run. If only she could catch the car before it disappeared. What a ridiculous hope! She looked down the road where the car had gone. There was no sign of it.

She swallowed her disappointment. For a moment relief had seemed so close. To make her feel worse she had lost a button from one shoe and she had a blister on one heel.

She came up to some children playing hopscotch and asked them the way to the shops. They stared at her as if she had spoken a foreign language.

The biggest boy said, 'Ho, do HEXCUSE me, H'IME LORST,' and they all toppled about laughing.

By accident or design the flat stone which was being used in the game skidded over the pavement and caught her on the ankle. The unexpected pain made her wince and the children shrieked with mirth.

Lacie picked up the stone. Evidently this was regarded as an important possession for at once their hilarity changed to concern.

' 'Ere. Give us that.'

'No.'

The leader of the gang stepped towards her. Lacie's hand lifted itself, fingers tightening over the stone.

One child yelled, 'Look out, she's going to chuck it.'

Lacie said nothing as the leader took a purposeful step towards her.

He moved closer.

Suddenly Lacie flung the stone behind her over her shoulder into somebody's yard.

There was the sound of breaking glass.

All the children fled.

Lacie stood still, struck with unbelief. She, Lacie Lindrick, had picked up a stone in the street and flung it through somebody's window.

She dared not look behind her to find out the damage she had done. She would just have to stay and face the consequences. She couldn't run in her buttonless shoe. What would happen now? Would somebody fetch a policeman? Would she be arrested?

She *must* run. But her feet would not move.

There was a sound further up the street. A familiar sound – the chug-chug of a motor bicycle. A horn hooted.

The motor bicycle stopped.

'Lacie!' said Mr Springles pushing up his motoring goggles. 'What on earth's going on? What are you doing here all by yourself? I thought you were supposed to be shopping with Chloë.'

Lacie just looked at him.

'Never mind,' he said. 'Jump in the side-car.'

'I – I'm afraid I can't,' said Lacie. 'I – you see – I've just broken somebody's window.'

'What!' He got off the motor bicycle and came towards her, a strangely contorted expression on his face. Was it a dreadfully serious matter, then? He couldn't be going to laugh.

'I saw those kids,' he was saying.

'They didn't do it,' said Lacie. 'I did. It was my stone. At least it was theirs – but I threw it.'

'Well – let's have a look then.' He went to look over a wall into a yard. 'I can't see any broken windows.'

Lacie took heart and went to his side.

'There you are,' he said. 'Look at that. You've broken somebody's old jam-jar. Now you can get in the side-car.'

And Lacie got in.

'We'd better get a move on,' said Mr Springles as he started up the motor bicycle . . . 'or Chloë won't like it at all. Tell me where you left her and we'll just hope she's still there.'

And Chloë was still there – with Gertie – pacing up and down outside the Penny Bazaar.

9

Profit and Loss

MR SPRINGLES managed everything beautifully. The apologies and explanations could come later, he said. He calmed Chloë's nerves, got her into the side-car with Lacie, put Gertie on the pillion, then whisked them away to the River Rover café where he had already ordered tea.

At last they were all sitting down at a table in the window and a supply of good things began to arrive . . .

It was a pleasant occasion . . . but for Lacie there was a cloud at the back of it all. The day had been rescued from total collapse and yet – it had seemed like perfection this morning.

Perhaps it was the disappointment of losing perfection that made her silent and unable to eat very much. She even refused a cream bun.

Chloë looked at her with mild reproach and Lacie was conscious of a slight fall from grace. There was a lump in her throat and she stared at a bit of tablecloth in front of her. When she looked up again she saw that Mr Springles was watching her, and as they all got up from the table he patted her hand, and whispered, ' "*Courage, mon amie, le diable est mort*," in other words, Cheer up !'

Chloë glanced through the window, and remarked to

Gertie, 'I thought you said your father wasn't coming into Hawksop, today.'

Gertie also looked through the window, then with a piercing yell of, 'Medad! It's me dad!' so that everybody in the café looked round and stared, she rushed into the street and dashed at her father who nearly fell over in surprise.

While Mr Springles paid the bill Chloë and Lacie stepped into the street just in time to hear Mr Sprott say, 'No, you can't go home with me. I've got to go somewhere else first.'

'Why can't I go with you?'

'Because you can't,' said Mr Sprott. 'That's why. I'm going somewhere you can't go. Now shut up and be quiet,' and with a hurried nod in the direction of Chloë he dived off into the crowd.

Gertie with a rebellious thrust to her jaw stared after him.

'Hullo!' remarked Mr Springles coming up. 'More trouble?'

'There'd better not be.' Chloë frowned at Gertie who was saying in a loud voice that she'd a good mind not to go home at all now, never!

Mr Springles nodded to somebody passing by and remarked that all Owsterley seemed to be in Hawksop.

'And they'll all see how badly behaved you are,' Chloë told Gertie who did not care a scrap.

'Cousin Nora's here too,' said Lacie, amiably trying to take attention from Gertie. 'At least I'm almost sure I saw her.'

Chloë was most surprised.

'I think it was Nora,' said Lacie. 'She was in a little red car and wearing that red bandeau thing.'

'Sounds like her,' said Chloë. 'Well! Well!'

She looked thoughtful.

Bertie Bisset came out of a shop across the road and stood for a moment to glance at a newspaper he had bought.

'Bertie!' yelled Gertie. 'It's me! I'm here!' and she darted across the street.

Chloë, Mr Springles and Lacie made their way more cautiously through the traffic.

Mrs Bisset was in the market hall. Bertie had just nipped out for a newspaper – he could only afford one on Saturdays but believed in buying what he considered the best – and was now going back to help his mother to pack up their market things.

'Let's go and see Missy Bissy,' shouted Gertie, pulling at Chloë's arm. 'You promised we could.' So they all went to the market hall, Gertie following closely at Bertie's heels.

'Bertie's a very clever boy,' Chloë whispered to Lacie. 'It didn't take George long to see that. He soon had him sitting for a scholarship – and winning it too. It was the first in Owsterley and all through George.'

Mrs Bissett looked delighted to see her visitors, although Gertie's yell of 'Missy Bissy!' had startled her just as she was taking her first sip of some very hot tea.

'Why, it's Gertie,' she gasped, mopping up tea and knocking over a couple of baskets, 'and if it isn't Chloë Campion and Mr Springles. Well, well – and the little visitor.'

When all the greetings were over and she had got some breath again she turned to Gertie and asked, 'What are you doing in Hawksop on a Sat'dy afternoon? Is your dad here as well?'

Gertie's face clouded over. 'I don't know where he is,' she said.

The situation was explained at the same time by Chloë and Gertie in two different versions. Chloë bought some eggs and cream cheese, went behind a screen of piled up baskets for a few words in private with Mrs Bisset, then came out again smiling, and nodded to Mr Springles.

After a few minutes Mrs Bisset asked if Gertie and Lacie would give a hand with putting the unsold goods back in the baskets – only a few eggs and lettuces and some flowers – but a long job was made of it through Mrs Bisset wanting things first in one basket then another.

'What does it matter?' cried Gertie at last, then the two girls looked up and saw that Chloë and Mr Springles were not there.

'They won't be long,' said Mrs Bisset. 'They've just gone round the corner.'

Gertie saw a cream cheese sandwich and said she was hungry.

'You could have it if it was mine,' said Mrs Bisset, 'but it's Bertie's. He hadn't time to finish his tea.'

'Go on, eat it,' said Bertie, so Gertie demolished it as if she hadn't eaten a crumb the whole day. Mrs Bisset gave her a Bisset-grown tomato as well.

Soon Chloë and Mr Springles returned, looking as if they were sharing some pleasant secret.

'There's these crates to put in t'trap love,' said Mrs Bisset to Bertie, 'then we've just about finished.' She turned to Mr Springles. 'He's worked so well he deserves a medal.'

'Bertie always works well.' Mr Springles directed a

look of approval to his former pupil. 'That's why he's got where he is.'

Lacie was aware that he meant Hawksop Grammar School, not Hawksop market.

'And,' added Mr Springles, unknowingly echoing Bertie's last school report, 'he'll go further yet, much further.'

Mrs Bisset beamed.

Bertie, meanwhile, was counting the money which had been taken in the day's business.

'We've nearly sold out,' said Mrs Bisset, 'except for an egg or two, but we can eat them for our breakfasts, and there's a few lettuces and flowers left over. That's all.'

'Excellent!' said Mr Springles, awarding her full marks too as if she were another industrious pupil. 'Very good indeed.'

There was a general move, then Gertie suddenly flung herself at Mrs Bisset, almost knocking her over for the second time, and cried, 'Can I go home with you, Missy Bissy, oh let me go home with you an' Bertie in pony and trap.'

Mrs Bisset hesitated and looked at Bertie. She knew he was looking forward to reading the news when he got home, after he had seen to the pony and trap and the fowls and the pig and any other little matters which might have accumulated for him in his absence. He gave his mother a resigned nod, however, and Gertie was in a seventh heaven. Having gained one point she proceeded to press another.

'Can I stay all night?' she pleaded.

'But your dad won't know where you are,' Mrs Bisset objected.

Gertie said that her dad wouldn't care where she was.

'That's not true!' Mrs Bisset was most indignant, 'and you know it isn't,' then she said, 'I suppose Bertie could cycle over.' And Gertie began to dance about.

Chloë put in a suggestion.

'We'll tell Fred. If he's still not at home we'll leave a note.'

'He's been out for the day, has he?' asked Mrs Bisset.

' An' he won't tell me where,' Gertie rushed in.

'He doesn't have to tell you where he goes,' said Mrs Bisset – 'or anybody else either.'

'Shall I tell him you'll be home tomorrow?' Chloë asked Gertie, who shrugged her shoulders and said she'd go home when she felt like it.

'You'd better feel like coming to school on Monday,' Chloë reminded her. 'It's the last week of the term and your last week in the Little School.'

'Is she really going up at last?' asked Bertie.

Gertie looked serious, almost awestruck, at the thought.

Bertie came to Lacie with a bunch of roses and long-stemmed daisies.

'Ma says you and Miss Campion are to have these.'

Mrs Bisset smiled in the background. All the goodbyes were said.

'Goodbye Lacie,' said Bertie again.

'Come on! Come on!' shouted Gertie, and the two of them went off, Mrs Bisset following them.

Chloë sighed and Mr Springles said, 'Well! There goes Gertie!'

'She never even said "thank you" for the tea,' said Lacie.

They went the short way home, the field way by the side of the river bank, over the pot-holes and the hump-back bridge at Two Drains.

'Hold tight!' cried Mr Springles as they flew over the bridge.

'Whoops!' screamed Chloë, and laughed as she bumped in her seat. 'Some day somebody's going to fly right out going over that!'

When they arrived at School Cottage it was Lacie who remembered the note to Mr Sprott. Chloë had been laughing and talking so much she had forgotten all about it.

The Sprott house was in total gloom. There was not a flicker of life anywhere.

'No use knocking the door down,' said Chloë to Mr Springles. 'He hasn't come back from wherever he's been.'

She gave a little shiver as she looked at the dark windows and higgledy-piggledy roofs.

'I think I'd like to go to bed if you don't mind,' Lacie said in School Cottage.

'What! No supper?' said Mr Springles.

'She doesn't need any after that huge tea,' said Chloë. 'I'm sure I don't.'

Lacie felt the remark was rather uncalled for. She had not eaten a particularly huge tea.

'You've got a letter to write tomorrow,' said Chloë. 'Don't forget.'

Another unnecessary remark!

'Off you go then,' she added as Lacie hung about the door. 'We'll forgive you.'

'Sleep well,' added Mr Springles.

For what was she being forgiven? Lacie wondered as she went upstairs. Just for going to bed when Chloë and Mr Springles obviously didn't at all mind being left by themselves? No, Chloë must have been referring to the escapade of the afternoon. Lacie knew she had been wrong to rush away by herself and she hadn't really explained. She would go down again and make matters, if not right, at least better, by saying she was sorry.

Just as she opened the living-room door Mr Springles leaped in the air and landed at the other side of the room. He had been putting his arm round Chloë.

'Well, what is it now?' Chloë sounded annoyed.

'I'm sorry,' said Lacie.

'What about?'

'About this afternoon. Everything.'

'All right!' said Chloë. 'There was no need to come down again just to say that.'

Lacie had been thinking that if she could explain about Gertie's careless words in the Bazaar, Chloë would be sure to understand.

It was no use.

She swallowed any further attempt to explain and went back to her room but when she put her head on the pillow her heart was swollen with the enormity of the world's capacity for misunderstanding.

10

'See How They Twinkle'

'I'VE something to tell you,' Chloë said the next morning at breakfast, looking as if the sun were shining specially for her.

'I know,' Lacie smiled, 'you're engaged.'

'Well!' Chloë took a deep breath. 'You might have let me say it first.' But she looked pleased, and held out her left hand. 'There it is.'

An elegant ring was on the third finger. Diamonds!

'See how they twinkle,' Chloë said.

After a time she asked, 'How did you know about George and me?'

Lacie smiled. It had all been so obvious.

'Lots of ways,' she said. 'Gertie knew too. We were just waiting for you to tell.'

'Gertie!' said Chloë. 'I hope she's not spreading it all over the place. I'd like to be the one to announce my own engagement if you please ... not Gertie Sprott.'

'Gertie says – ' Lacie hesitated, then went on – 'Gertie says that there's still a bit of iron in him somewhere, left from him getting blown up, nearly. She says nobody could get it out. She says ever so many doctors – '

'That child!' Chloë was exasperated. 'Really!' She paused. 'He did have quite a bad time – but he's all right now.' She poured out a cup of tea. 'He's much better since he came to Owst'ley. Since the war ended he's got quite strong. There's nothing to worry about.'

'It's a pity he couldn't be like Mr Sprott,' said Lacie. 'He's strong. He was in the war but he didn't get hurt.'

Chloë sipped her tea, looked at her ring twinkling, and said, 'We got it yesterday. Don't you think I'm lucky?' Lacie did think so. She was growing very fond of George.

The church bells were ringing.

'I'll go and get ready,' said Chloë. 'If I wear my ring in church it will be one way of telling everybody about it. And we'll have a little drive to Nettlewood this afternoon and show it to Nora.'

Lacie had mixed feelings about visiting Nora and about going to Nettlewood again, but she said nothing, only rattled some pots as she washed up and broke a saucer.

Later she stood watching the river and listening to the church bells.

Mr Sprott was on the waterside dabbling paint on the *Wobbler*. He saw Lacie and moved his hand slightly in acknowledgement of her existence.

'Off to church?' he asked.

Lacie nodded, then said, 'Is Gertie home?'

'No, she isn't. Can't you tell?'

Everything certainly was very quiet around the Sprott house. 'She ought to have her ears boxed,' said Mr Sprott, 'spoiled little monkey. Anyway, she's got a long walk home when she does decide to come. She's got her new shoes on too. She'll know about them before she gets here.' And he grinned.

Chloë came out of School Cottage. Lacie moved away from the river and went to her.

'Haven't you any gloves?' Chloë asked.

'They're in my pocket.'

'Put them on then, it's Sunday. That hat doesn't look too bad.'

It was one of Nora's, slightly altered.

Lacie sighed.

'Gertie Sprott's not going to church – and she doesn't have to wear gloves or a hat.'

'Well, you're not Gertie Sprott,' said Chloë. 'Thank goodness, here's George coming. We'll be lucky if we get in church before the last bell stops.'

As they drew near to the church they saw a pony and trap coming towards them.

'It's Gertie Sprott!' cried Lacie. Bertie Bisset was driving the pony at a spanking pace and Gertie had her nose stuck in the air.

George drew up off the track so as to give the trap plenty of room to pass.

'Whoa!' said Bertie, and brought the pony to a standstill.

Gertie's hair had been well brushed and was tied up with a pink ribbon. To make sure it was noticed she tossed her head in a proud way.

'Very nice, Gertie,' remarked Chloë. 'Somebody's been making you look smart.'

'It was Missy Bissy,' Gertie replied. 'She got the ribbon off a choc'late box, and she's give me a great big pie for medad's dinner.'

'Sssh!' said Chloë, 'don't tell everybody in church.'

While George Springles was exchanging a few intelligent words with Bertie as to the quantity and quality of his homework at the Grammar School, Gertie was indulging in some horrible grimaces to Lacie, a sort of secret language which Lacie understood to mean, 'Has she said anything yet?'

'I shan't tell you,' thought Lacie, and stubbornly refused to answer the grimaces until Gertie could bear it no longer, and twirling an imaginary ring around her finger – on the wrong hand – she let the question out with a loud hiss, 'Has she got the ring on?'

Lacie looked as if she didn't understand, Bertie said 'Gee up!' Gertie pulled a face and the trap went on its way.

Chloë remarked to George that it was extraordinary how kids knew everything these days.

Lacie turned to look after the pony trap with more than a twinge of envy. Gertie did seem to be having a good time.

Chloë and George were already walking towards the church.

'Come along, Lacie!' called Chloë. 'Don't stand dreaming. That's the last bell and the organ's nearly finished the voluntary. I know when Jessima Throssel's got to the end of it. She plays all wrong notes.'

The service that morning was being taken by Mr Bindle, one of the two young curates attached to the mother church at Hawksop. They took it in turn to bicycle through the fields, Sunday by Sunday, to attend to the souls of Owsterley, or at least to those souls which had persuaded their bodies into church.

It wasn't long before all knew about Chloë's engagement ring. From the moment she took off her gloves the message from the little bits of diamond flashed its way into the dimmest corners of the church.

In the side-pews under the windows were the Sunday-school children. They knew. Miss Epiphany Throssel was in charge of them. She knew. Lacie saw her look in Chloë's direction, stare, send a telepathic telegram to post office Jessima at the organ, then rattle the knuckles of two little boys with her spectacle case.

After the service Mr Bindle sprang from vestry to porch and was waiting for the congregation to emerge. When Chloë came up to him he wagged a finger at her.

So *he* knew.

Outside church a little crowd gathered around Chloë. She was prevailed upon to exhibit her diamond ring. Both Miss Throssels came pattering up and gave it a shrewd examination, and only by an afterthought added their good wishes.

Mr Bindle was to eat his Sunday dinner at George's lodgings. The piece of beef he was to eat was being roasted as he stood outside the church. The pudding was being turned at that very minute.

Suddenly, as if by an ethereal message from beef and pudding, Mr Bindle cut short the conversations he was holding with his flock, jumped on his wheels and set off through the fields in the direction of Owsterley. At the same moment George detached Chloë from the ring's admirers and detractors, and got her and Lacie into the side-car.

They soon passed Mr Bindle who was pedalling strongly in the direction of his dinner.

From the village an odour of roast beef floated out as if in greeting to the church-goers.

At dinner the grown-ups were jovial. With George carving the meat and Chloë serving the Yorkshire pudding it was almost as if they were married already.

George went to a cupboard and brought out a bottle of red wine.

'Oh dear!' said Mr Bindle. 'Oh dear, dear, dear! Dare I?' Then he dared because it was such a special occasion. (Chloë had reminded him of it by flashing her ring.)

He refused a second glass, reminding them all that he had still a lot more bicycling to do that day. There was a bicycle ride back to Sunday school at three o'clock, another ride to the Misses Throssel for tea, another ride to church for evening service and after that the long haul to his lodgings in Hawksop.

He was extremely active both spiritually and physically on his Owsterley Sundays.

The theme of his conversation over dinner was that of 'lucky chaps'.

George was a lucky chap, the luckiest of chaps, while he, poor Bindle, wasn't half so lucky. He was a fool, an idiot who took too long about things and missed his chances. He looked at Chloë so mournfully that she immediately refilled his plate with pudding. He sighed after he had eaten it, and yawned. It had been a very large helping and a very heavy pudding.

On the way to Nettlewood, George said to Chloë, 'Do you know, I think Bindle's been a bit sweet on you.'

'What?' shouted Chloë, so George had to shout it again.

'He never said anything to me about it,' said Chloë. After a time she began to laugh. George wanted to know the joke.

'I hope he's got over the wine,' she said. 'He's going to tea at the Throssels — and they don't believe in wine.'

Hawksop was wrapped in its Sunday calm and George moderated the noise of the engine somewhat until they had gone over the bridge.

The river rippled and glinted in the sunshine.

Soon they turned off the main road and went along the bumpy lane that led to Nettlewood.

They had to proceed more slowly because of the pot-holes. The air seemed gentler here and blew lazily. Lacie took off her hat. Chloë's long scarf floated behind her, her hair was softened and some of it escaped its pins. She began to sing.

George joined in and they sang in duet.

One more week.
One week more,
Only one more week of
S-C-H-O-O-L

Lacie had never seen grown-ups — and certainly she had never seen teachers — behave in such a way.

Still singing, George drove across the rickety bridge over the empty moat and still singing, rattled the motor bicycle and side-car around the gravel path before drawing up at the bottom of the front steps. Then Nora whirled out of the gloom of the hall ex-

116

claiming, 'What on earth do you think you're doing? I thought it was a circus.'

After a moment she calmed down and took them to her private sitting-room, promising that they should have tea presently. She was free for an hour as Granny Betts was sitting with Mrs Mountsorrel.

When the ring had been shown and the engagement discussed Chloë wanted to know how Nora was getting on with everything?

Nora shrugged her shoulders and lit a cigarette. She was wearing a white dress, and the red bandeau around her hair – it *was* her yesterday, thought Lacie – and didn't look at all like a nurse.

Chloë wanted to know where Nora's bedroom was and whether it was damp. It was along the corridor, on the ground floor, near the oldest and sealed off part of the house, and it was damp.

'Oh dear! And where's Mrs Mountsorrel?' asked Chloë.

Mrs Mountsorrel's room was facing the river on the east side of the house and that was damper than anywhere else.

Oh dear!

It was the old school room. All the upstairs rooms were unusable. Then Nora went on to say that all the kitchens but one were out of use, most of the roofs had fallen in, the stairs were in danger of imminent collapse, and, in short, the whole place was likely to fall down at any minute – 'and if you say "Oh dear!" once more I'll scream,' she finished.

'Oh dear!' said Chloë.

Nora looked at her, then laughed. They all laughed.

'I wish I could get into the old part,' George began.

'You can't. I've told you it's sealed off,' Nora interrupted him.

'Pity,' said George, 'those underground parts are where you'll find the history of Nettlewood.'

Lacie's thoughts had been going their own way. 'Find what?' she asked. 'The monster?'

George was mystified. Chloë and Nora laughed.

'It lives in the tunnels,' said Nora, 'and frightens naughty children.'

Her eye fell on Lacie who immediately felt indignant.

'What rubbish!' George was quite annoyed. 'How people will distort simple facts. Those secret cells and tunnels were almost certainly hiding places and escape routes for the monks. This place has seen troubled times.'

'What place hasn't?' asked Nora, looking bored.

Suddenly she sprang to her feet and went to fetch tea.

'She won't stay,' Chloë said.

'You never can tell with Nora,' George replied. 'She may be enjoying herself for all we know. Anyway, she doesn't look too fed up, if you ask me. She's got a sort of look about her — '

Soon Nora was back with the tea and cakes.

Delicious cakes. Chloë was surprised.

'Rose Fennell made them,' Nora said. 'She comes in every day and does the meals and the baking.'

Chloë was pleased. Such a nice girl, Rose, a relief from cross old Granny Betts with her bonnet of bees.

Lacie thought of the pink sunbonnet as the two sisters chatted and laughed. Talking of bees in bonnets what about the boy Tom? Poor Tom. Goodness!

The bees he had in his bonnet – never mind his bonnet, in his head! And as for Mrs Mountsorrel she'd stirred up a whole hive.

'I've never heard so many bees in my life,' Nora looked pathetic, 'and they're all buzzing around poor little me.'

'Bees don't only sting,' said Lacie in defence of bees in general. 'They make honey as well, you know.'

'I'm sure you mean something,' said Nora, 'but I can't think what.'

Then she laughed and said BUZZZ-BZZZ-BZZZZ – and spun about the room in a ridiculous manner as she handed round the rest of Rose Fennell's home-made cakes.

11

The Black Kitten

AFTER tea Lacie went with George to the wood and showed him the mysterious hillock. It was an old ice-house, he explained, where ice taken from winter ponds had been preserved in straw and earth for use in the summer. He tried to open the door but it was stuck fast and he had to sit down to get his breath back. No, he wasn't strong, not like some people. He wouldn't be able to haul boats across the ferry, for instance.

Poor old George. It wasn't fair that others, not half so pleasant, should be so much stronger.

He soon discovered the hidden stream, and when Lacie told him how long she had looked for it the other day he teased her and said that looking wasn't always seeing.

When they were back in the house Chloë suddenly announced that she and George were going for a little ride by themselves. Even George looked rather surprised. Nora stared, then said, Oh well, all right, but she was on duty in a minute and wouldn't have time for amusing anybody.

'Lacie doesn't mind amusing herself,' said Chloë.

'She's used to her own company. Aren't you, dear?'

Lacie supposed that she was used to it. She was certainly getting plenty of it nowadays ... but she didn't say that.

Chloë began to wind her scarf around her hair, and said to Nora, 'We'll pick her up in an hour.'

Lacie keep silent. It wasn't pleasant to feel like a parcel which was alternately deposited and collected. Soon she and Nora were standing on the front steps and watching George drive Chloë away. The machine whirled around the carriage drive, making a circle, then went over the wooden bridge, rattling all the footboards.

'Stupid thing,' said Nora. 'Driving over that bridge.'

She gave Lacie rather a severe look and said, 'Remember! No disappearing act this time!' Then she disappeared.

Lacie ran after her, not wanting to be alone.

'Oh dear!' exclaimed Nora. 'You're not intending to traipse after me everywhere I go, are you? I'm going into the sick-room in a minute.'

They went past a door which was half-open. Lacie peeped round it and saw a vast chamber with an arched roof, and ropes of cobwebs everywhere.

'That was the servants' hall,' Nora said. 'Poor devils. You'll get lost if you wander about on your own.'

They were now in one of the smaller kitchens which, as Nora pointed out, was at least clean, and if not exactly cheerful, was less dismal than it might have been. 'And that means a lot here,' she said.

There was a depressing mound of ashes in the grate, not a spark of fire, but that didn't matter. There was a spirit-stove in a little room next to Mrs Mountsorrel's where Nora could boil a kettle — so if Lacie should want some cocoa before she went home —

Lacie hastened to say that she wouldn't want any.

'That's the sort of thing that annoys me about you,' exclaimed Nora. 'How do you know now what you won't want later on?'

Lacie offered to wash up the tea-things but Nora told her to leave everything for Granny Betts or Rose Fennell and to go and amuse herself.

Yes. But how?

Nora disappeared and Lacie wandered back to the sitting-room.

A foot scrunched on the gravel under the window. Startled, she looked outside.

Poor Tom was there, staring at her. He was not wearing a corn scoop this time but there was something on his head, something vaguely familiar to her, but before she had time for another look he had gone.

'Wait,' she called and ran outside.

The terrace at the front was deserted so she went round a corner of the house.

Poor Tom was not to be seen. Disappointed, she turned back, then something made her look behind her.

He was there, looking at her.

'Hullo!' she said. 'You're Tom, aren't you?'

He shook a thatch of fair hair.

'But you are. You're Tom Betts,' she insisted. 'I know you are.'

'I'm Poor Tom,' he said, 'If you know about me you should know that. I'm Bad Luck,' he added.

'I didn't know that.'

'Well, you know now, 'cos I've told you.' He looked

doleful. 'My other name's Misfortune. Ask me granny.'

Lacie decided to change the trend of the conversation. 'You made me jump, just now,' she told him. 'I didn't know you were there.'

'I'm not there, am I?' he answered, ' 'cos I'm here.'

'You were there a minute ago, outside the window,' said Lacie. 'and you were wearing a hat, a straw hat.'

'You can't have that,' he said quickly.

'I don't want it.' She was about to say that she had recently owned one very much like it and had been glad to get rid of it, when he suddenly leaped from the terrace down the steep bank into the sea of long grass. It was called mowing grass — she had been told that afternoon — because it was to be mown for hay. You were not supposed to tread it down to spoil it for the mowers.

Poor Tom should have known that . . . but perhaps nobody cared about the grass at Nettlewood, whether it were long or short . . . and who would be the mowers anyway?

He stood knee deep in it and beckoned to her. She took a deep breath, flung herself down the bank, then waded through the grass till she stood beside him. He put his finger on his lips, then making a sign for her to follow him, made his way along a narrow path only as wide as the sole of a foot.

He stopped, and crouched. Deep in the grass, in a comfortable nest, was a sumptuous black cat lying at ease amongst four black kittens.

'Nice cat,' said Poor Tom. 'Tiss! Tiss! Tiss!'

As he touched her she began to purr. Lacie knelt down amongst the clover and sorrel and moonpennies

123

and trembling grass. She put out her hand, then drew it back again. Two red weals across her wrist had reminded her of the cat of yesterday in Hawksop.

Poor Tom saw the scratches, took her hand and with it stroked the cat. 'Friends now,' he said, taking his hand away, and Lacie went on stroking.

The kittens were quite old enough to leave their mother. Poor Tom took one of them, the prettiest, Lacie thought, and holding it against his chest, got up to go.

She followed him into the courtyard behind the house. He went into a scullery and came out with a saucer of milk which he put down in front of the kitten. It began to lap immediately as if there were nothing in the world but lapping milk.

After a time she said that she must be going.

'Where to?' asked Poor Tom.

'Well – to Owsterley eventually,' she replied.

'My! That's a bad place,' said Poor Tom.

'Is it?' Lacie was surprised. 'I don't think it is.'

'A very bad place,' went on Poor Tom, 'there's lads there that throw stones at folks and take folks' hats and throw 'em in a ditch – and they throw folks in too, even if they're just a little lad.'

'They – folks wouldn't do it now,' said Lacie, who had understood what he meant – 'Not now you – not now folks are grown so much bigger.'

'Oh, wouldn't they?' said Poor Tom. 'I wouldn't put it past 'em. Anyway I'm not going to find out . . . I'm staying here. And if folks want me to go away . . . I'll hide myself and they'll have a job finding me. Don't tell on me, though.' He looked at Lacie in sudden fear.

124

'I shan't tell anybody anything.' she said. 'I'm very good at secrets.'

'I'm all secrets,' he said, 'I reckon I'm made of 'em.'

He fondled the black kitten which had finished all the milk.

'There was just me granny and me once,' he said, 'for a long time. We was all on our own, and everything was all right. Just Granny and me . . . then folks started coming, badgerin' and botherin'. Oh, I'm in a muddle.'

'So am I,' said Lacie, 'often.'

'I'm always in one,' said Poor Tom, 'specially now. It's because the world's too wicked for me. At least, that's what Granny says.'

He picked up the empty saucer.

'But I shan't go,' he declared. 'I shan't go anywhere with anybody.'

'I don't suppose anybody would want you to,' Lacie tried to soothe him.

'Oh, wouldn't they?' said Poor Tom, 'What do you know about – about – HER . . . ?' He jerked his head towards the house.

Did he mean Nora?

'She'll have a job to get hold of me . . . 'cos I'll be missing. Nobody'll find me. I'm not going to let anybody take me to It'ly.'

'You can't mean Mrs Mountsorrel, surely?' said Lacie.

'Oh, can't I?' Tom replied. 'Who else talks about me dressing different and talking different and being improved? Not me granny Betts. She likes me as I am.'

'But she's so ill – Mrs Mountsorrel I mean. She can't do anything.'

'P'raps she can't now,' said Poor Tom. 'But what about when she's better? But don't you worry. I've got somewhere to go where nobody'll find me.'

'My goodness, he has got a bee in his bonnet,' thought Lacie.

'Don't tell anybody,' he said, again.

'No I won't. I've promised you that.'

He was pleased with her answer and picked up the kitten which was playing with a feather.

'Shall I take the saucer into the house?' Lacie asked.

But he kept the saucer, and held out the kitten, saying, 'It's for you.'

Pleasure and doubt conflicted in Lacie. She hesitated.

'Don't you want him?' asked Poor Tom.

She put her cheek against the kitten's fur.

'Oh yes! But perhaps they won't let me keep him.'

'They!' said Poor Tom. 'I know THEY. THEY's always spoiling things. That's all THEY ever do.'

Lacie gently hugged the kitten.

'I'll try to keep him,' she said, 'if I'm not allowed to I'll give him back to you.' And saying goodbye to Poor Tom, she left him and went back to the house carrying the kitten and breathing against its fur.

At the front door she hesitated. The house seemed full of darkness.

The kitten mewed. She stroked it and felt reassured. She moved slowly across the hall and somehow found her way to Nora's sitting-room.

Nobody was there. It was very gloomy.

'Of course you can see quite easily,' she said to the kitten.

It was too dark to read. She had no idea where there was a lamp or a candle.

'We'll just sit in the window-seat and hope somebody comes soon,' she told the kitten. She could feel its plump little stomach. At any rate it was not hungry.

The kitten however was feeling adventurous and did not want to stay in Lacie's arms.

'If I put you down p'raps you won't come back to me,' she told it. 'Still, if you run away you are in your own house. You'd soon find your way back to your mother . . . I wish I could.'

The last thought came so quickly it took her by surprise.

She put the kitten on the floor. It scampered off, she couldn't see where.

It was disconcerting to sit in a strange dark house and wonder if she would be forgotten !

She was forgotten !

No. Footsteps.

Nora came in.

'All in the dark ? I'll get a light.'

She disappeared and soon came back with a lamp which she put on the table, then went to close the windows saying that moths would get in.

Lacie shivered. She had come in a coat, and Nora told her to put it on so as to be ready to go when the motor bicycle came.

'They're late,' said Nora. 'I knew they would be. What about some cocoa ?'

Lacie thanked her and said no – and then was sorry.

'There you go again !' Nora said, 'of course you'd like some. I'm going to make some anyway. You can come with me if you like.'

So Lacie followed along corridors of musty smelling darkness until Nora opened a door into a small room which seemed dazzlingly cheerful in contrast to the gloom outside it.

Although there was a narrow bed in it the room was not Nora's bedroom. That was on the other side of the house near the oldest sealed-off part. This was just a little service room where Nora could rest – if she got a chance – when on long duties. The sick-room was next door and Mrs Mountsorrel was asleep.

Nora was reaching for cocoa and cups. A kettle was already singing on a spirit stove.

It all looked quite cosy. The cocoa was made, but before they had finished drinking it there was the sound of a motor bicycle coming up the drive.

'Thank the Lord!' said Nora. 'I thought they were never coming.' She dashed off to the hall and Lacie ran after her.

Outside the front door somebody was standing with a torch.

'Who is it?' cried Nora.

'Don't be alarmed, Miss.' The light shone into the hall. 'I'm a police constable.' Nora gasped, and the voice went on, 'Are you a relation of a Miss Chloë Campion?'

'I'm her sister,' said Nora. Lacie's heart was already bumping.

'I'm afraid I have to tell you that there's been an accident,' said the policeman. 'I think I'd better step inside.'

12

Accident!

NORA took a step forward.

For a moment she looked as if she were going to rush off there and then but she pulled herself up and led the way into the sitting-room.

The lamp had been left there and was burning low. She turned up the light.

'I should sit down, Miss, if I were you,' said the policeman. Nora sat down.

The accident though 'nasty' was not fatal. At least the policeman didn't think so, it hadn't been fatal when he had been despatched to tell the news, but of course he couldn't really say how things had been going on since he left.

It was all through that blasted motor bike, Nora said. She had known something would happen.

Where had it happened?

'At Two Drain Bridge,' the policeman said. 'A nasty spot, that. They ought to do away with it before anything else occurs.'

Something had happened to the side-car. He thought it had broken loose, he couldn't be quite sure. The lady had been thrown out.

'How badly hurt – is she?' asked Nora.

It wasn't for a policeman to say.

'I'm only here to tell you of the occurrence,' he said in an official voice, 'and that the accident wasn't fatal, at least it wasn't . . . when I last heard of it.'

Nora sprang to her feet.

'I must go at once,' she cried, then she sat down again. 'But I'm on nursing duty here and . . .' she looked into the shadows and remembered Lacie – 'I'm in charge of this child.'

'Dear oh dear l' said the policeman looking at Lacie, who looked round the room and hung her head. She felt almost ashamed to be there.

Nora looked at Lacie.

'You'll have to stay here,' she said.

Lacie's heart dropped.

'It's not so bad,' said the policeman. 'It could a been worse.' He had already said it several times.

Lacie heard Nora draw in her breath.

The policeman moved his feet two steps nearer the door.

'I shall have to fetch Granny Betts,' Nora said to Lacie. 'She'll grumble, I dare say, but she loves emergencies. You're the problem. You'll have to look after yourself, that's all. All right, officer – ' She remembered the policeman, 'I've got a car. I'll drive myself to the hospital as soon as I've arranged everything here.'

The policeman went away on his motor bicycle.

'I shan't rest till I've found out what's happened,' Nora was saying. 'You'll have to sleep in my bedroom for tonight. You'll be all right. Just try not to think of anything till morning.'

They were already hurrying along a corridor so dark that Lacie had no possible chance of keeping track of the way.

'Here's my room.' Nora at last opened a door, then rushed about opening drawers.

'Here's a nightgown . . . water in a jug over there – soap and towels. You'll soon be asleep.'

She waited at the door as Lacie stood bewildered in the middle of the room. They were two shadows talking to each other.

'You won't be alone in the house,' Nora said, 'because Granny Betts will be here.'

'B-but I won't know where to find her if I want her,' quavered Lacie.

'You'd better not want her,' said Nora. 'You'll just know she's there. That's sufficient.'

She almost shut the door then opened it again. 'Here's a torch,' she said. 'Put it by the side of your bed. If you do need a light – I don't see why you should – well – it'll be there.'

Lacie began to shiver. Her breath hissed through her teeth.

'I hope you're not going to make everything worse than it already is,' said Nora, 'things are bad enough already.'

With an effort Lacie tried to stop her teeth chattering.

'I hope Chloë . . .' she said. 'I'm sorry,' then could not go on.

'We're all sorry,' said Nora, and was gone.

Lacie went to the window and looked out through the green twilight over the expanse of long grass where the cat had its nest. Behind that was the wood, a band of deeper darkness where the owls were already sending their cries to each other.

She threw off her clothes as quickly as she could — she tore off at least one button — and dived into bed, covering her head with the bedclothes and shivering as if she had just jumped into water. She breathed under the sheet and tried to make a little tent full of warm air. She wished she could go straight off to sleep in it but she heard her heart thumping and had to put her head outside the covers again.

If only she had the black kitten with her. How comforting it would be now, how useful, as good as a hot water bottle.

The owls were so close. They were shrieking at her outside the window.

She still hadn't written her answer to the letter her mother had sent.

'The kitten would be so warm . . . I wouldn't mind the owls so much, the *hiboux* . . . iboo . . . iboo . . . iboo,' and she drifted into a troubled sleep which was full of motor bicycles and owls and flashing lights and bridges with humps on them like camels.

She was in a car or on a bicycle . . . or was she running? — and just about to rush over a particularly humpy bridge when she saw a black cat sitting on it. 'I can't stop! I can't stop!' she cried to the cat . . . no, it was a kitten and it answered with the most pitiful mew.

Miaow!

Lacie sat up in bed.

'I couldn't stop,' she cried.

There was a cat, a real cat, no doubt about it. There was a cat in the room close at hand. Its cry was a young cry.

She was sure it was the black kitten.

A feeling of relief flooded through her as she jumped out of bed. How nice it would be to have the warm little kitten. How good of it to come!

'Puss! Puss!'

No answer . . . then a mew again, fainter this time.

What did Poor Tom call it?

Tiss. Tiss. Tiss.

She hunted all over the bedroom which was now filled with a greeny-greyness as if light, in passing over the leaves and grasses outside, had absorbed some of their colour and filled the room with it.

She went to the window. Yes, outside all was a soft pussy-willow grey. The summer night was draining away.

She wondered if the mother cat were snug in bed with the rest of her family in the grass nest . . . if she were missing her wandering young one.

The kitten's mew sounded further away, not as if it were in the room . . . but somewhere near.

She remembered the torch and went to fetch it from under her pillow. With a needle's beam of light she explored the room again.

How cold and harsh it looked, with its dull, heavy furniture. She crawled about the floor once more, poking the torch everywhere but the kitten was nowhere to be found.

Suddenly it mewed again.

The sound seemed to come from behind a washstand which had been placed so as partly to conceal another door.

The kitten cried again. So it was behind there!

She began to move the heavy piece of furniture inch

133

by inch — the kitten's cries seemed to add to her strength — and at last she was able to get to the door.

She had to turn the knob with both hands, it was so stiff and rusty, but it moved, and she went through the door.

At the other side was absolute darkness and she had to squeeze herself back again to pick up the torch. With the aid of its thin beam she tried to make out where she had got to.

She was in a long narrow room. All the windows had been boarded up. That explained the darkness.

There were pictures on the walls.

She flashed the torch ... pictures and pictures ... no, they were portraits.

Ah! Here were the ancestors.

'Puss! Puss!'

There was no furniture here for the kitten to hide behind. She walked the length of the room. The door at the end had been bricked in.

This was the sealed off part of the house, then.

Puss! Puss!

The kitten answered with another miaow.

She walked back again flashing her torch along a line of portraits. White blurs of faces looked at her.

There was another whimper from the kitten. This time it seemed to be coming from the other side of the wall.

Even cats can't get through solid walls, not real cats, and this was certainly a real cat's kitten.

She shivered and wished she had put on something warm over Nora's nightgown.

Suddenly, as she moved the torch, she thought she caught a glint of light from behind one of the portraits.

At the same time the kitten cried again. It was somewhere very near.

She went close. Lifting up her torch she saw a portrait of a young man with fair hair curling loosely about his face. He had ruffles of lace at his neck and wrists and there was a bright-coloured bird perched on his shoulder.

He reminded her of somebody but there was no time to stop and think about it, the kitten gave a most plaintive moan.

It was somewhere here.

The eyes of the portrait looked down at her as she shone the torch ... and again she fancied she saw a gleam of light from behind them.

Curiously she stepped up to the picture and put up her hand to touch it, then —

Whoosh!

Before she realized what was happening the frame had swung inwards as if it were a door and she had stumbled through it.

She dropped the torch. As she bent to grope for it something soft touched her bare toes.

'Miaow!'

She scooped up the kitten.

'Oh, Puss! Oh, you wicked little thing.'

She was so thankful to feel it close to her. The kitten seemed thankful too. Its heart was thumping as rapidly as hers was.

Now she had found the kitten she had better go back, quickly.

She felt around the floor for the torch but could not lay her hands on it. Nora would be annoyed if it were lost.

135

Further ahead there was a touch of – she hardly called it light – but the darkness was not so dark.

She hesitated, pressing the kitten closely to her. It purred ecstatically.

'We must go back,' she whispered, yet the strange thing was, though she firmly intended to turn round and find her way back through the wall, her feet were already going forward as if having decided to do so all by themselves.

Was this one of those famous Nettlewood underground tunnels?

There was a carpet – or at least matting – on the floor. When she put out her hand and touched the wall she touched wallpaper, and although there was the damp odour of shut-up unused places it didn't smell of under the ground, wet, mouldy, cavey – it smelled of . . . surely not . . . but yes, it did . . . it smelled of coffee.

COFFEE.

She took some more paces forward then went down some steps, she was lucky not to fall down those! Then she went some more paces forward and down some more steps (she was ready for those). Then forward again, she turned a corner. It was dark now. Down some more steps, then straight along towards a strip of light which was coming from a partly open door.

Holding the kitten so tightly that it mewed, she cautiously pushed the door open and saw a room.

A small lamp was burning and there was a fire, a very untidy one, full of ashes. The hearth certainly needed a hearth brush.

A pan was bubbling on the hob. So that was where the smell of coffee was coming from.

Who lived here?

Could this be the abode of the mon – She tried not to think of the word.

If it were it must be a very human monster.

She had said it – aloud! It didn't sound frightening, at least not very, just rather silly.

How could this weird but interesting place belong to anything that wasn't human?

Why, it even smelt like the cosy café in a High Street.

But somebody lived here in a higgledy-piggledy sort of way, somebody who wasn't at all tidy, who liked cases of stuffed birds and animals and old birds' nests and fishing rods and cricket stumps and lumps of rock.

This somebody liked carving pieces of wood and never swept up the shavings, and hoarded piles of rusty old skates and croquet mallets. This somebody owned a beautiful life-like fawn whose moveless eyes of brown glass still had an echo of a loving look in them, and upon whose head somebody had put a hat, a yellow straw hat crushed and faded, with a bit of blue ribbon still attached to it and a few washed out daisies still clinging to the brim.

'It's my hat!' breathed Lacie. It had gone into the river at Hawksop. Why, it was still damp.

The kitten struggled to free itself. This time Lacie was firm. 'I'll never find you again if you run off now,' she told it, and held it tightly.

There was a door by the side of the fireplace. She could hear somebody moving behind it. Suddenly, it all became too much for her. Her nerve broke and, dropping the hat, she fled.

She ran up the passage, up all the steps, blundered round the corner, ran up steps. Her foot trod on the torch. She stooped to pick it up, then flung herself at the end of the passage. The wall swung outwards and she was in the picture-room, the picture-door falling into place behind her.

She wasted no time in getting back to Nora's bed-room, and shut the door but could not turn the key to lock it, her fingers were trembling so. Yet she managed, with a strength which amazed her, to drag the wash-stand back into its place. There! That would keep out anything, anybody, whatever, whoever it was.

It was nearly light.

Still holding the kitten, and half terrified and yet — strangely — near to laughing, she jumped into bed and pulled the covers right over her head.

13

Secrets

COFFEE!

Lacie could still smell it in her dreams.

She was in a large bed in a strange room, there was a kitten mewing and a new voice, a pleasant one, said, 'Are you awake yet? The kitten wants to come out.'

Somebody tapped at the door and came into the room.

'I thought you were in my dream.' Lacie looked at a new face which smiled at her.

'No wonder you're in a bit of a mix-up,' said the owner of the face. 'I'm Rose. Rose Fennell. I come here to give a hand to your cousin and Granny Betts. Mother said it wouldn't hurt me to do 'em a favour.'

She bustled about the room picking up the clothes which had been thrown off in such a hurry. Coming to the wash-stand she gave it a push back to the wall. 'Clumsy old thing!' she said.

She opened the window.

'Another grand day,' she announced, putting her head right outside. 'Ee! That grass wants cutting.'

Lacie sat on the edge of the bed rubbing her eyes.

'I was dreaming of coffee. I can still smell it.'

'That's not in your dreams,' Rose was laughing.

'It's in a jug. Your cousin Nora sometimes has coffee for her breakfast.'

Nora. Chloë.

Memories of the night's happenings came flooding back.

Lacie's face clouded over and she told Rose about the accident.

'I know,' said Rose, 'but I don't know the ins and outs of it yet. Your cousin Nora didn't get back from the hospital till this morning. She'd just gone to bed when I came. She might have mentioned something to Granny Betts but all she says is, 'What can you expect from them motor bikes?''

Lacie began to dress. There was nothing to be done but the things everybody expected her to do ... like getting up and dressing.

Suddenly she gave a cry. 'My black kitten's gone again !'

There was a hollow place on top of the bed with a few black hairs clinging to it. 'It slept here.' She patted the place. 'It's still warm — or I'd begin to think I'd dreamed that.'

'It's gone back to its mother,' Rose told her. 'I saw it going off into the mowing grass when I opened the window.'

Lacie went to look outside.

The lawns rippled in waves like the river. She thought of being a kitten in a nest in the grass with the tops of flowers waving above it. 'I thought they were rather a secret,' she said.

'They're a secret everybody knows, then,' said Rose, 'gallivanting all over the place and getting under everybody's feet. As for secrets,' she went on as she turned the sheets over the end of the bed, 'there's no place like Nettlewood for secrets – only everybody knows 'em.'

Secrets.

Lacie thought of the hidden room. Better not mention that. Goodness knew whose secret that was.

'What do you call secrets?' she asked Rose, 'just things people ask you not to talk about?'

'Ee, I talk too much,' said Rose, 'no use telling me any secrets,' and she laughed.

Poor Tom walked by. He was made of secrets. That was what he had said.

'Are the kittens his?' asked Lacie.

'Everything's his. All the livestock, cats, fowls, pigeons. Woe betide anybody who lays a finger on 'em.'

'He gave me a kitten.'

'Think yourself honoured then.'

Lacie said, 'It would be nice to take it back to School Cottage.'

'You won't be going back there for a while,' Rose replied. 'Still, I don't know. It's not for me to say. Nobody's told me anything but if Miss Campion has to stay in hospital it stands to reason you can't be in School Cottage by yourself. If you don't come and eat your breakfast it won't be worth eating.'

She went out of the room. Lacie ran after her.

'Where do you live, Rose?'

Rose said she lived at a farm, Lark Grange.

'It sounds nice. Are there larks there?'

'Millions of 'em,' said Rose. 'All kinds of 'em,' she added with a grin. 'I'll take you some day, if you're good and let me get on wi' my work now.'

In the kitchen a fire was burning. In front of it,

141

fastened to the bars of the grate was a dutch oven in which, hanging from little hooks, strips of bacon were grilling themselves in the heat. The fat dropped on to a little tray. On the fender were a long toasting fork and some slices of bread.

'Bacon's overdone,' said Rose, 'but it's your own fault for making me gossip. Not that I mind though,' she said. 'It's not my nature to be dumb.'

Lacie was hungry and was enjoying her breakfast when Granny Betts showed her head. There was no sunbonnet on it this time – just a little white bun of hair on top of it.

'H'm. Not lost her appetite then by the look of her,' she remarked to Rose, then disappeared.

'I can't help being hungry,' thought Lacie, 'even if Cousin Chloë is hurt.'

Her cast-down look must have been noticed by Rose who said, 'Don't take any notice of Granny Betts. You make a good breakfast. We've all got to eat while we're still alive. That's nature. Even after a funeral people enjoy their tea. Especially after – now I come to think of it.'

Lacie grew cold. 'You don't think there'll be a – a funeral for Cousin Chloë?'

Rose was embarrassed. 'Goodness, no. What can I a been thinking about,' she exclaimed, 'I only meant – ' She broke off as there were footsteps outside the door and Nora came in. She put a cup and saucer down on the table. She looked tired and yawned several times. Lacie ventured to say, 'Is – is Cousin Chloë – ' then stopped.

'Oh,' said Nora, 'I'd forgotten about you.'

She accepted another cup of coffee from Rose and

began to describe the accident. Chloë had been thrown out of that stupid side-car – one wheel was loose or something. She had fallen on the grass, fortunately, and just missed being hurled on to the bridge wall. She had a broken collarbone and bruises. She was lucky not to have been killed.

Rose shuddered.

'That Two-Drain bridge. It ought to be pulled down. Everybody keeps on about it but nothing's ever done. How's Mr Springles?'

Nora was sipping coffee. He was all right. He had left hospital and gone back to school.

'It's the last week,' Rose said, 'they'll soon be having their holidays, that's one good thing, but whatever will they do without Miss Campion till Friday?'

'They'll have to do without her,' said Nora.

Rose smiled at Lacie and said, 'I was at school when her dad' – she looked at Nora – 'was headmaster. I'll not forget Mr Campion. He wasn't half strict – but fair,' she added hastily, 'I'll say that for him. He wouldn't cane you for nothing like some of 'em did.'

She went into the scullery with a tray of pots.

Nora looked at Lacie.

'Well, here you are and here you'll have to stay. There's no use arguing – ' for Lacie had opened her mouth to speak. 'I don't know what you'll do with yourself, I won't have any time for you.'

Next to Nora's bedroom was a box-room. Rose would get it ready and Lacie would have to sleep there.

'We'll just have to make the best of a bad job,' said Nora, and by the way she spoke, it was plain that she considered it a very bad job indeed.

She was on her way out of the kitchen when Fred

Sprott came in with a basket of groceries from Owsterley. He was most concerned about the accident.

When Nora gave him a list of Chloë's injuries, he shook his head and said, 'Eh dear, dear, dear!' then added, 'Something funny seems to happen to motors if they're left about here.'

'What do you mean?' asked Nora.

'Well, there was your car ... now the motor bike.'

'George Springles can't understand it,' Nora looked thoughtful. 'He said it was impossible for it to happen ... but it did.'

They were agreeing quite well today. Presently Nora asked if he would be going over the river some time in the afternoon. Yes, he was going to take the washing to the washerwoman in Owst'ley. Certainly Lacie could go at the same time and collect some clothes from School Cottage.

Nora thanked him politely. Lacie still could detect no undercurrents of their usual hostility, and thought how pleasant it would be if they were always so agreeable to each other.

He had a bit of gardening to do for Granny Betts but would be waiting for Lacie at three o'clock. When he got to the door he stopped and remarked that Gertie was tickled to death. She was sure there would be no school now Miss Campion was away — 'and if school's closed it won't be our Gert's fault for not going, will it?' His grin was just like Gertie's as he disappeared.

George Springles turned up later in the morning in a hired car from Hawksop. He looked very shaken up and had bits of sticking plaster on his face ... and he limped. Wincing, he said, 'Otherwise I'm all right,' in spite of the fact that nobody had asked him.

144

Lacie felt a sense of injustice, and smiled at him.

He smiled back. Rose brought forward a chair. He lowered himself into it and did nothing but breathe for a few minutes.

Nora came in, and gave him a brief nod.

He had called a meeting of the school governors. The infant school was being closed until after the holidays.

So Gertie was right about that. Granny Betts, who was making one of her frequent perambulations across the kitchen, paused to listen.

'I had some trouble collecting the governors,' George went on. 'Old Bonem was digging a grave and Bindle had got a funeral.'

'Who's he buryin' today?' Granny Betts was most interested.

'Nobody in Owsterley – it's in Hawksop,' replied George.

Granny Betts looked disappointed.

'If Bonem's diggin' a grave there's somebody goin' from here,' she remarked, 'unless he's diggin' it for his sen,' and she scuttled away laughing to herself.

George came to the end of his tale at last.

'Eventually I got authority to close the Little School.'

He was completely exhausted.

'They'll get five weeks' holiday instead of four,' Lacie remarked.

'It never happened when I was at school,' said Rose, 'I'd have been glad if it had.' She lowered her voice so that Nora, who had gone into the scullery, could not hear. 'Her dad was a Tartar!'

George remembered an attaché case he had brought with him.

'Here's your things,' he said to Lacie. 'Chloë told me to bring them. I hope they're what you want . . . and I thought you'd like to have this.' He took an envelope from his breast pocket.

'My letter!' cried Lacie.

'And some books,' George was saying . . . 'I know what it's like to be marooned somewhere with nothing to read so "*Courage, mon amie, le diable est mort*". You'll find that in here.' He patted a copy of *The Cloister and the Hearth*.

Stifling a groan he got out of his chair, but Rose made him sit down again, saying that he was not to move until she had made him a cup of tea.

'Now I won't have to go over the river with Mr Sprott.' There was satisfaction in Lacie's voice. 'I've got everything I want.'

'Everything she wants!' Nora had come in and overheard her. 'She must be the only one in all the world.'

She lit a cigarette but put it out again and made her exit from the scene.

14

Poor Tom

THE next day Rose said to Fred Sprott who was hanging about the kitchen, 'You'll have to let your Gertie come over here a bit more often.'

'Oh, shall I?' he replied. 'Why?'

'She'll have nothing to do all day now she's not at school, and she could help her granny a bit.'

'Oh, could she?'

'And she'd be a bit of company for Lacie,' Rose went on. 'These are long days for her all by herself.'

'I thought there was a bit more to it than meets the eye,' said Fred Sprott looking at Lacie. 'Moping about is she? There's nothing like a bit of hard work for passing the time. Give her some scrubbing and cleaning to do.'

'I'd like that,' said Lacie, 'especially scrubbing.'

'I can't be at our Gertie's beck and call,' Fred Sprott ignored Lacie and spoke to Rose, 'gettin' her over t'river and back, morning, noon and night.'

Rose replied that his Gertie could get herself over the river, he knew that well enough.

'Oh, do I? Well, I don't then. What I do know is

that she's been showing off a bit too much on that river. She needs watching at it.'

'Well, watch her then.'

'I've got a lot of things on my mind just now.' He was looking at Nora polishing her nails. 'She's not neglected, if that's what you're getting at. She's very well looked after, at present, I can promise you that.'

'Who's looking after her?' asked Rose.

Nora laughed.

'The fat little Bisset, of course,' she said.

'Better a plump hen than a lean cat, any day,' replied Fred Sprott, and Rose laughed.

'It's as good as a pantomime to hear you two when you get started.' She clattered some pots together and began to look as if she were busy.

Nora stood up, and remarked that the place was supposed to revolve around a sick-room, and that it certainly wasn't a holiday home for spoiled kids.

'Nobody's spoiled around here,' retorted Rose, 'least of all kids. Anyway,' she persisted, 'that poor old soul is running off her feet. Gertie could help her, and as for going back and forth over the river, what's to stop her sleeping at Granny Bettses?'

'What's this about Granny Betts?' came from under a pink sunbonnet in the doorway.

'Oh, Lord,' said Nora, 'it's here again!'

Fred Sprott suddenly had a change of mind.

'If our Gertie wants to come over here she can – if that's all right with you . . .' He looked at Nora, who looked uninterested.

Granny Betts was carrying a tray. She put it on the kitchen table, and indicated the remains of Mrs Mountsorrel's breakfast.

'Only peckin' at it. That's all she's doing.' She looked round accusingly. 'Who's talkin' about Granny Betts?'

There was a silence, then Rose said, 'I only said that Gertie could sleep at your place – if you'd let her of course – if she was here.'

'Where is she, then?'

'At Celery Cottage,' said Fred Sprott.

'Then why should she sleep at my place?' asked Granny Betts.

'I meant, if she was here, instead of there,' Rose said.

'What on earth is everybody jabbering about?' Nora burst in impatiently.

'Aye what?' asked Granny Betts. 'That's what I'm trying to find out. It must be important if you don't know yourselves.'

Rose took a deep breath.

'I was only saying,' she began slowly and carefully –

'I'm not an ijiot,' said Granny Betts, 'I can understand sense when there is any.'

'It might be a good thing,' Rose went on, 'if Gertie came over here and stayed with you a while to give you a bit of help and be company to Lacie as well.'

And she sat down as if overcome by the effort of packing all the gist of the conversation into a nutshell.

'Very kind of you, I'm sure,' said Granny Betts, 'to mind my business for me.'

'Don't mention it,' muttered Fred Sprott. Granny Betts turned to him. 'And as for thee, Fred Sprott, go and dig that bit o' garden. It's taken thee three days already to get started. If it takes thee much longer I'll dig it mesen.' She looked at Nora. 'And mebbe you'd be interested to know t'doctor from Hossup's been here for ten minutes, but don't bother about him, I can soon tell him you've not finished gossipin'.'

Nora rushed away and Granny Betts moved after her. At the door she paused. 'The bairn can stay wi' me if she likes, as long as she behaves her sen. As for helping me – when I need any help, I'll ask for it.'

'No, you won't,' said Fred Sprott. 'You never do.'

'And another thing,' Granny Betts ignored the interruption, 'folks who talk about me behint my back should make sure I don't hear 'em. I'm not deaf, remember, no, an' I'm not daft, neether.'

With this parting shot she scurried after Nora to take up a listening post outside the sick-room door.

Fred Sprott muttered something, and went off to do the digging.

When she was alone with Rose, Lacie asked if she could do some scrubbing. Rose didn't see why not – but on another day, she was behindhand now through all that gossiping and had to see to the dinner, which was at twelve o'clock. Tea was at four, supper at eight. Lacie sighed. There seemed to be such a lot of time in between.

She asked why Rose couldn't stay at Nettlewood, why must she go home?

'Ee, I've got a young man,' cried Rose, 'we don't see enough of each other as it is. It's a long walk from Lark Grange to Birdhill.'

'Birdhill,' said Lacie. 'What's that?'

'Birdhill Farm, where Dick lives ... it's not far from Bridgeover.'

'Dick's a nice name,' Lacie said. 'Is he nice?'

'Of course he is,' said Rose, 'or he wouldn't be my young man, would he?'

Lacie wanted to know all about him.

His name was Dick Stilbush and he was mad about horses. 'And about you,' said Lacie. Rose smiled.

Dick rode over every night just so that he could see her for a few minutes. She couldn't miss that, could she?

Lacie agreed that Rose mustn't miss seeing Dick every night and asked her if she would like being Mrs Stilbush.

'I'm sure I will,' Rose said, 'seeing that I like both him and his name so much. But I'm not getting my work done. Stop hindering me, there's a good girl. Go and finish that letter you're supposed to be sending your dad.'

But the letter was written. It just needed a stamp, a special one for going abroad. Nora would have to be asked about that. She was regarded as an authority on all foreign affairs.

Rose escaped, saying that there wouldn't be any dinner if she didn't hurry up.

As Lacie went across the hall she saw a pony and trap outside. It belonged to old Doctor Plumtree of Hawksop, the senior partner who didn't like motor cars.

She was making friends with the pony when Nora and Dr Plumtree came out of the house.

Nora told him who Lacie was and he said, 'Hm, rather tall for her age, isn't she? We mustn't allow her to shoot up too high, must we?'

As this seemed to be one of those questions which never expect an answer, neither Lacie nor Nora gave it one.

'Still,' Dr Plumtree looked at Lacie, 'I do know one

good reason why you won't grow into a telegraph pole.'

'Oh?' Lacie was interested. 'Why?'

'You're not made of wood,' he replied and still chuckling he gee-upped the pony and went away.

There was something Lacie could do, Nora said, as she was only hanging about.

Lacie quickly said that she'd do anything.

'Mrs Mountsorrel is feeling much better,' said Nora, 'and she wants to see Tom.'

'Tom?' repeated Lacie.

'Poor Tom then,' Nora said. 'God knows he's poor enough. See if you can find him and tell him to go to his granny at once.'

'Do you mean Granny Betts?'

'Who else should I mean?' Nora said. 'She'll see that he makes himself tidy, I suppose.'

She went back into the house. Lacie was glad to find a purpose for roaming about and set off to look for Poor Tom.

He was not at the front of the house, nor in the region of the cat's nest nor in the courtyard. She put her head in at the kitchen door. Rose had not seen him. She was making a bread and butter pudding and lavishly sprinkling it with sultanas. She gave Lacie a handful, telling her to try the barns or the fowl-house.

But he was not in the barns nor in the fowl-house. Lacie could hear the sound of a spade behind the walls of the kitchen garden. The door in the wall was open. Fred Sprott had his back to her and was working hard. She decided not to disturb him. Poor Tom was not there.

She went to the riverside. He was sitting on top of

the bank, staring down into the water, a fishing-rod beside him.

He was wearing a crushed faded straw hat with a vestige of blue ribbon dangling behind.

Her hat! Again. She stood watching him, not wanting to startle him. He went on staring into the water.

'I know who's there,' he said, without turning his head. She went up to him and sat on the grass.

It was some time before he spoke again. The silence was one of those silences, which, as they go on, become more and more difficult to break, and Lacie, in her mind, turned over several opening remarks, while she looked at her hat. It had survived its voyage pretty well. One thing was clear to her now. The secret chamber belonged to Poor Tom.

Still he was silent.

'There's not much of a monster about him,' her thoughts ran on. 'If he's the only mystery about those underground places there's no need to be nervous.'

Should she tell him she knew about his room and the long corridor and the picture that opened? Or would it be better to wait for him to tell her?

She was so deep in her thoughts that she jumped when he did speak.

'Some folks would say I'm a fool,' he said.

'Do you mean in that hat?'

'In it or out of it.' Poor Tom turned to look at her. 'What do you think?'

She decided to stick to the hat as a topic of discussion. 'It's a bit unusual, perhaps, on you.'

'I don't mind about that,' he said. 'It just fits. That's a bit o' luck, isn't it?'

'Why aren't you fishing?' asked Lacie.

'Because I don't want any fish,' he said.

'Why the fishing-rod then?'

'I'm thinking of fishing. And if I forget, it reminds me again.'

'But – do you have to think of fishing?' she asked. 'Couldn't you think of something else?'

'Not here,' he replied, 'not when I've got me fishing-rod.'

'Are there a lot of fish here?' asked Lacie.

'Ask Fred Sprott. He catches 'em. He doesn't mind pulling 'em out, all jumping and slithering, on the end of a hook.' Poor Tom clutched his throat. He opened his mouth, then snapped it shut again. 'The hook gets inside here you see.' He opened his mouth and pointed inside, then suddenly took the fishing-rod, broke it in two and threw the pieces in the river.

'Now they'll know I'm not going to catch 'em,' he said.

'I don't see why you had to do that,' Lacie objected.

'I thought you liked chucking things in the river,' he answered. She stared at him. Did he mean the hat? And how did he know that she had thrown it in? If he did know.

She stood up.

'I came to tell you something. You must go in now. Mrs Mountsorrel is asking to see you.'

'What?' He looked up. 'Me? Why?'

'I don't know.'

'I know.' He jumped to his feet. 'It's about being improved, talking nicer and dressing nicer and all that.' He jammed the hat further on his head. 'Or else it's

about goin' to It'ly. I'll tell you something about her —
she's not right up here.' And he touched his head.

There was a pause, then he said. 'Who do you live
with when you're not here?'

'My father and mother . . . when — when everything's
all right.'

'I don't think I ever had either o' them . . . only
Granny Betts. She's all I ever had.' He looked at Lacie.
'You can tell her I'm not coming. Go and say Poor
Tom can't come, he's all of a tremble.'

It was true. His hands were shaking. So were his
shoulders. So was his chin. His teeth chattered.

He urged her away and she began to walk back to
the house. When she had gone a little way she turned
to speak to him again.

He was gone.

In the distance near the kitchen garden she saw the
pink sunbonnet. Did it know everything that was going
on?

At that moment the sound of the gong boomed
through the air and she slowly went in to dinner.

15

'Look Who's Here! It's Gertie!'

LATER in the afternoon Granny Betts was seen leading
Poor Tom across the courtyard. His shock of hair had
been brushed as flat as it would go. He looked tidy
and chastened. His head was cast down and he walked
with lagging feet.

'Like a lamb to the slaughter,' said Fred Sprott
taking a cup of tea from Rose.

Rose objected, 'Nobody wants to do him any harm.
The old lady's only taking a decent interest in him.'

She cut him a large piece of sponge cake. He bit into
it, and said, 'Pity it's taken her so long. She's left it a
bit late, hasn't she?'

Lacie remarked that it was only four o'clock, and
they both laughed.

Nora came in.

'What's funny?' she asked, taking hold of the teapot.
'People stuffing cake into their mouths with both
hands?'

'No, you sitting down in the kitchen and taking tea

with us servants,' replied Fred Sprott, dropping crumbs.

Rose was indignant. 'I'm not anybody's servant. I'm just doing a favour, don't forget that.'

'Do us another favour then, and pour some more tea.' He passed his cup via Lacie. 'Wake up, Miss Head-in-the-clouds.'

'Stop bothering the child,' said Rose.

'Me?' He seemed surprised, and asked Lacie if he did bother her.

'A little bit,' she admitted.

'Dear, dear!'

'She's all at sea with nobody but grown-ups around her all the time, and no wonder,' Rose said.

'Oh Lord!' Nora exclaimed. 'All this gabble gets on my nerves. It's like the monkey house at the zoo.'

She went out, taking a cup of tea with her.

'So now we know,' said Fred Sprott. 'To her we're monkeys.' And he went out but through a different door.

'Thank goodness,' said Rose. 'They snaggle at each other like cat and dog. We can have a bit of peace now they've gone – and finish the cake.'

But Lacie didn't want the cake.

'Sure?' said Rose. 'Oh well, then – ' and took the last piece.

The next day after dinner Lacie went into her own room for something. The letter she had written to her parents was propped up on the chimney shelf and still waiting for a stamp. Somehow she had not yet managed to ask Nora's advice about it.

Now, however, a slight sound in the room next door

reminded her that Nora had an hour off this afternoon while Granny Betts sat with Mrs Mountsorrel.

Before she had time to stop herself Lacie tapped at her cousin's bedroom door.

Nora was lying on the bed reading a novel. She had changed into a pretty kimono, her hair was held back in a band and she had cold cream on her face.

She sighed and said, 'Well?' over the top of the book.

Lacie asked her about the stamp.

'I don't know how much it will be.' Nora looked as if she were really trying not to be exasperated. 'Give the letter to Fred Sprott. He'll take it to Owsterley and Jessima Throssel will stamp it for you and send it off.' She went back to her book, then had an afterthought. 'If you need any money . . .'

Lacie thanked her quickly and said, no, she didn't need any, and was turning to go when something about the room caught her attention. For a moment she couldn't think what it was, then she said, 'Oh, you've moved the wash-stand. It was silly having it in front of that door, wasn't it?'

'Why?' asked Nora.

Lacie was beginning to realize by now that whenever she asked Nora a question she usually got another one in reply.

'Well, it made it so difficult to get through the door,' said Lacie.

'Who wants to go through it? Do you?' Nora raised her eyes from her book.

'N-no,' stammered Lacie, 'of course not.'

That was true, anyway.

Nora sighed. 'I was trying to get a bit of peace.

Goodness knows, I don't get much of it.' She looked at Lacie who was still staring at the second door, and said, 'That's the old part of the house through there. It's sealed off. I told you about it.'

She was on her feet and, untying the band from her hair, went to the looking-glass and used a hairbrush vigorously.

Lacie felt uncomfortably involved in an act of deception about that door. Ought she to tell Nora about the passage that led to the secret room? Warn her?

But it was Poor Tom's secret . . . and Nora at the moment was certainly looking as if she didn't wish to be told anything.

'I'm not nervous, if that's what you mean,' she said, banging the hairbrush down on her head with every stroke, then stopped. 'Good Lord! you're not still thinking about that Nettlewood monster,' she laughed. 'Don't worry – if it pays me a visit one night, I'll give it a good clonk on the head with that.'

'That' was a croquet mallet in a corner.

'Now, my free time is over – such as it was – and I have to dress.'

Lacie apologised for giving her so much trouble and left.

Rose came to the rescue about the letter. She took it to Dick who would get it properly stamped, and post it. The next morning when she came to work she smiled and nodded. Dick had given his word to post it in Bridgeover that afternoon.

Lacie felt as if an achievement had been made and when Rose asked her to go and find a few eggs in the fowl-house she took a basket and set off with a light heart.

As she went across the courtyard the mother cat strolled from around the corner with her four kittens. Lacie stopped to fondle them. The black kitten – her black kitten – sprang back from her hand on all its four paws, its back arched and its tail waving. It must have forgotten that it was supposed to be hers, yet when she stood up to go it suddenly pounced upon her foot and began to play with the shoelace. She had quite a business to persuade the silly little creature to follow its mother who had set off to the mowing grass.

In the end Lacie had to pick it up and set it down in the grass where it spent some moments mad with excitement, spinning itself round and round.

The fowl-house was as big as a cottage and had furniture in it. There were old chairs, old tables, old sofas, old pots and pans, old packing-cases, old clothes-baskets, old hampers and an old grandfather clock. They all made marvellous nesting places for the hens.

The cockerel rushed at her as she opened the door. She didn't like him and let him go outside where he paraded haughtily up and down the yard.

Some of the hens came clucking around her feet, some sat up high in the rafters, and some were still sitting on their nests. Lacie looked into their anxious little eyes and passed on.

The clock had its door swinging open from a broken hinge, and looked as if it were a good place for a nest. It was. She put her arm deep inside and brought out three eggs. Once she slipped her hand under the soft breast of a speckled hen and felt the warm oval of a new laid egg.

'You can sit on it for a little bit longer,' she told the hen, 'but you'll have to give it up in the end. Somebody will boil it and have it with bread and butter and I'm afraid that somebody may be me.'

Soon the basket was full.

Outside, the cockerel was making his way into the water meadow.

'He'd better keep his eye open for the fox,' she thought, rather uneasy about him. She would be sorry if anything happened to him but she would understand the fox.

Suddenly she heard a shout.

'Hey! Hey! I'm here. It's me!'

She looked around.

Only a few steps away from the fowl-house, so close to the barns and outhouses that it was almost a part of them, was Granny Betts' cottage and in its open doorway stood Gertie Sprott.

'Hey!' she shouted again. 'I'm here. There's no school. Little School's got an extra week's holiday.'

'I know,' said Lacie going nearer.

'Where did you get them eggs?' Gertie immediately demanded. 'You'd better not let me granny see 'em. She's the boss of the fowls.'

'I thought Poor Tom is.'

'Well, she's the boss of the eggs. I've come to help her,' Gertie said. She was encased in a vast apron made of sacking which had been made to fit her by means of enormous safety pins. Her hands were red and looked as if they had just come out of hot water.

'This is me apron,' she went on, 'and yon's me scrubbin' brush an' pail.' She sounded proud of them. 'Medad brought me this mornin'.'

'Are you staying here?' asked Lacie. 'I mean sleeping?'

'Medad says I've to be at t'ferry at seven o'clock sharp an' if he's there he'll take me home. An' if he's not I've got to come an' sleep here at me granny's. I've brought me belongings in case I don't go back.'

Lacie was silently sorting out her feelings about Gertie's arrival – her company would help to pass the time but –

'Still stuck up,' said Gertie. 'You're not a bit diff'rent.' Before Lacie could reply Granny Betts put her head out of one of the bedroom windows.

Lacie immediately felt guilty about the basket of eggs.

'I can hear thee a mile off, Gert Sprott,' said Granny Betts. 'Tek the little lass inside, don't keep her standin' on t'door step like a beggar,' and she drew in her head.

'You'd better come in,' said Gertie, very much surprised. 'She don't like folks comin' into t'house.'

Full of curiosity but a little nervously Lacie followed Gertie into the cottage. Its downstairs windows were never opened and were crowded with pot-plants which blocked out the light and produced an atmosphere of stuffy fragrance. There were scented geraniums and musk, busy lizzies and mothers-of-thousands and a big fuchsia that drooped from the window-sill over a horse-hair sofa.

'This is t'best room,' Gertie still spoke in a whisper. 'Nobody ever comes into it, well, hardly ever.'

In the middle of the room was a round table covered with a cloth of green plush, and in the middle of that was an aspidistra. Lacie had already heard it spoken of at Nettlewood. Granny Betts, it was said, gave it drinks

162

of cold tea and washed its leaves as if she were bathing a baby.

There were pale brown photographs on the walls.

'They're me granny's dead 'uns,' Gertie said. 'She's got a lot on 'em, han't she? A'most everybody's dead except me and medad and our Tom.'

She conducted Lacie from one photograph to another. 'That's medad's mam. She's dead. An' that's his a'ntie Molly. She was our Tom's mam. She's dead. An' him – he's medad's grand-dad when he were young. He died 'cos a tree fell on him when he were chopping it down.'

Granny Betts' far off husband. Lacie stared at the faded picture and tried to think of Granny Betts as having been young. ' An' that's her,' said Gertie, 'in her wedding clo'es. But come on – ' she turned away from the gloomy display – 'let's go into t'house.'

'But we're in the house already,' said Lacie.

'I mean in here.' Gertie led the way into a back-room where the main fireplace was, the hearth-stone, the heart of the home.

'This is t'house,' said Gertie, 'the house-place, me granny calls it.'

'I'd call it the living-room.' Lacie was looking around with interest. Suddenly –

'Get off that floor!' screamed Gertie. 'I've only just scrubbed it. D'you think I did it just for folks to walk on?'

Lacie hastily jumped on to a bit of matting.

'Do you like scrubbing?' she asked.

Gertie didn't mind it, except for the bit of floor underneath the mangle in the back kitchen where the bricks were all broken. Ugh!

163

Her apron had wet patches on it. She always managed to get wet, somehow, did Gertie!

'Gertie!' It was Granny Betts' voice. 'Gertie! Come you here!'

Gertie pulled a face, but at once moved towards the stairs which rose straight up from the living-room. When she was half-way up Granny Betts cried, 'Don't come up empty-handed, bairn, bring them sheets wi' thee. They're on the mangle in t'back kitchin.'

Gertie came back for the sheets, then went upstairs with them. When she came down again she was taking off her apron.

She looked subdued, but — 'Me granny says I can go out now,' was all she said until she and Lacie were some distance away from the cottage. She looked glum and Lacie asked what was the matter. Gertie stopped walking. She was full of doubts about staying with her granny, and hoped her dad would arrive at seven o'clock to take her home. She only liked being at home or at Missy Bissy's.

Her father was not waiting for her at seven o'clock, nor could she find him wherever she went looking. She sat patiently waiting on the river bank while the evening dew fell on the grass around her, and owls began to call. With a melancholy look she sat and stared at her home across the water. She was homesick already.

She peered across the river and saw *Wobbler* moored at the bottom of the steps, and began to wonder where the other boat was. Her dad must have gone somewhere, but where? And why hadn't he told her?

After a time she said, 'I wish I could get hold of that *Wobbler*, I'd go home by meself.'

'Then it's a very good thing you can't get hold of it,' said Lacie, 'because you've been told to stay here.'

She got up from the damp grass. 'Look, Granny Betts is coming to look for you.'

'I'm gettin' me feet wet,'. cried Granny Betts, 'traipsin' about t'grass lookin' for thee. If thou's goin' to be all this trouble, me lass, I'd sooner thou'd stayed at home.'

'Gertie will agree with her about that, anyway,' Lacie said to herself as she went back to Nettlewood.

16

The Rose Days

It was surprising how quickly they all settled down into a routine. Chloë was not forgotten, but in that country place – and time – things to do created themselves minute by minute and day by day.

Rose, Tom, Lacie and Gertie made their own little world with the grown-ups on the outside of it. Rose was grown up in years of course, but in spirit, and in presence as often as she could, she joined the young ones. Poor Tom was young, eternally, irretrievably young.

So began what Lacie was always to remember as the Rose Days, the days of Rose and roses, of sunshine, hay and summer, and Rose again. She played such a part in that world. She shone into it with her gladsome heart and filled it with her kindness. Soon the dark corners were lit up and the silent places sounding with laughter. She settled arguments, soothed hurt feelings, restored lost pride. Poor Tom trusted Rose more than he trusted any other person on earth except Granny Betts.

'Rose wouldn't harm folks. She wouldn't pester 'em to look different and talk strange. She wouldn't bother about improving 'em and takin' 'em travellin' where they don't want to go. Rose wouldn't set traps for 'em.'

'Eh, Tommy,' said Rose, 'I couldn't set traps for anything, not even mice though they do make me squeal.'

Mrs Mountsorrel got better, then got worse, then got better again.

Dr Plumtree came and went in his pony and trap. He always looked out for the two little girls, and whenever he saw them together, never failed to remark on Lacie's height and Gertie's red cheeks. As the days passed he began to look approvingly at Lacie's colour and say, 'H'm yes, getting quite a nice pink, that's better, poor little town bairn.'

Gertie was usually busy at Granny Betts' cottage in the mornings, and quickly learned to take charge when her granny was out.

There was not much to do in that poky hole, not like there was at home when she was looking after her dad. So she had said the morning after her arrival, as she hung up her sacking apron behind the scullery door. She could do it all with her hands tied behind her back. Then she wanted to know if Lacie had done any scrubbing yet.

'Not yet,' Lacie had to confess.

There was no cooking for Gertie to do. She was to have her dinners and teas with Lacie and Rose. What about puddings, she wanted to know, how often were there puddings?

'Every day.' Lacie replied, 'Rose makes them.'

'What sort?'

'Various sorts.'

Gertie pressed for details.

'Ever get Spotted Dick?'

'We had that yesterday.'

'Damn,' said Gertie, 'what else do you get?'

'Lemon pudding, bread and butter with lots of currants, treacle sponge –'

'Oo! Go on,' breathed Gertie.

'Treacle tart, golden pudding, raspberry pudding' – Lacie paused.

'Go on,' urged Gertie again.

'Roly-poly – I can't think of any more but they're all nice.'

'What about rice? D'you get rice puddin'?'

'Never,' said Lacie.

'Good!'

'Up to now, that is,' said Lacie.

'I hope we don't go an' start gettin' that now I've come,' Gertie remarked.

'And there's scones and tea-cakes and curd tarts and things for tea,' Lacie added.

'An' bread as well? Bread an' jam?'

'Bread and butter and jam,' said Lacie.

'Ee! I'm glad I've come,' sighed Gertie, 'I could eat some o' them puddings now. How long is it till dinner-time?'

But neither knew the time. Granny Betts' clock had stopped long ago. She got up and went to bed when she felt like it. She had no need of clocks.

She didn't need locks either, and the back door of her cottage was never barred.

'Let's go an' look for findings,' was Gertie's suggestion, one day.

'Findings?'

'Things what you find, silly, when you go lookin' ... specially things nobody else knows about, like – ' but Gertie stopped.

'Like secrets, you mean?' asked Lacie.

'What do you know about secrets?' Gertie said quickly.

Lacie hesitated. 'There's supposed to be rather a lot around here,' she said, 'at least, I suppose so.'

'I s'pose,' Gertie heavily exaggerated the word, 'I s'pose you haven't found any yet? But I s'pose you wouldn't tell me if you have, that'd be just like you.'

Lacie shrugged. She was feeling rather awkward about the secret room.

'I'm sure you've found something,' shrieked Gertie, 'you've got a secret, I can tell by your face. Go on, tell us.'

It was a good thing that Poor Tom popped up just then or there might have been an argument and Lacie might have told his secret. 'After all, they're cousins, or nearly, at any rate, family – but I'm glad I didn't tell.'

She was thankful that she had escaped temptation.

In his hand Poor Tom was carrying a wounded thrush which one of the kittens had mauled.

'I hope it wasn't the little black one,' cried Lacie.

'It's natur',' said Poor Tom, 'but I wish it wasn't.'

'It'll die,' pronounced Gertie after one expert look.

A spasm crossed Poor Tom's face.

'I think I can mend it,' he said, 'but it'll never make much of a flyer.'

He went off in the direction of the wood.

'Silly fool,' said Gertie, 'he should let it die. If it

169

can't fly it'll be no good. Something else'll catch it and eat it.' She paused. 'I'll tell you something you don't know.'

'What about?'

'Him. You know your hat, that straw thing wi' daisies on, the one you chucked away – I know who's got it.'

'So do I. Tom has.'

'How did you find out?' cried Gertie.

'It was on his head the other day,' Lacie replied. 'He must have fished it out of the river. There's nothing very mysterious about that.'

Gertie looked disappointed at having her mystery so quickly dispelled. She had found the cat's nest but, as Lacie pointed out, the kittens couldn't be counted as secrets, they were jumping out all over the place.

'I've got a secret though,' Lacie said, 'and I'll tell you.'

Gertie's eyes brightened and she put her ear closer to Lacie.

'One of those kittens is mine,' said Lacie, 'the little black one.'

'They're all black.'

'The blackest ... it's the prettiest and cleverest as well.'

'It would be,' remarked Gertie.

'Poor Tom gave it to me. I'll probably take it home with me when I go.'

'She won't let you.'

'SHE is the cat's mother and SHE won't mind. She hardly cares about them now.'

'You know who I mean,' said Gertie, 'that long-legged nurse called Nora. That's what me granny calls her. You can stick your nose in the air as much as you like but NOWT will make me say I like her.'

The gong boomed from the kitchen door. Dinner-time.

'Do you think there'll be Spotted Dick again?' asked Gertie.

The days became hotter. The evenings were soft as velvet. The passing of time was only noticed as day slipped into evening and evening into night. Every morning was the discovery of new joy.

Tom shared his duties and his pleasures with Lacie and Gertie, and with Rose, too, whenever she was free of the house. They helped him to feed his hens and pigeons, and gather kindling for the fires.

They went with him around the woods and fields to see the favourite haunts of wild birds, and by the sides of stream and river to watch for water-fowl and voles. Once, once and only once, there was the jewelled flash of a kingfisher. Like a sharp pain of delight it came and went.

One day Tom said mysteriously, 'Come wi' me, I'll show you summat. Rose too,' and Rose at once stopped what she was doing, saying that she'd finish it after-wards, even if she had to work late. Dick wasn't coming till tomorrow, anyway.

Tom took them into the barn. Telling them to be quiet, and with an air of secrecy, he closed the door, then stood looking up into the rafters. Sunlight filtered through the broken parts of the roof in golden-dusty beams so that the darkness all around seemed even darker.

He pursed his lips and made a chirruping call.

171

'Prrrip . . . prrr . . . rr . . . pp . . . prrr . . . Tw . . . Tw . . . Tw . . . Prrrip.'

A feather slowly dropped from above, circling down through a sunbeam. Then — without a flutter, or scurry or sound of wings, a baby owl flew down and perched on his shoulder.

'I thought he was asleep,' Tom said, then whispered in its downy ear, 'Iboo! Iboo! This is little Iboo.'

Lacie was startled at the way the word had come up again.

'Is Iboo its name?' she whispered.

'They're all iboos, you silly,' he said, 'every man jack on 'em.'

When at last he sent the owl back to its sleeping place in the roof Lacie asked him how he knew of the word 'iboo'.

'Fred Sprott told it to me when I was a little lad,' he replied. 'I've allus called 'em "iboos" ever since.'

'It's French for "owl",' Lacie told him and spelled '*HIBOU*'.

'Aye, Fred Sprott's clever,' he said, 'I shouldn't put it past him to talk French.'

Gertie looked proud.

'Fancy medad talkin' French,' she said, 'and not telling me.'

'He doesn't have to tell you everything,' said Rose. 'You always find out for yourself soon enough.' And Gertie laughed, for somehow from Rose no remark was ever unkind.

Gertie did find something one morning.

She had finished her tidying-up in the cottage earlier than usual and had called for Lacie.

Granny Betts saw them as they were strolling away and called from the back-kitchen door, telling them to collect the eggs.

They soon filled a basket and Gertie began rummaging around. Whenever Lacie found something she stumbled upon it but Gertie went searching like a bloodhound for *her* discoveries.

Some idea or other led her to move boxes and packing cases away from the bottom of an old treadle sewing machine she was interested in — and she found a box.

Lacie hurried to look. A large stone was on top of the lid.

'That's been put there a purpose,' said Gertie. 'Somebody's hid it.' She looked up, her eyes shining. 'We've found summat at last.'

It was a heavy box. Together they lifted the lid.

Hidden treasure found at last!

Coins were mixed up with marbles — glass ones of all colours and many sizes — and buttons, and beads and pebbles.

A look of doubt was replacing Gertie's expression of joyful surprise.

'It's funny money,' she said, dropping coins from her fingers.

'It's foreign,' said Lacie.

'Isn't it any good?'

'Not much. Not here anyway, and its only small change. There's centimes — and francs. They're French, and look, it says lira on this. That's Italian. I suppose Mrs Mountsorrel brought it.'

'Can't we spend it?' asked Gertie.

'It isn't ours, is it?' said Lacie. 'Anyway, of course

we can't, unless we go to France or Italy. You'd better put it back again, and put the stone on the lid.'

'It must be our Tom's,' said Gertie. 'Well, he can have it for all I care,' and she hid the box all over again.

At dinnertime there was treacle sponge pudding. Gertie was revelling in it when Rose suddenly said, 'Let's go to Haw'sop.'

'When?' asked Lacie. Gertie could not speak at the moment but she looked up.

'Now,' replied Rose, 'as soon as dinner's cleared away and washed up. It's Wednesday, so its market day. There'll be ever such a lot going on. They have roundabouts and things, first week in August.'

Gertie gave a choked cry of excitement modified by treacle.

It wasn't a fair. Just rather a special market day that's all. They could walk through the fields. Rose had a bit of money to spend.

'What about them curd tarts?' asked Gertie, for Rose had been baking, 'if I don't have me tea here I shan't get any, there's sure to be none left tomorrow.'

'We'll take our tea,' cried Rose, 'and eat it on the way. Make haste and finish your pudding.'

She got up from the table and began to clear away. Her eyes sparkled and her feet flew from kitchen to scullery and back again.

'Will it be all right?' Lacie asked as she dodged back and forth trying to keep up with the flying Rose. 'I mean, what about *them*? The grown-ups?'

Rose stopped for a second. 'They won't mind as long as I'm with you,' she said, 'besides they're not taking much notice of us these days. Look sharp and get ready while I put some curd tarts in a bag.'

Outside, they came across Tom. 'Where are you off to, all on you?' he asked.

'Haw'sop!' cried Rose, 'Come with us!'

He hung back. 'I dunno,' he said, 'it's, it's the world, Haw'sop is . . . it's bad for Poor Tom.'

'Not it!' said Rose, 'you'll be all right if I'm with you . . . Besides the world's not all bad.'

'P'raps it'll be better if you're there,' said Tom. 'All right. I'll come . . . but don't go an' leave me, will you?'

Rose promised on her heart that she would not leave him for one minute, then asked him to get a bit of a wash and comb his hair.

So Tom washed under the pump in the back kitchen.

'I don't know what me granny will say,' he said, as he tried to straighten his hair, 'when she hears I've gone off into t'world.'

'She's sitting with Mrs Mountsorrel,' said Rose, 'and the other one – your Cousin Nora – ' She caught Lacie's eye – 'is having a rest somewhere. Leastways I haven't seen her for an hour or two. I don't know where she's eaten her dinner but it's not my fault if she hasn't had any.' She looked at Poor Tom. 'Don't worry, I'll make it all right with your granny when we come back. She won't miss you while you're gone. She hardly ever knows where you are in daylight, anyway.'

'No, nor in moonlight, neether,' said Poor Tom with a smile.

Just as they were ready to go he planted down his feet, and asked if he could fetch his hat.

He was away rather a long time and Rose began to fidget. Gertie was dancing about with impatience and was just going to look for him when he came back, wearing the straw hat. Lacie turned away to hide a smile, and Gertie grinned.

Rose stared.

'Don't you like it?' He looked at her. 'I won't wear it if you don't want me to.'

'I don't mind,' said Rose, recovering from her surprise. 'You wear it if you like, Tommy. We'll put some real daisies in it on the way.'

'These are all right.' He took off the hat and looked at it. 'I like it just as it is,' and they all laughed as he stuck it at a jaunty angle on his head.

'Stop a bit,' said Rose, 'you're covered with bits of straw.' She brushed her hand across his shoulders. 'You looked all right a few minutes ago. Eh dear-a-me-today, what a boy you are!'

'Just what me granny says,' Tom said, delighted, and crinkled up his face into such a droll expression that they all burst out laughing, and laughing they set off to Hawksop.

17

The Liberator

THEY were laughing most of the way.

Once out of the wood and in the open fields they could feel the sun burning down on them and Rose said she envied Tom his hat. He took it off immediately and offered it to her and, delighting him, she put it on and wore it.

'We'll all be as brown as berries,' she said and when Poor Tom said 'as brown as owls' they all laughed as if they would never stop, and began hooting and tu-whit-tu-whooing and repeating 'as brown as owls' in different voices, and staggering about on the grassy track, and bending double with the pain of laughing.

From owls they got to cuckoos and for some time were baffled by cries of 'cuckoo', sometimes faint and far away, and sometimes so loud that they sounded just around the corner – but there was no corner. There were no trees near by, and no hedges.

'Wheer is it?' cried Gertie, tired of running here and there. 'I never heerd such a bird.'

'Neither did I,' said Rose, then burst out laughing again as she caught Tom's eye.

'Is it him?' Gertie gave him a thump. 'It sounded just like a real 'un.'

'You oughter known,' Tom told them. 'It's August now.'

'Only just,' said Gertie.

'Well, go he must,' said Rose.

'How does the cuckoo know he must go in August?' asked Lacie.

'He does know,' Rose replied, 'that's all.'

After some more walking Gertie wanted to know when it was teatime.

'Shall we have it on the way back?' Rose suggested. 'We don't want to get to Haw'sop ever so late . . . what about those roundabouts? Look! I can see Haw'sop bridge already. Tom, you can have your hat back now.'

They could all see the bridge and they walked forward at a good pace. Soon the Nettlewood lane joined the road into the town.

There was a lot of traffic. People were still coming in from the farms. Rose nodded several times to people she knew, but looked rather disappointed.

'Are you looking for Dick?' asked Lacie.

Rose blushed.

'P'raps I am,' she said and smiled.

'Oh go on,' cried Gertie, 'you are! So that's why you wanted to come to Hossup.'

'We-ll,' said Rose. 'All right. I did think he might be here, but he wasn't sure, and – ' she smiled – 'if I do see him . . .' Her expression grew dreamy and she seemed to forget what she had been going to say until the girls prompted her.

'If we do see him,' Rose came back to earth, her face

pinker than ever, 'p'raps we can all have tea at the River Rover.' She, too, knew of the famous cream buns.

'Oo! Better than curd tarts,' shouted Gertie, 'and milk out of a medicine bottle.'

'You may be glad of that yet,' said Rose.

Poor Tom had looked uneasy at the thought of Dick joining the expedition. Rose sensed this.

'Now, Tommy,' she said, putting her hand on his shoulder. 'Dick's just as nice as – as nice as you think I am ... you won't mind him being here one little scrap once you've met him.'

'You won't go and leave us though, will you?' asked Tom, and Rose made her promise all over again.

Before they crossed the bridge she stopped and gathered the three around her.

'Now, see here,' she said, 'I want you to listen to me. There's such a lot of folks here, you never know, some of us may lose sight of each other. If anybody's lost – separated – I should say,' she looked at them seriously as if she meant to be obeyed, 'whoever it is must come over the bridge and wait here. Our side of the bridge.'

'Do you mean me?' asked Gertie, for Rose was looking at her. 'It wasn't me who got lost last time.'

'Never mind that,' replied Rose, 'I mean whoever it is that gets separated – I hope nobody will – but just in case of emergencies.' She was looking at Tom.

'I'm not going to get separated, am I?' he asked anxiously.

'Of course not,' said Rose, 'you stick to me.'

'Aye!' Tom said in relief. 'I will.'

They walked over the bridge amongst the gigs and pony traps, bicycles and people, and a few motor cars, into Hawksop.

After a time Lacie whispered to Rose, 'I think people are staring at us.'

It wasn't that Tom's was the only straw hat in town, and it certainly wasn't the only battered-looking one, and as for the daisies in it, a dray-horse was wearing a hat which was covered with daisies, real ones, and poppies as well.

'It's not the hat exactly,' Rose whispered to Lacie, 'I don't know what it is. He's not doing anything to be noticed, not half as much as you are.' This was to Gertie who was bouncing up and down from the pavement to the road.

All went well, however, until they got into the streets leading to the market where there were drays and carts carrying penned-up animals. Lacie had experienced qualms about Gertie going near the market and expected her to begin bothering about the Bissets, but it was not Gertie who caused the fuss.

When Tom saw the animals he frowned and looked troubled. Rose put her hand on his arm and hurried him on.

'If this is what folks call the world,' he kept saying, 'I don't think much of it.'

'He knows when things are going to be killed,' said Gertie in her loud voice, 'and he can't stand it.'

'Ssh,' said Rose, 'we know all about it. Don't I know if I want a fowl for dinner at Nettlewood I have to bring one from home? Just keep quiet for a bit.'

Lacie thought that it was a pity they had come so

close to the market but of course that was where Dick would be.

Rose was looking about, but there was no sign of him and they set off in search of the roundabouts. Strains of music soon proclaimed their whereabouts.

'I told you it wasn't the fair,' Rose said as Gertie looked scornful. 'You'll have to wait till October for that."

But Gertie wasn't going to wait until October for a roundabout ride, even if this was only a poor little affair of painted horses and dragons propelled by the hand of a bored-looking youth with a pink muffler around his neck.

Lacie chose a horse, and Gertie a dragon with its paint peeling off because — she said — it looked like Miss Throssel, and they waited. The youth was evidently not going to work the machine for the two of them and several minutes went by before he considered the number of customers to be worth the effort of turning the wheel.

At last the ride began and a wheezy little tune came out from somewhere.

Tom stood and watched the handle being turned. He begged to have a go at it, promising that he would put it round at a rare old gallop.

The youth very coarsely told him to clear off and mind his own business.

Rose was thankful when the ride was over and hurried them all away.

Presently they saw a gaily painted barrow which was presided over by a plump woman in a white apron.

Fanciful yellow lettering on a red background proclaimed that —

181

PIZZUTTI'S ICES ARE BEST

A flash of presentiment went through Lacie. She nudged Rose and whispered, 'Isn't it Italian?'

''Course it is,' answered Rose, 'that's why it's the best ice-cream in Haw'sop.'

'I don't think we should tell Tom, though,' Lacie said. 'He seems to get upset about Italy.'

The ice-cream was safely bought, however. Gertie was served first with two ha'penny cornets. Her agile tongue, licking alternately around them, diminished them at a perfectly equal rate. She had half finished them before Rose had received her wafer.

'I'll pay,' cried Tom, and, putting his hand into his pocket, brought out plenty of coins which he held out to the woman behind the barrow.

The woman looked surprised, then glanced at Rose.

'Go on,' Tom said, 'take it. Take all of it.'

The woman turned over a coin with her finger.

An amiable woman, she looked at Poor Tom and shrugged.

'What's the matter?' asked Rose.

'It isn't proper money,' whispered Lacie.

'No English money?' The woman asked Tom. 'Only Italian money?'

'It'ly?' Poor Tom stepped back. He looked at the money in his palm.

The woman might have thought he was a foreigner. 'No good in England,' she said. 'Only in Italy.'

'It'ly?' Tom repeated, and dropped all the coins as if they stung. 'I don't want It'ly money,' he cried and turned out his pockets, there and then, on to the pavement. Some children appeared as if by magic and crawled about picking up the money.

Rose hastily paid for the ice-cream and bustled Poor Tom away from the scene. Lacie and Gertie followed.

'I hope he doesn't chuck his ice-cream away,' muttered Gertie, her cornets only a memory, 'if he doesn't want it he can give it to me. I don't mind it being I-talian.'

'I suppose it was the money from the fowl-house,' Lacie said. 'He must have gone to fetch it when he went for the hat.'

Tom was a bit unsettled. In a cheerful voice Rose suggested that it was time to go to the River Rover.

'Come on, then,' shouted Gertie, dragging Tom by the hand, 'it's this way.'

But they never reached the River Rover.

'Watch that child,' Rose said to Lacie. 'We'll lose her if we're not careful. Watch the top of Tom's head.' It was a good thing he'd got the hat on !

Crowds of people kept getting between it and them but they managed to keep it in sight as it bobbed along.

'That's not the way,' cried Rose, 'she's taking him back to the cattle-market. We must catch up with them.'

She was bustling along so quickly that her face was red. Lacie was almost running but people kept blocking their way and the straw hat always kept ahead.

Then they lost it for a minute or two. It was some time before they caught sight of it again, in the middle of a thicket of people.

Suddenly the thicket broke up. There was a lot of squealing and shouting. Everybody was moving. Somebody shouted, 'He's let them pigs out.'

A little pig ran squealing past Lacie's feet. She jumped aside just in time to save herself from falling. Some people had fallen and were getting up again looking angry.

Piglets were all over the place.

Rose had reached Tom who was smiling in satisfaction to see them escape. She grabbed him by the arm and began to walk rapidly away, almost pushing him before her. Lacie and Gertie followed at a trot.

'It was that shock-headed chap,' a man shouted. 'That one in t'straw hat. I saw 'im let 'em all out.'

'Hurry!' urged Rose. Tom broke into a run and she sped after him.

Lacie lost sight of her and of Tom's hat. Perhaps it had been knocked off his head. She lost sight of Gertie, too.

Once more she was without companions in the streets of Hawksop. She was luckier this time and ran in the right direction towards the river. Soon she saw the bridge. Nobody was chasing her so she stopped for breath.

A cuckoo called very close to her – and again.

She knew that cuckoo and walked over the bridge.

At the other side, hiding behind the stonework, were Rose, Tom and Gertie, all red in the face and laughing, though Rose said ruefully, when she could get it out, that she never thought she'd be running wild through the streets of Haw'sop and if anybody she knew had seen her, Dick would be told, and whatever would he think? But she went on laughing as she wiped her hot face with a handkerchief and straightened her hair with her fingers. Nobody had a comb.

Tom put on his hat again. It was more squashed than ever as Gertie had just been sitting on it.

As they all stood up to go Lacie said, 'Look at the river! It's gone again!'

'What d'you mean, gone?' Gertie was scornful. 'Tide's out. That's all. You ought to know that by now.'

Lacie did know, but somehow when the water had run out she had a sense of unease, almost of loss, and longed for the river to be full again.

The river. Rising, falling, flowing fast or with infinite leisure, its presence always charmed, or alarmed and mystified her.

She would never understand it as Gertie did, nor be familiar with it.

Rose said reproachfully, 'Oh, Tommy, you shouldn't have let all them pigs loose. That was wrong.'

'They shouldn't a been fastened up,' he answered. 'That was wrong. The world's a wicked place just like me granny says it is.'

'I don't know about that.' Rose replied. 'All I know is, I can't help living in it 'cos here I am.'

After the heat and excitement of the day they were almost too tired to crawl the last miles home. Gertie said that she was too famished to walk another step without having summat to eat.

'Don't say summat,' Rose corrected her, 'say something.'

'All right,' said Gertie. 'As long as I get summat I'll say owt you like. Summat — I mean — something.'

They climbed to the top of the river bank to eat the curd tarts and drink the milk which Rose had been carrying around in two large medicine bottles.

'It's sour,' cried Gertie, spouting milk.

'It's been churned with all that running and jumping about,' Rose said. 'It's buttermilk now. It'll do you good. Drink it, and see what you'll find.'

In each bottle when the milk was gone was a pearl of butter. Gertie spent a long time trying to get one out with a twig.

As they went over the rickety bridge at Nettlewood owls were calling and some were flying across from the woods to the barns.

Rose slept at Nettlewood that night.

'Can I sleep here, as well?' Gertie begged. 'I know me granny'll shout at me for being so late.'

'I won't let her shout at thee,' promised Tom, and hanging on to his arm, she went off with him to the cottage.

The lamps had not been lighted and Rose and Lacie went into a dark house. Rose said she could make up a bed for herself in the sitting-room and didn't need a candle. 'I'm good at finding my way about in the dark,' she said, but added, 'I'm glad I'm not walking back home tonight for I'm dead beat an' that's the truth.'

Lacie discovered that Nora's room was empty. Rose could sleep there, as Nora must be spending the night in the little room next to Mrs Mountsorrel's.

But Rose said that she would be perfectly all right on the sitting-room sofa. She and Lacie were flitting softly about like moths. Just before they bade each other goodnight Lacie said, 'Poor Tom doesn't seem to get on very well in the world, does he?'

'What can you expect,' answered Rose, 'when he's been out of it so long?' She began to brush her hair. 'If you ask me, that's all that's wrong with him. He ought to get out and see more of it.'

She brushed vigorously for a few minutes, then went on, 'We'll have to try and get him out of his shell a bit, while I'm here.'

'Would you take him out again?' Lacie was surprised.

''Course I would. It'll do him good. Going out is just what he needs. I'll tell you this, if I'd been shut up in Nettlewood all my life with nobody but Granny Betts I'd be a bit dotty, I'm sure.' She sighed and said, 'It would ha' been nice if we'd seen Dick. This makes two whole days I've not seen him. Eh dear, dear, dear!'

Then she went to wash under the back-kitchen pump, and Lacie went to her own room.

18

Mowing

THE next day the sun was hotter than ever.

Nora came yawning into breakfast. Rose was yawning too. So was Lacie.

'What happens to you these days?' asked Nora. 'I don't seem to be seeing much of you.'

'Just what we've been thinking about you,' Rose told her, but in such a pleasant way that Nora did not resent it, and only laughed and said that her hands were full of Mrs Mountsorrel at the moment.

'And it's the weather as well,' she added with another yawn, and went away again.

What had the weather got to do with it, Rose wondered.

Gertie did not come in for dinner.

'Did her granny tell her off, d'you think?' Lacie asked.

'What if she did?' said Rose. 'It won't bother Gertie for long. Anyway it's too hot for rows.'

In the afternoon she and Lacie went to lounge about in the garden, where Fred Sprott had fixed a swing in the alder tree, with long strong ropes from his boatyard.

Lacie was swinging lazily at first, then with mounting excitement she went higher, then higher . . . She could see over the river, over the trees, over the church, over the moon!

After a time Poor Tom appeared. He walked around the sea of grass and gave Rose a basket of raspberries.

She began to eat some and told Lacie to come down to earth if she wanted any.

Gertie soon joined the party. She had raspberry juice around her mouth and her fingers were stained a bright pink.

Her granny had been making jam. She and Tom had been picking raspberries for her and Gertie was sick of the sight of them.

'Then you won't want any of these,' Rose said, but Gertie had her share just the same.

It wasn't long before she was in the swing and going higher than anybody had ever gone before. She made the branches of the tree rattle together and leaves showered down.

After a time she said she felt 'funny' and began to 'die down'. She got off the swing without being told to, sprawled in the mowing grass and was unusually quiet for a while.

Butterflies danced over the grass and bees, heavy with pollen, lurched through the air.

Tom had disappeared. Rose closed her eyes and lay back in the grass. Only Lacie sat up, her chin propped upon her knees, and looked at the drowsy world.

Suddenly she gasped. Rose woke up with a start. Gertie rubbed her eyes.

Tom's head was sticking round the corner of the house, well above the height of the ground-floor

189

windows. He was making faces at them and calling 'cuckoo'.

Rose sat up and stared as he came round the corner into full view. He was now about ten feet tall.

'Stilts !' shouted Gertie dashing up to him. 'Where did you get 'em.'

'Keep off, blunderbuss,' he cried, 'you'll knock me over.' But Gertie would not keep away and chased him all over the garden.

'You're not supposed to run about in that long grass,' called Rose, but they were laughing so much they paid no heed to her. Soon Lacie joined the chase and all three of them were rushing about on the lawns. Gertie at last managed to get at the stilts and tipped Tom over. They rolled in the grass screaming with laughter. There were groans from Tom, and Rose had just gone over to see if they were mock groans or real ones – Gertie was very rough and might have broken his legs as he kept crying out that she had – when Fred Sprott appeared, in a rage. He was all ready for mowing with a scythe in his hand.

'Get out o' that grass !' he bawled. 'All the lot o' you or I'll cut you in two.'

He accompanied his threat by furious movements with the scythe and a variety of adjectives, some of which Lacie had heard him use before, and some of which she had not, but all of which she was sure were not to be used in polite society, though Rose was still laughing.

'It should a been done a month ago,' he said, 'now it won't be worth cutting with you daft lot rolling about in it. You ought to have more sense. Especially you.' He looked at Rose.

'Go on, you old misery,' she said, 'who cares about a bit o' grass?'

He began mowing and they helped him to rake the grass into heaps, but no sooner had somebody piled it up than somebody else jumped in it and scattered it all over the place. Fred Sprott said he could manage better by himself, then, as they took no notice of him, he said he would chuck 'em in the river if they didn't give over playing the fool and throwing the hay about.

'It isn't hay yet,' cried Rose.

'And never will be by the way you're spoiling it,' he said. Then Rose picked up an armful of whatever it was, hay or grass, and threw it all over him so that he stumbled and fell. In a second they had buried him and Gertie was firmly sitting on him and refusing to let him get up.

Nora came to see what all the noise was about and just as he was struggling to get up, she threw another armful of hay over him, and they all joined in burying him again until he begged them to stop fooling and Gertie sat on him and pushed grass into his mouth.

'Where've you been our Dad?' she kept shouting, 'I've not seen you for ages. It isn't fair. Where've you gone and been?'

When most of the grass was cut and the heat of the sun had lessened, Fred Sprott wiped his face and said it wasn't half thirsty work.

Rose immediately offered to go and make some tea, saying it was long past teatime anyway, but Fred Sprott said, no, he'd got something better than tea.

He went away and came back with some dark brown liquid which spouted and foamed from tall bottles.

'What on earth is that?' asked Nora.

Saying that it was herb beer which he had brewed himself, and that something better would take a lot of finding, he poured some into a glass for her.

He looked at her as she tasted. She said it was horrible – then drank it right off.

Gertie was swilling beer as fast as she could until her father said that she would go off bang like a burst balloon. Rose said, 'No, don't go off bang, go off to the larder and bring back a seed-cake and the rest of the curd tarts if you haven't pinched 'em already.'

'I haven't,' replied Gertie, ''cos I dursn't – not here.' And she looked under her eyelids at Nora, who suddenly seemed to become oblivious of everybody, and strolled to the swing, and languidly went up and down with her gaze far away.

When the cake and the tarts arrived Rose called to offer her some but got no reply.

'She's forgotten us lot down here,' said Fred Sprott, 'or she wants us to think she has.'

After tea – after beer rather – the air grew cooler and they all livened up again.

Nora went into the house and came out with a croquet mallet and a couple of balls.

Tom cried, 'Wait a minute,' and rushed away. When he returned he was struggling with an armful of mallets and hoops and a box of balls.

'Croquet!' cried Nora. 'Put the hoops in, Fred.'

Everybody blossomed in the sun of her good mood and soon a game was in progress, but try as she would she couldn't make it a proper game. Gertie and Tom – and Rose was as bad – were rushing about with mallets hitting balls through any hoop they fancied. Fred

Sprott was laughing his head off at Nora's attempt to enforce the rules.

'It's sillier than the croquet in *Alice*,' Lacie said to Rose who was giggling so much as she tried to get a ball through a hoop that she only said, 'Alice who?'

They went on playing with a kind of inspired lunacy. Fred Sprott, crawling about on his hands and knees, tried to push a ball through a hoop with his nose. 'It's been knocked on one side once before,' he said. 'Mebbe another knock'll put it straight.'

'I'll knock it for you with a mallet if you like,' Nora offered and everybody but Gertie thought it was funny – then Gertie smiled, and yelled, 'Yes, go on hit him,' and held her sides laughing.

For a brief spell of time it seemed that nobody could be cross, nobody hated anybody. All were joined in happiness.

A white blur appeared at one of the windows overlooking the lawn. It was Mrs Mountsorrel wrapped in shawls and recalled to life by the sound of ball on mallet. Rose nudged Nora who shrugged her shoulders and said, 'Leave her alone. It won't make any difference,' and went on playing.

The next time they looked the blur had disappeared.

Tom was wild with excitement and joy. He kept saying, 'Isn't it good? Isn't everything good? This is better than being in t'world, isn't it?'

'Where did you get all these from?' Gertie brandished her mallet at him – 'and them stilts and the racquets and things?'

'You'd like to know, wouldn't you?' he said. 'Mind your own business, our Gert.' He suddenly looked worried.

'Is it a secret?' she teased. He wouldn't tell — but Lacie knew.

They played until the sun had gone down. Even while it was still shining, at the other side of the sky the moon had risen. It looked as if it were made of white air.

'Make a wish!' Nora looked at the moon, then at Fred Sprott, but he shook his head, and Gertie said scornfully that wishing was only at new moons.

'Wishing's only for fools,' said Fred Sprott. He threw back his head and looked at the sky, saying, 'When that moon's out and the next one's full, this weather will have broke.'

'Listen to old Misery again!' cried Rose. She stretched her arms above her head and breathed in deeply the scent of the new-mown grass.

'I do love summer,' she said.

'And summer loves you by the look of you.' Fred Sprott smiled at her, then turned to Nora. 'Doesn't it?' But Nora was going into the house.

'And I'm going home,' Rose said. 'I've a good walk ahead of me. I'll be so late they'll think I've got lodgings.'

Gertie was rolling about on the cut lawns.

'You'll smart tonight,' her father warned her. 'Them grass stalks sting like nettles.'

Lacie said that her arms were already smarting, and so were her legs, but Gertie ran about shouting, 'I don't care! I don't care!' until her father grew impatient with her and told her not to be such a daft little monkey.

'Good night,' called Rose, coming from the house with her basket.

The girls clamoured to walk a little of the way home with her.

194

'Haven't you had enough for one day?' asked Fred Sprott.

No, they had not had enough. Their appetite for pleasure was never-ending. Who wanted to go in on a night like this?

Fred Sprott gave them his permission to go as far as the Three Willers, then they must turn back or he'd come and fetch them.

Nora put her head through a window and called from the house to Tom who was picking up the mallets and balls, 'Put those things in a corner of the hall somewhere. We may want to use them again.'

She drew her head inside. Lacie saw Tom's indecision and felt indignant.

'They're not hers,' she thought. 'They belong to Tom. Well, to him more than to anybody else. They're certainly not Nora's.'

'Go on, then,' said Fred Sprott to Tom, 'do as she says, but be sure and stack 'em up where folks won't break their necks over 'em. The hoops can stay where they are.'

Lacie went up to Tom and whispered, 'I wouldn't if I were you.'

Tom said, 'I don't mind . . . as long as folks are enjoying themselves. I like to see 'em laughing.'

'It's getting late,' Rose called to Lacie. 'I shall have to be going.'

As Lacie hurried over the wooden bridge she looked back and saw Tom carrying the croquet things away, while Fred Sprott strolled about the lawn and smoked a pipe – a clay pipe, of the sort that cost only a penny in Hawksop Penny Bazaar.

'What's the Three Willers?' Lacie asked Rose as they went along.

'She don't know what a Willer is!' Gertie was full of scorn.

Rose sang, 'I'll hang my harp on a weeping willer-tree.'

'Oh, willows!' said Lacie.

'Everybody says willers around here,' Rose told her. 'They'd think you were daft if you talked about the three willows.'

'I see. It's like the Biggills,' Lacie said. 'Local pronunciation.'

'What's she mean?' asked Gertie.

Lacie ignored her and asked Rose if she would see Dick that night.

Rose said that she hoped so even if it were only for one tiny little minute, then she told them to listen for the sound of a horse's hooves, for he might come on Warrior to meet her as he often did when she was late on her way home.

But although they kept listening they didn't hear a horse's hooves and were disappointed.

Lacie wished they could have seen Dick – he sounded so exciting.

'My, he is that!' Rose was in heartfelt agreement. 'But you shall see him . . . one day . . . perhaps sooner than you think.' She added that she'd soon be telling them something, yes, something nice.

Lacie and Gertie clamoured to be told more – but – 'I'm not making any promises, then I won't have to break any,' was all Rose would say.

They walked a little further.

'Here's Three Willers,' she said, 'so you've got to turn back. No arguing. You promised.'

Neither Lacie nor Gertie showed any signs of arguing. The three willows cast trembling shadows in the moonlight and shone silvery white. Lacie certainly didn't wish to go past them and Gertie willingly planted down her feet and stopped.

'Aren't you scared?' she asked Rose, who only laughed and said, 'Who, me?' and set off in a run in the direction of Lark Grange. Lacie and Gertie began to run back to Nettlewood.

As they drew nearer to the trees Lacie for the first time felt positive pleasure at the presence of Fred Sprott. They heard him before they saw him for he called to them from the edge of the wood, and as he stepped out of the shadows Lacie felt, rather than saw, that he was smiling.

'So you did turn back at the Three Willers,' he remarked.

'I was rather nervous,' Lacie replied. 'Willows — willers, I mean,' she quickly corrected herself, 'willers always remind me of the Erl King. They're so creepy and shivery.'

The words had slipped out.

'Who's he when he's at home?' asked Fred Sprott.

'It's a song, I mean a legend, "O who rides here on a night so wild, it is a father with his child." The child sees the Erl King who brings death, and the father tries not to believe it's the Erl King . . . it's a shadow, a willow tree . . . but it *is* the Erl King and the child dies.'

There was a pause then — 'You do know some stuff,' said Fred Sprott.

'Why did you come an' meet us?' Gertie was always ready to direct conversation back to herself.

'I thought you daft little things might not like the

197

idea of coming back through the wood by yourselves. It seems I was right,' he said, 'what with this Earl or King or whoever he was, eh Miss?'

'I wish you wouldn't say that!' Lacie felt sad that somehow she could never get on with him – or rather that he would not get on with her.

'Say what?'

'"Miss", I hate it.'

'Oh! I thought you'd like it.'

'Well, I don't. And what's more – ' she stopped.

'Go on,' he said, 'what's more what?'

'What's more,' she spoke firmly though her heart was beating quickly, 'you know very well I don't like it and I believe that's why you say it.'

He laughed.

'Eh well!' was all he said.

When they got over the bridge the scent of the new-mown grass met them in an intoxicating wave. Gertie snuffed it in, went galloping over the lawns and promptly fell over a croquet hoop.

Her father laughed at her as she sprawled in the grass, and told her that she shouldn't act so wild.

He stopped in the middle of the lawn, and threw back his head.

'Listen to them owls,' he said.

'*Hiboux*,' said Lacie, watching him. She drew a blank. He went on looking at the woods, the sky, the looming house.

'What?' he asked.

'*Hiboux*. It's French for owls.'

'Oh, is it? Thanks for telling me. I am learning summat tonight.' Then he called Gertie, who came back to him, rubbing her knee and grizzling.

198

'Shut up, you monkey, You're making more row than them what-did-you-call-'ems just now?'

'*Hiboux*,' replied Lacie.

'Hear that?' said Fred Sprott to his daughter. 'What do I keep telling thee? Keep thi ears open and thou might learn summat.' Before she could get a word out in reply he shut her up. 'Now get off wi thee to thy granny's.'

Gertie asked if she could go home with him.

'I'm not goin' home. I'm not there much now. I . . . I'm busy.'

'I know,' cried Gertie. 'You're working wi' the celery for Missy Bissy again.'

'No, I'm not. I never set eyes on her. Oh, shut up and go to your granny's.'

So Gertie went to Granny Betts', Lacie went into the house, and Fred Sprott disappeared upon his own affairs.

19

Lark Grange

'PERHAPS they're getting to like each other better,' Lacie said to Rose as they watched Nora showing croquet strokes to Fred Sprott.

Nowadays peaceful airs were flowing through Nettlewood. Mrs Mountsorrel was gaining strength. At any rate Nora was giving herself more time out of the sick-room and Granny Betts more time in it, an arrangement which was suiting them both.

'She's peckin' better and sleepin' better,' said Granny Betts of the invalid, making it clear that she regarded herself as having something to do with the improvement. 'When you've sat by as many sick folk as I have,' she went on, 'you get to know a thing or two as isn't writ in books.'

Lacie and Rose were waiting near the wooden bridge for Gertie and Tom. The four of them were going to Lark Grange that day. This was the 'something nice' which Rose had told them about.

Fred Sprott called across the lawn.

'Our Gert's got to scrub her granny's floor. She won't be long.'

'Don't lift your head when you hit the ball,' Nora told him, 'and keep your mind on what you're doing.'

'That frock,' Rose said looking at Nora, 'is only two bits of white silk sewn together, yet anybody can tell it never came from Hawksop.'

Gertie came galloping up by the side of Poor Tom's long legs.

She was red in the face already, and Rose told her to ease up a bit.

'What if we're late for dinner?' Gertie asked. 'Will they save us some?'

'Of course not, they'll eat up every scrap.' Rose laughed at Gertie's long face, and added, 'I told Mother to get us a cold meal. It'll be a sort of mixture of dinner and tea, so if we're a bit late it won't matter.'

As they began their long walk she told them that Dick was to be there, she hoped in time for dinner. It would be like a party if he were.

The day was everything a day of high summer should be. The wood was cool, the fields were hot. Pheasants strutted through the grass, hardly ruffling a feather at the sign of intruders. Partridges burst from cover in the leaping corn. The sun blazed in a blue sky.

'I've never seen so much sky all at once,' said Lacie. 'There seems more sky than earth.'

The warm wind raced from one side of the horizon to the other.

'There's plenty of air to breathe,' said Rose, 'nobody can deny that.'

Their faces were blooming like the poppies which Gertie was picking.

'Don't smell 'em,' warned Rose, 'you'll get a headache.'

For miles there was nothing to be seen but the wide fields with here and there a farmhouse, or a cluster of cottages or a distant windmill.

It was so hot and yet — Rose sniffed the air — autumn was round the corner. She could smell blackberries.

Gertie threw down her poppies and was ready to go blackberry picking at once.

'We're coming to a good place for 'em,' Rose said, 'but don't go and get yourself all torn and tangled.'

They had to cross a stretch of heath where there were plenty of brambles. Tom roamed about, eagerly followed by Gertie, and quickly spotted the ripest berries. He always got the best ones, Gertie said. He could go blackberrying with his eyes shut.

Rose accepted a handful from him. 'Ee! Look how ripe they are,' she said, 'and it's not the middle of August yet.'

He walked beside her. Lacie was at her other side. Gertie was running and skipping about, sometimes ahead of them, sometimes behind.

'You're a bit quiet,' Rose said to Tom after some time had passed in silence except for occasional whoops from Gertie. 'What's the matter?'

At first Tom said nothing was the matter.

Gertie ran up, laughing. 'Yes there is,' she cried. 'It's Mrs Mountsorrel.'

'You shut up, our Gert!'

'He's scared that the old Missis is going to get better,' shouted Gertie, then ran off. Rose looked at Tom.

'It's true,' he said, beating his hand upon his breast, 'I know I'm bad ... and I'm scared o' being punished for it, but bad thoughts come an' I can't help 'em coming.'

'Tell me,' said Rose in a gentle voice, 'pr'aps they're not so bad after all.'

At her other side Lacie was treading over the grass as softly as a bird.

'If she'd get better an' go away,' said Tom, 'I'd be glad she'd got better. But I'm feared – '

'Go on,' said Rose, 'you're not frightened of telling me.'

'If she gets well she might start it all over again.' He stopped.

'Start what?' Rose asked.

'All that about me going away and bein' made different. "Improved" she calls it. While she was so badly she couldn't go on about it . . . and I was pleased. That's wicked isn't it?'

'You're not wicked,' said Rose.

'If I am,' he said, 'I'm sorry for it. But I can't help it. If she's goin' to get better and begin all that about me goin' away . . . I'd rather she didn't get better at all.' He took a deep breath. 'I'd rather she got worse.'

He looked at Rose who hadn't turned a hair. His confession hadn't disturbed her apparently.

'Folks shouldn't interfere with other folks,' she said, 'even if they think they're doing good by it. 'Cos they don't always know what's best even if they think they do.' She thought for a while. 'Don't you worry though,' she said, 'your granny Betts would never let go of you.'

'She might not be able to help it,' Tom said. 'She mightn't be able to stand against t'other 'un. Other 'un's clever and knows how to talk her way round everybody . . . an' I'm Bad Luck, remember. I've been forgettin' it lately, since you came, but now I'm remem- berin' it again. Tom's a poor misfortunit boy.'

'Poor Tom,' said Rose. 'But never you mind, we'll think of something.'

'Will us?' he asked, brightening up.

'Pr'aps she'll die,' Gertie shouted in his ear, then darted away again.

'Oh, hush!' cried Rose. 'Oh dear!'

Tom gave a great sigh and hung his head.

'Cheer up,' Rose said. 'Remember, you can always come and talk to me.'

'Aye, I will,' he replied, 'if you'll be there.'

'I'll be there,' Rose said several times, and Tom began to look happier.

'I'll come an' tell you if it starts goin' wrong. Yes. I'll come an' tell you and you'll tell me what to do.'

Gertie came galloping back to them shouting that she was hungry.

'There it is!' Rose pointed into the distance where a farmhouse lay at the end of a green track. 'That's Lark Grange.'

'I don't call that nearly there,' said Gertie, 'my legs are tired.'

'No wonder! They've come about three times as far as ours have,' Rose said. 'Think of that dinner Mother's got waiting.'

Gertie immediately began to rush forward as if re-inforced.

Tom was pushing ahead by himself. 'He knows these parts well enough,' Rose told Lacie. 'Mother and Dad have often seen him wandering about but speak they ever so kindly he'll never come in, no, nor even look. He just goes off like something that's scared o' being caught. But he'll be all right today . . . at least I'm hoping so.'

He came back to her looking anxious. She reassured him by saying that he wasn't going amongst strangers, but amongst friends who knew him, and he walked quietly beside her.

No wonder it was called Lark Grange. So many larks were singing all at once.

'Somebody's coming!' There was a note of alarm in Tom's voice and he stepped back behind Rose.

She shaded her eyes with her hand.

'It's Dick!' she cried, 'it's Dick on Warrior! He said he'd meet us if he could.'

Both horse and rider were growing bigger every second.

Rose could not control her feet. They flew off with her to meet the horseman.

He was a big chap. Sitting at ease upon his black horse he looked as high as a house. He pulled Rose up to the saddle – there was a lot of laughter – and rode with her the distance back to Poor Tom and the girls.

Rose was beaming. Her hair was falling about her face and she was trying to pin it up again.

'Here's Dick!' she cried. 'This is him.'

He dismounted, then lifted her down and she introduced him to the others.

'Careful!' he warned as Tom went up to stroke Warrior's nose. 'He's got a bit of the devil in him. Whoa! Steady now.'

But Warrior, as if he were a pet sheep, put his nose into Tom's hand.

'Well! I'll be blowed!' said Dick. 'He's never done that before to a stranger.'

Tom walked by Warrior's head and, after a time,

held the reins while Rose and Dick were together on the other side.

Lacie and Gertie, suddenly shy and prone to giggles, held back for a time and dallied together some distance behind.

'D'you like him?' whispered Gertie. 'I mean Dick . . . not t'horse.'

'Oh yes!' Lacie whispered in reply. 'Do you?'

Gertie sighed, 'Oh, aye!'

They walked in silence and looked at Rose and Dick who were oblivious of them. Tom, with his head close to Warrior's ear, looked as if he were whispering too.

Lacie's imagination had leapt into the future. 'If I get married,' she whispered to Gertie, 'I'd like it to be somebody just like Dick.'

Gertie said that she'd like to get married to Dick.

A spasm of annoyance ran through Lacie.

'You're miles too young,' she cried, 'even to think about it!' Then she brought her voice down again.

'I'm ten next month,' retorted Gertie, 'and I shall grow up quick when once I start!'

'Rubbish!' said Lacie, 'it'll take you just as long as it takes everybody else . . . besides he wouldn't fall in love with you even if you were grown up.'

'Yes he would. But I s'pose you think he'd like you best.'

'Yes, he would! Well, he might.'

They were almost quarrelling. Their voices were shrill. Rose looked back in surprise and asked what was the matter.

'Nothing,' replied Lacie, and Gertie sighed again and said, 'I wish I was as old as Rose. I've never see'd anybody as nice as him.'

'What about your dad?'

'That's different.'

'Well, what about Bertie Bisset?' Lacie said.

'Oh, him! He's only a kid!' replied Gertie, then added in the same breath, 'Don't go an' tell him I said that, though.'

'You'd tell him if I'd said it,' Lacie remarked, 'but I don't tell tales, so I won't.'

Rose remembered their existence again and asked them what they were whispering about.

'Nothing!' they said.

'Anyway,' Lacie still whispered, 'Rose has got him, so it's no use quarrelling.'

'Oh, you two!' cried Rose, 'I don't know what's got into you!'

They laughed — and began to run about picking flowers to give to her mother.

They all had a delightful day. It *was* like being at a party.

When Gertie first saw the meal which was spread out upon the white-clothed dining-table in the biggest of the kitchens she grabbed Lacie's arm in a spasm of speechless delight. Lacie had the fingermarks for several days afterwards.

The table was as big as Granny Betts' cottage. At one end was a great ham, at the other a round of beef as big as a barrel. There were dishes of chicken and tongue and bowls of salad from the garden and tomatoes from the greenhouses and raspberries from the copse. There were jugs of cream as thick as custard and of custard as smooth as cream . . . and there were tartlets and pielets and buns and cakes on every available inch of space.

Mrs Fennell had to preside over the teapot and cups at a side table, there simply wasn't room on the big one.

'Come along, my duck,' Mr Fennell said encouragingly to Lacie, 'you can eat a few more of these rasps,' and Rose poured cream, refusing to take 'No thank you', as an answer.

And as for Gertie! When Mrs Fennell said, 'Now love, is there anything else you could fancy?' even Gertie for once had nothing to suggest, and to Rose's sly suggestion about a bit of Spotted Dick she could only give a faint smile and shake her head.

'Spotted Dick!' exclaimed Mrs Fennel. 'Well – if that's what she'd like she can have it, I'm sure. We had one yesterday and there's half of it left in the dairy.'

'Oh, Mother!' Rose laughed, and Gertie blushed and shook her head again.

At last they all left the table.

The afternoon they spent riding in the paddock on a comfortable mare, Tom taking so naturally to the saddle that Dick said it was a crying shame that the lad had never owned a horse or pony of his own.

'Not even a donkey?' he said in disgust, 'somebody should ha' seen to it for him. There's plenty of stable room at Nettlewood. He's not been treated right, poor chap.'

'There was only Granny Betts, I've told you,' Rose said to him in a low voice, 'and she wouldn't think of horses.'

Poor Tom had ridden up to them and had heard something of what they said. His face was flushed and his hair flying about it. He looked extremely happy. 'She said she'd get me a horse,' he said, 'her, you know. The other one.'

'Did she?' cried Dick, 'then it's as good as done. Leave it to me. I'll find one for you. I'll be looking around pretty soon anyway.' But Tom shook his head and turned the mare about and rode to the other end of the paddock.

Rose quietly told Dick that Tom was nervous about Mrs Mountsorrel and wouldn't want any favour from her.

'Why ever not?' asked Dick, 'especially if it's a horse?'

'He's got a bee in his bonnet about her. He thinks she might want to send him away from Granny Betts, somewhere he could be . . .' Her voice became too low for Lacie to hear all that was said but she did hear Dick say again that it was a crying shame. Rose murmured, 'Everybody knows that Mrs Mountsorrel is . . .' then caught Lacie's eyes and did not finish the sentence.

'It's a funny business,' said Dick, 'upon my word, it's a funny business.'

Several times during that afternoon Lacie heard those words. 'Yes, a funny business,' and 'a crying shame,' from Dick and from Rose's parents too. She supposed that they meant about Tom being Poor Tom and destined to be young and pitiful for all his life.

At the end of that perfect afternoon they set off on the return journey to Nettlewood after receiving many-times-repeated invitations for another visit to Lark Grange.

'There's always a welcome for you here,' said Mr

and Mrs Fennell, looking especially – so Lacie thought – at Poor Tom. 'Treat it just like your own home.'

Rose's father several times during the afternoon had been heard to wonder if Poor Tom couldn't be found a job – 'For everybody's better wi' something settled to do.'

He'd got such a way with the animals, added Rose's mother. It was wonderful to see him with them little pigs.

Rose explained that though Tom was certainly good with animals he wasn't to be relied upon when it was time to send them to market or to the butcher. She shuddered at the thought of what Tom might do then.

Mr Fennell replied that, well, all right, never mind the pigs and such, Tom would surely make a good shepherd. He'd like that, just tending sheep all day.

'Such nice peaceful creatures,' put in Mrs Fennell.

'He'd get to know when they were intended for mutton chops,' said Rose, 'and then – my word!'

Her parents tut-tutted and shook their heads in puzzlement.

'Leave him be,' said Rose at last, 'that's best, and that's all he wants.'

The long walk home was in moonlight. Rose and Dick went part of the way and Tom was allowed to ride on Warrior at a walking pace with Dick by his side.

'I've never seen anything like it, bless my boots I haven't,' said Dick. 'He's never taken to anybody else but me as he's taken to that lad.' He was silent, then said to Tom, 'If you ever want a job with the horses, lad, you come to Bird Hill and I'll find you one. In fact ...' he thought again for he was not one to speak without plenty of thought, 'you shall all come to Bird Hill and have a day there, then Tommy-me-lad can look about him and see the stables an' all. And then — well, we'll see, we'll see.'

20

Bonfire

B<small>UT</small> the day had not yet ended . . .

'We'll go as far as the Three Willers with you,' said Rose, 'then we'll have to turn back.'

'Not just yet,' pleaded the two girls as the three willows came in sight, 'come as far as the wood,' and Tom, sedately riding Warrior, said, 'Yes, come as far as the wood,' and he whispered secretly into Warrior's ear.

'My poor legs!' cried Rose, 'I've been on 'em from morn till night.'

'You'll be riding home, my pet,' Dick told her. 'Once we turn back you shan't walk another step. Me and Warrior'll see to that.'

He called out to Tom, 'Watch him at the Willers, he shies at his own shadow sometimes,' but Warrior, under Tom's magical hand, went safely through the quivery shadows of the willow trees without a tremor, even though some of the leaves fell softly on his head.

'Look how the leaves are falling!' Dick brushed some from Rose's hair. 'It'll be autumn before we know about it.'

The tang of the woods was in the air. 'Autumn

always comes to Nettlewood before anywhere else,' Rose said.

In a voice that echoed through the wood Gertie said that Oo! she liked autumn.

'Ssh!' said Rose, looking over her shoulder.

'Why should I sssh!' cried Gertie, 'there's nobody listening.'

'Everything's listening,' Tom said and let Warrior canter gently forward.

'He's a living wonder on that horse,' murmured Dick.

'I knew it'd do him good to get out a bit more. I said so, didn't I?' Rose asked the two girls. 'He's come out of his shell today, and no mistake.'

'I've never seen him so happy,' Lacie agreed.

The cool breath of the woods was around them like a warning of the end of summer. Gertie stayed with the theme of autumn. It would soon be bonfire night, then there'd be parkin and treacle toffee.

'Talking of bonfires,' Dick said, 'somebody's got one.'

They were nearly through the trees now and ahead of them was the glow of a fire.

Sparks were flying upward and dancing about in the upper air before they danced into nothing.

'Wonder what they're burning,' said Dick. 'They've got a good old blaze on.'

Instinctively they all hurried forward till Rose said, 'Well, it's not the house afire, and it's not the stack-yard because there isn't one. Fred Sprott's been gardening. He's burning rubbish, that's all.'

Gertie was snuffing the air like a champion racer, then bolted in the direction of the flames.

Tom had brought Warrior to a standstill and was staring ahead.

'Turn him round, lad,' Dick said. 'We'd best be going back now.' So Tom dismounted.

Dick lifted Rose up to the saddle in front of him and soon they were disappearing into the dimness.

Tom stood looking after them for some minutes until Lacie pulled at his arm and reminded him that they had better go in. They scrambled across the moat, rustling knee-deep in dead leaves, then made their way over the grass to the back of the house.

The fire was on the waste ground between the barns and the kitchen garden. Gertie was already there, standing as close to the flames as she could without roasting herself. As she saw Tom and Lacie she shouted, 'Hey, Tom! Come an' look what somebody's been an' gone an' started burning.'

Something in her voice made Tom hurry forward and sent a tingle along Lacie's spine like a warning of disaster.

A sound broke from Poor Tom.

Now Lacie could see what was burning — some trays of butterflies, wooden cases with glass fronts all smashed and their contents already half consumed, a stuffed owl, a fox with a bird in its mouth, a battered straw hat with daisies on it, a mountain of old birds' nests and on top of all (Lacie felt a long sigh emerge from her as if it came from the deepest part of her being) on the very top, striding the flames, its patient brown glass eyes shining straight at Tom, was the pet fawn.

Nobody spoke — then a strange sound lifted itself up to the moon, a long howl of rage and anguish as

Poor Tom rushed to the fire and began to kick it apart.

He looked as if he were going to throw himself into the centre of it to drag out the stuffed fawn, but the flames suddenly leaped even higher and fiercer and Lacie and Gertie pulled him back.

The treasures of the secret chamber were dissolving into ash and smoke.

Rigid as a statue Tom stood and stared.

'Oh, Tom!' Lacie whispered. 'Oh, poor, poor Tom! Everything's gone.'

Gertie chimed in with a mournful voice, 'All the findings. All them things you didn't want us to know about.'

Nora and Fred Sprott appeared from the kitchen garden. They were laughing and tousled, and carried garden rubbish with which to feed the flames.

'Been clearing out a bit,' Fred Sprott called. 'We haven't half been busy while you lot have been gallivanting about.'

He threw an armful of thorns on to the fire and stirred it with a rake, then stopped, as if becoming aware that something was wrong.

Poor Tom suddenly awoke from his spellbound state and rushed away to the house.

Nora threw some more thorns on to the fire and the fawn sank into a mass of leaping sparks. Its head was still looking out from the heart of the flames when Poor Tom came staggering back. He was carrying a jumble of old tennis racquets and stilts and croquet mallets, and as if he could no longer bear the sight of his old pet, he hurled the lot over it.

The fawn collapsed and sank and was consumed.

This was too much for Lacie. She broke.

'Oh no! Oh, don't!' she cried, covering her face.

'For God's sake!' said Nora. 'What now?'

'What the hell did you do that for?' shouted Fred Sprott. 'That's all good stuff. You needn't have chucked all that on.'

It was all good stuff and it was burning madly. They waited in silence, a sort of awe around them as the flames ate up the last recognizable trace of Poor Tom's earthly treasures.

'Well, that's that,' said Fred Sprott.

After a last look into the fire Poor Tom turned his face to the woods and walked away.

'What's the matter with him?' asked Fred Sprott. Then, as nobody answered, 'Did he really care about that old junk?'

'Shall I fetch him back?' Gertie asked uneasily.

'Nay, let him go. He'll get over it.' Fred Sprott poked the fire again with a rake. 'Can't keep things for ever,' he muttered, 'there isn't house-room for 'em.'

'I'm going in. It's turning cold,' Nora said. 'By all the fuss, anybody would think we'd burned a body. You'd better come too,' she nodded at Lacie, 'as the entertainment seems to be over.'

But Lacie did not wish to go in with her.

'I'll come in a minute,' she said and Nora went away by herself.

Gertie stayed and watched the fire die, but as soon as Nora had disappeared Lacie went into her bedroom where, without undressing, she lay for a long time on her bed grieving not only for Poor Tom and his destroyed treasures, nor for the mallets and racquets and the lost pleasure they represented, but for the spoiled happiness of the day.

Poor Tom went to ground. He all but disappeared. He was seen occasionally crossing the lawns, silent as a shadow and keeping as far as possible from the house.

'What's got into him?' asked Fred Sprott. 'Still sulking about that old rammel that got burnt, is he? If I'd known he was so set on it I wouldn't ha' bothered with it, be damned if I would. Not worth the fuss and bother, it wasn't.'

He looked at Nora and she looked somewhere else.

'Somebody should ha' told me,' he went on. 'Anyway, I'll make it right wi' him when I see him, whenever that is. He slips out of sight as soon as he sets eyes on me.'

'No wonder,' said Granny Betts. 'You just let him be, Fred Sprott. You've caused enough damage as it is, you and ...' She snapped her jaws together as if she had bitten off the end of her tongue and glared at Nora who was eating thin pieces of bread and butter.

Rose was away, and everybody was missing her, even Granny Betts, though all she said in a querulous voice was, 'When's that pesky girly goin' to hurry up an' come back?'

Rose was doing the housekeeping at Lark Grange. Her mother had gone away to a sick-bed.

'There's a sick-bed here,' snapped Granny Betts, 'though there's only me as seems to remember it,' and again she glared at Nora who was calmly pouring out another cup of tea for herself. Fred Sprott was also sitting at the table at the opposite end and he was drinking tea.

'I've nivver seen anything like it!' muttered Granny Betts as if to herself but making sure that she was heard, 'it's tea, tea, tea all mornin', noon an' night.'

She looked from one end of the table to the other.

'H'm!' she said. 'H'm. Some are dragged up and some are dragged down . . . and them as stand watching see most.' Still nobody answered her, and she walked to the door saying that she was going home whether folks liked it or not, then, though she was wearing her carpet slippers, she made off for her cottage, going across the courtyard in a manner that expressed good riddance to everybody.

For the next few days she made herself scarce. Gertie, too, was less conspicuous. It seemed that a division had fallen between the two parties. The dividing line had been unwittingly drawn by Poor Tom. Granny Betts and Gertie had gone with him to one side of it and put up an invisible barrier.

Lacie wished that she could burst through it and join them. Nora was so busy and bad tempered. She missed both Rose and Granny Betts although she never admitted it. She just snapped and groaned more than usual. Lacie helped her as much as she was allowed to, though trying to help Nora was like trying to touch fire without getting burnt. No matter how careful not to draw attention to herself Lacie tried to be she still got burnt every now and then.

Yet time passed without any major explosion. There were irritated remarks, of course, like, 'For heaven's sake child, can't you look where you're going?' or 'Must you always be under my feet?' And so on, as Lacie fetched and carried like a good-tempered little slave.

In one of the back kitchens she found a rough apron of sacking, tied it around herself and scrubbed a floor. It took her a long time and she became very wet, and somehow the floor, too, stayed wet for ages and folks began to paddle across it just as Gertie said they always did over wet floors. There were a lot of feet-marks on it when it finally dried.

Fred Sprott came in and out, looking surly. Sometimes when he spoke to Nora she seemed to look right through him as if he were made of thin air – or so Lacie thought – or as if he were not worth treading on, never mind speaking to, as he said once in Lacie's hearing.

'You can please yourself whether you speak or not,' he shouted after Nora when she had ignored him, 'I don't depend on you for pleasant company,' and he banged out of the kitchen, knocking his shin against a chair on which he had put some cabbages.

'Cabbages!' said Nora kicking them across the floor.

'She's not getting on very well with him,' Lacie thought, and felt a pang for the golden age which had just passed.

There was plenty of time now for the books which George Springles had brought her, and there was plenty of time for thinking. Too much.

'You're paler again.' The doctor from Hawksop watched her as she stroked the pony he always preferred to a car. As he stepped into the trap he said, 'Not too much reading, now, and not too much alone. Find some companions.'

As the pony trotted away with him Lacie wondered once more where her companions had gone for now she never saw them at all.

She went to the swing in the alder tree and amused herself for a time. When she had tired of swinging – and somehow today she wasn't really interested in anything — she got down, sat on the grass and opened a book. It was *The Cloister and the Hearth* and she remembered George's voice, teasing and affectionate. '*Courage, mon ami, le diable est mort.*'

Ami. Amie. Her thoughts went idly on. *Ami* would have an 'e' on it if he were speaking to her, but in the book . . . She began to turn over the pages, then sighed, not really wanting to read. Soon the open book was lying on the grass beside her and her chin was propped upon her knees.

A pheasant honked in the wood and made her jump. It sounded just like a motor horn. She wondered if Poor Tom were near. There was no sign of him though she kept looking into the trees, just in case —

Her thoughts rambled from him to Gertie. It seemed from what she had said on the night of the fire that Gertie, too, had known of Poor Tom's secret room. At any rate she had recognized the things which were burning just as Lacie had.

What had Rose once said of Nettlewood's secrets? 'Everybody knows them.'

Well, Lacie hadn't told any. She felt pleased about that anyway. There wasn't much to be pleased about these days.

The pheasant honked again, nearer this time. It was like a motor horn. It was a motor horn.

George Springles came rolling up on the renovated motor bicycle and side-car. He saw her, drove over the wooden bridge, and stopped.

'What d'you think of her, eh?' He smiled at Lacie as she ran up to him, then gazed fondly upon his beloved machine. 'She's as good as new now, you know. Been completely overhauled, every nut and screw's been tested. Nobody can understand – ' he lowered his voice – 'how such a catastrophe could happen to MY bike.'

Forgetting her boredom and her book Lacie climbed into the side-car and he whirled her around the carriage drive to the bottom of the front steps.

'Good, eh?' he beamed. 'That is, unless you're nervous of her.'

'Her? Who?'

'It, then. The bike.'

She had been thinking of Nora.

George had come with the news that he was going to take Chloë out of the hospital and back to School Cottage that afternoon.

'If she'd fallen another inch or two further away she'd have struck her head on the bridge.' He grew pale. He still couldn't bear to think of it.

They couldn't find Nora and went into the sitting-room. Lacie was just suggesting that she go and make George a cup of tea when Nora came in.

She was wearing the white silk dress, a white woollen jacket slung over her shoulders. The red silk band was around her head and she was smoking a cigarette from a long holder. She looked even less like a nurse than usual.

'Hullo, Nurse!' George greeted her and got out of his chair.

'Hullo, Schoolmaster!' she replied, a slight frown jagging at her eyebrows.

After George had told her his news she looked pleased but then frowned again as she asked if he were going to take Chloë home in that thing?

'That thing!' echoed George. 'If you mean my bike,

let me assure you, it's been thoroughly overhauled. There's nothing wrong with it now. Nothing whatsoever. But as a matter of fact I've hired a taxi in Hawksop. Mrs Bisset is at School Cottage and she'll stay for a day or two to see to things, then if Chloë feels up to it I shall take her to stay with Mother for a time.'

'How exciting!' said Nora, 'for all of you.'

George looked at Lacie.

'I've been wondering if you'd like to come over and see Chloë? You could stay for a few days while Mrs Bisset is there.' He looked at Nora. 'If that's all right with you, of course?'

But she didn't care one way or the other.

A woman was to come in from one of the outlying cottages to help with the household work at Nettlewood. She wasn't at all like Rose. She was cross-grained and had a rough voice and was at that very moment drinking tea in the back kitchen before setting off on her long walk home.

Lacie ventured to remind Nora of the new arrangement. 'There's Mrs I don't know her name yet. She says she'll come tomorrow and every day if you want her to.'

'I'll get Chloë settled in School Cottage,' George said, 'then I'll pop over on the bike and fetch you . . . unless,' he turned to Lacie with a smile, 'you'd rather Fred Sprott take you over the river.'

'Oh no! You know I'd rather go with you!' she cried and flew to hug his arm.

Fred Sprott came in. It was the first time that Lacie had seen him appear in the sitting-room and she was surprised. He looked out of place in it but he looked

222

as if he didn't know it. And Lacie knew that if he had known it he wouldn't have cared. He would have laughed, as he was laughing now, only louder, and would have rolled up his rolled-up sleeves still further.

She gritted her teeth. Resentment burned at the bottom of her throat so that she could hardly swallow. She was full of confusion. Couldn't Nora see the impertinence of him? He was walking about the place as if he . . . as if he were quite at home in it, as if he had the right to be wherever he wanted to be.

This was Nora's sitting-room, her private sitting-room. People should wait to be invited into it . . . at least Fred Sprott should.

After exchanging greetings with George he looked at Lacie and said, 'What's the matter with Miss Highty-Tighty? She looks as if she's swallowed a fish-hook.'

'Well, I haven't,' said Lacie. 'I'm going back to School Cottage.'

'Oh? When?' He looked at Nora. Something made Lacie say quickly, 'But perhaps I won't go. Perhaps I'd better stay here after all. There's such a lot to do.'

'Nay, don't worry about that,' Fred Sprott replied in a jovial voice. 'We'll have to try and manage without you.' Again he looked at Nora.

Lacie turned away from him.

'What are you doing with yourself these days?' George asked him.

'Oh, dodging about.'

'Busy with the wireless? I see you've put up an aerial here.'

'Aye.' Then the two men began to talk of wireless and motor bicycles and George grew so boring about his marvellous machine which had been taken apart and put together again so that it was now as good as new, if not better, that Lacie went outside to get away from the conversation.

To her surprise she saw Poor Tom.

He was standing by the motor bicycle staring at it, his face haggard and despondent. Something in his look gave Lacie a disturbing thought. Her knees shook with it and she had to sit down on the steps.

Poor Tom looked at her. Between them a question was silently asked and answered, then he hurried away.

Tom. The motor bicycle. The accident. The three came together in Lacie's mind.

George came out of the house with Fred Sprott who began to look inside the engine.

This time it was George who said, 'What's the matter, Lacie?'

Fred Sprott again made a remark about swallowing a fish-hook.

Lacie said nothing.

'Are you worried about going in the side-car?' George asked her, and assured her that it was perfectly safe. 'Ask Fred,' he said.

Fred Sprott lifted his head.

'Eh? Aye. It's safe enough if you drive it right.'

'The mechanic in Hawksop,' George went on, 'was certain that it would never have let me down like that –' he dropped his voice – 'unless it had been tampered with. The wheel nuts had been deliberately loosened on the wheel of the side-car. They held until we went over Two Drain Bridge – then –' He stopped for a moment's emotion, then said firmly – 'In short, somebody did it.'

Lacie's heart gave a thump just as if she had been that somebody.

Fred Sprott was on his knees.

'Oh, aye,' was all he said.

Lacie's lips felt cold. She forced them to move. 'If somebody — ' she stopped and gave an involuntary look around, 'I mean, if it was done on purpose will — will anybody get into trouble?'

George looked at her, then laughed and ruffled her hair. 'I don't think you did it,' he said. 'No . . . it's too late now to start investigating. I'll have to let it go. But if it happens again, I'll leave no stone unturned,' and he looked very serious.

'It'll not happen again.' Fred Sprott got to his feet and wiped his hands on a rag he took out of his pocket.

('But perhaps it's his handkerchief,' thought Lacie.)

'You know what they say . . . lightning never strikes twice in the same place.' He dusted bits of gravel from his trousers.

'Yes. They did a good job on it, George,' he said, 'nearly as good as I'd have done it myself.'

There was some more conversation about motor cars and motor bicycles then George rode away and Fred Sprott went into the house, through the front door.

Lacie waited outside on the steps.

She had seen Poor Tom at the edge of the wood. He was watching George drive away.

So it was Poor Tom who had tampered with the motor bicycle.

But why?

She ran down the steps and across the lawn to the bridge but he had disappeared amongst the trees.

Going into the wood she called his name. She

wanted to tell him that she was trying to understand, that she would keep this secret as she had kept the other. She wanted to tell him that he could talk to her, now that Rose wasn't there. 'I'd be better than nobody, surely,' thought Lacie, 'though not as good as Rose.' She wanted to tell him that there would be no trouble about the motor bicycle's accident, not this time.

He had gone, disappeared quickly and completely as if he had sunk into the ground.

She gave up searching for him and went back across the bridge, picked up her book from beneath the alder tree, then went into the house.

21

Discoveries

LACIE looked for Nora but could not find her and supposed that she had gone to Mrs Mountsorrel.

The new helper had just been speeded upon her homeward way by Granny Betts who was still gazing after her out of the back-kitchen window, and said as Lacie came in, 'I thought she was never going. I'm glad to see the back of her.'

She watched the back go out of sight then unfixed herself from the window and took a cup and saucer to the sink.

She glanced into the cup.

'H'm. Trouble an' sorrow an' a deal o' hard work,' she said. 'Well, that's true anyhow. There's not much fortune in store for that lass,' and she rinsed the ill-boding tea leaves away. 'She's Jake Trudgitt's grand-daughter, and he never amounted to much. None o' them Trudgitts did. Five bairns she's got, she telled me. Just like Trudgitts.'

Lacie was not quite sure whether the last remark meant that the five bairns looked like Trudgitts or whether it was a Trudgitt habit to have five bairns. She asked who would look after them if their mother came to Nettlewood.

Granny Betts gave a screech, then a cackle.

'Look after 'em? Why, lass, they'll have to look after their sens, same as she and her brothers and sisters did when they was little 'uns ... same as Trudgitts always does. I shan't fancy any pudden she makes I can tell you that.'

'What's her name?' Lacie asked.

'Eh, I don't know. I never asked her. She's not a Trudgitt now I reckon, not by name anyhow. But she's a Trudgitt whatever her name, and Trudgitt's good enough for me.'

Lacie was beginning to feel sorry for the former Trudgitt.

'She'll bake as heavy as lead as sure as I'm standing here,' Granny Betts was going on. 'Still, she's the best we'll get so we mun put up wi' her.'

She paused and Lacie got in with her news about going back to School Cottage, and thought how glad she was to be escaping the puddens – amongst other trying things.

Granny Betts was most interested, and – when Lacie had explained – graciously expressed pleasure at the news of Chloë's recovery.

'She was allus the best o' the two,' she said, 'if it had to be one of 'em it should ha' been her,' but Lacie could make nothing at all of this remark, examine it how she would. She gave it up, storing it away for later reflection, and said that she had just seen Tom, but that he had gone before she could talk to him.

Granny Betts made no reply and her face closed up. She began to beat up some eggs in a concoction for Mrs Mountsorrel.

Lacie realised that she was not going to be given any information about Tom and asked about Gertie.

She was cleaning; turning out a bedroom and making herself useful for once.

Lacie thought that was unfair to Gertie but only asked to be remembered to her.

Granny Betts nodded and added brandy to the eggs.

No wonder Mrs Mountsorrel was getting her strength back.

'Aye, she's pickin' up,' Granny Betts said. 'I've brought 'em back to life from death's door before now although I've none of them what-d'you-call-'ems like she reckons she's got – *tifficates.*'

Nora's nursing certificates seemed to be a sore point with Granny Betts.

Lacie said that she was looking for Nora, and supposed that she had gone back to be with Mrs Mountsorrel.

'Nay, she's not. I've been with the old Missis, and have been all this day. I've only just popped out to make a drop o' something strengthening and to have a look at that Trudgitt.'

The drink was ready on a tray and Granny Betts was tying the strings of a dazzlingly white apron behind her back.

'I was brought up to stick to my job if I took one on –' she gave a contemptuous look that seemed to pierce the walls and go up the corridors in search of Nora – 'even though I haven't got some bits of paper wi' writing on to say I'm a nurse.'

She was ready to go to the sick-room.

'Mind you give my remembrances to your cousin Chloë,' she said, 'and tell her I'm glad she's better.

You'll be good company for her, you're not a bad little lass.' She went some way up the corridor then stopped and called back, 'If you're going past her bedroom, don't go empty handed, take some clean pillow slips with you from t'kitchen dresser. She wants some on her bed.' SHE and HER in that tone of voice always meant Nora.

She was not in her bedroom. Lacie put the pillow-slips on the bed and was just leaving to go to her own room when she noticed that the other door — the one she always referred to in her own mind as the 'secret' one — was open.

Perhaps Nora had gone through into the picture room.

'I must find her before I leave,' Lacie thought. 'She may be offended if I don't say goodbye.'

A medley of other thoughts rushed through her brain, thoughts of the picture room, of a picture which opened, of the mysterious corridor and of the secret chamber which was Poor Tom's secret no longer.

Her feet kept pace with her thoughts for now she had gone through that other door, she was in the picture room, and standing before the portrait of the boy who reminded her of somebody. He had the same kind of thick, fair hair, the same shy gaze. Change the bright-coloured bird on his shoulder for a baby owl — it could be a portrait of Tom.

She stretched out her hand, no, it stretched out by itself without waiting for her permission. The picture swung inwards. Before her lay the long brown passage.

She was not frightened, not now that she knew where the passage led. She could hear birds singing outside. Light oozed in from somewhere. Her heart was thumping, nevertheless, as her feet went on.

On, on, on, then several paces forward, then down some steps. On, on, on, then down again and forward, then turn a corner, down more steps then on to Poor Tom's no-longer secret room.

The door was ajar. She had the sense of somebody being there. Was it Tom? Had he come back? She hoped so. She would be able to talk to him at last.

She pushed the door further open, but gently so as not to startle him.

It was not Poor Tom she saw. She saw Fred Sprott.

He was sitting with his back to her and he was wearing earphones and working on a wireless set.

Lacie stared, scarcely able to believe her eyes. Now there was plenty of light – where was it coming from? – and she could see that the room had been scoured and cleaned, trimmed and tidied almost beyond recognition. The fireplace was free of ashes. A fire was laid ready for the match. There were two comfortable chairs, a sofa, some pictures and books and a bench full of tools and pieces of wireless apparatus.

A white woollen jacket was slung over the back of a chair. So was a red bandeau.

Behind the fireplace was a sound. Somebody was moving in the other room.

'Hey!'

Fred Sprott called out so suddenly that Lacie jumped.

'Hey!' he called again, 'come and listen to this. It's London calling.'

And from the room behind, as mild as milk, came Nora.

She went up to Fred Sprott and put a hand upon his shoulder. He took off the earphones and put them on her head.

Then he took her in his arms and kissed her and she ... she wound her arms about his neck and fastened her hands in his dark hair and laughed until he kissed her again.

Lacie suddenly heard her own breath. She put her hand over her mouth, then silently, swiftly, so swiftly that she later felt she must have flown over the ground, she went up the passage, up the steps, and round the corner and up the steps, and up the steps until she was in the picture room and the portrait had closed behind her.

She went into her bedroom, sat on the bed and stared at the wall for a long time, then put her head down on the pillow and cried and had no idea why she was crying.

There was the sound of a motor horn. George Springles was back from Owsterley and she wasn't ready. Quickly she tidied herself, packed up a few of her personal things, then thankfully and without saying any more goodbyes slipped out of the house.

Soon she was sitting in the side-car, the wind blowing through her mind as if it would blow the dark thoughts out.

George smiled down at her. She smiled at him but could not think of a single word to say.

At School Cottage Mrs Bisset had already created an atmosphere of calm and comfort.

Tea was ready. A kettle was singing at the side of the fire and she was just putting the finishing touch – a rose picked by George from the garden – to a tea-tray which was to be taken into the front parlour where Chloë, in layers of delicate shawls, was reclining in state.

A sofa had been drawn up to the window so that she could see what was going on outside. She had seen the arrival of George and Lacie but now nothing was going on and she wanted to be near the fire. She was lying back on a heap of cushions and looked pale, and rather fretful. She was pleased when Lacie came in and immediately wanted to hear all the news of Nettlewood.

'Tea first!' said George and firmly directed Lacie back to the living-room, insisting that he could move the sofa all by himself. As she closed the door she saw him bend his back to the task and sing into Chloë's ear at the same time, 'Give me a little cosy corner in an arm chair for two.'

'Listen to that!' There was a sigh underneath Mrs Bisset's smile. 'I must say it's nice to be made a bit of a fuss of.'

And George certainly did make a fuss over Chloë that evening, and so did Mr Bindle who arrived a little later on a new bicycle which he had pedalled at top speed from Hawksop. *He* fussed so much that Mrs Bisset said as she and Lacie sat a long time over the tea-table together in the living-room, 'If you ask me she could have been the parson's wife as well as the schoolmaster's.'

'Not both!' Lacie smiled at the thought of Chloë with two husbands.

'Seems a shame to have to let one go,' sighed Mrs Bisset, 'especially as some of us don't get the chance of one, let alone two. Still, she can't have 'em both and that's a fact. It's a law o' the land, this land any-way.' And she looked quite relieved as she stirred her tea.

'Mr Bisset must have been very fond of you,' Lacie remarked, wishing to remind his widow that she, too, had once been chosen.

'Aye, but it's such a long time ago.' Mrs Bisset sighed again. 'It's almost as if it never was – except for Bertie. And I'm not young any more and I'm getting fat.'

A phrase came into Lacie's mind and was out of her mouth before she thought twice about it.

'Better a plump hen than a lean cat,' she said.

'That's a bit of Fred Sprott!' Mrs Bisset twiddled her teaspoon, a flush rising in her cheeks.

Lacie wished that she hadn't remembered the remark for it made her think of Nora and Fred Sprott. The memory of those two together hurt her in some way and made her feel uneasy. It would be comforting to tell Mrs Bisset about them. She would be sure to say something sensible . . . but Mr Bindle put his head round the door and asked for some more tea-cakes.

Gertie Sprott appeared before the last one was eaten. The last but one, that is, for one had been put aside on the top of the oven for Bertie who was to come in later.

'How did you get here?' demanded Mrs Bisset when she had swallowed her surprise – and a three-cornered bit of cake which made her catch her breath – 'Did your dad bring you?'

'No, he didn't. I bringed myself.' Gertie's jaw was thrust out in a way which signified her present lack of amiability towards her dad. 'He don't know I've gone,' she added.

Mrs Bisset gave a cry. 'Have you taken the boat? How is he to cross?'

'He'd got both boats over there.' Gertie informed her. 'He's been painting or summat. I left *Wobbler* for him. I can't see as he needs two boats.'

Her eyes were on the tea-table and Mrs Bisset told her to sit down at it. Gertie obeyed immediately, her expression lightening.

'I don't think he's coming home tonight, though,' she said, her mouth already full of bread and butter. 'He don't seem to go home now.'

'Oh?' Mrs Bisset raised her eyebrows. 'Then where – ?' But she broke off as another thought struck her. What was Gertie going to do? Surely she wasn't thinking of sleeping at home all by herself. Gertie hadn't thought at all, but now said she would stay with Mrs Bisset.

'You can't,' said Mrs Bisset, 'it's not my house, and there isn't any room. Your dad will come over when he finds out you're gone, I suppose.'

Gertie said she didn't care what he did and Mrs Bisset looked quite stern.

After a time Bertie Bisset came in. He had ridden over from Celery Cottage on Mr Bindle's old bicycle. After the ride through the fresh air Bertie had a good appetite. When he had taken the edge off it he was able to tell his mother how things were at Celery Cottage, and they were all right. Ebenezer Bonem kept popping in to give a hand though his rheumatism was bad. Poor old Bonem! After a lifetime of planting celery in the damp river soil, and of digging graves in it, he was as stiff and creaky as an ancient oak.

When those who had to leave School Cottage were getting ready to do so Gertie again pleaded to be allowed to stay the night, and was again refused. She was furious at the idea of Lacie being left with Missy Bissy.

As Bertie said goodnight and began wheeling his bicycle out of the yard Gertie had a brainwave. She would go back with him. There was plenty of room at Celery Cottage.

'Ridiculous!' cried Mrs Bisset. 'Certainly not!'

Gertie wanted to know why not.

'Because – because Bertie's got a lot of jobs to do when he gets home.'

Gertie made light of that as an argument. She could work, too, couldn't she?

Mrs Bisset looked around as if for help. The sight of Bertie coming in again through the door inspired her. He had a lot of school work to do as well, she said.

'What! In the 'olidays?' Gertie was incredulous.

'Yes. He does homework every night, don't you, Bertie?'

Bertie nodded in modest appreciation of himself.

'And you certainly can't help him with that,' put in Lacie.

Mrs Bisset intervened in order to deflect Gertie's annoyance from Lacie.

'Now, now! Gertie!! Gertie! Don't get so wild. Your dad will come home. I'm sure he won't leave you in that horrible – in that house all night by yourself – whatever his faults.'

'Faults? What faults?' Gertie glared. 'Medad hasn't got no faults. You've no right to talk against him behint his back.'

'Behind,' murmured Bertie, 'not behint.'

Although flustered, his mother gave him a glance of approval, then sat down and fanned herself with her apron.

Gertie scowled at everybody. Her mood mollified however when, after a few moments for recuperation, Mrs Bisset got up and discovered another tea-cake in the larder. It was a *special* special one she had put away for Bertie to take home and it was for that he had popped into the house again.

He looked glum as he saw it disappear into Gertie's pocket.

'I'll make sure you get one tomorrow, love,' said his mother, 'I'll be baking again in the morning.'

She was beginning to sound tired.

'Tell you what,' she said, 'we'll all three of us walk with Bertie for a bit of the way. It'll freshen me up – I could do with stretching me legs – and on the way back me and Lacie will drop Gertie in at home and make sure her dad's in.'

So Mrs Bisset, Lacie and Gertie accompanied Bertie down the long village street until he said good night and set off across the fields.

There was a light in the Sprott house. Mrs Bisset was relieved.

'Come an' talk,' begged Gertie, 'just for a minute,' but Mrs Bisset said she must hurry back to School Cottage.

'You can give my regards to your dad, though – if you like,' she said.

Gertie was still aggrieved.

'I don't think it's fair. I've got more right to stay with you than she has.'

'Lacie has nowhere else to go,' Mrs Bisset replied, 'not at present anyway.'

And Gertie went into the Sprott house, at last, without any more argument.

22

Somebodies – and Nobodies

AFTER the recent constraints and silences of Nettle-wood, School Cottage was a paradise of comfort and good humour. Pleasant mealtimes punctuated the hours. Mrs Bisset's baking beggared description. Buns, pies, tarts, puddings. What Gertie was missing! Gertie *was* missing – she did not appear again.

By day, Lacie hung on to the company of the grown-ups and looked forward to seeing Bertie in the evenings. She had a number of congenial tasks to do and enjoyed being useful, yet troublesome thoughts were still at the back of her mind and when she was off guard they crowded forward and demanded attention.

She could not blot out the memory of Nora and Fred Sprott together in the secret room, and mixed up with it all was a confused feeling of deception, conspiracy even, for why had they waited until Poor Tom's back was turned before stealing his room and destroying everything that was in it?

Couldn't they have asked him if they had wanted the room so much?

And why had it been necessary to burn all those things?

'Cruel! Cruel!' thought Lacie. Tom would never trust anybody now. Just when everything, chiefly because of Rose, had begun to look so much better for him. She had been trying to draw him out of himself into the world, and for a time, when they were all at Lark Grange, it had looked as if she would succeed.

And she would have succeeded, but for Nora and Fred Sprott. Now they had spoiled everything.

'It isn't fair, it isn't fair!' was Lacie's passionate inward cry.

She kept thinking of Tom as he had held the little bird which the kitten had mauled, and felt again the sense of helplessness and injustice which had oppressed her then.

Once or twice she had been at the point of confiding in Mrs Bisset, who could perhaps explain certain puzzling things. For instance, it had seemed that Nora and Fred Sprott hated each other, and that they should hate each other was a much less hurtful idea to Lacie than that they should love each other.

Why?

Could Mrs Bisset explain it?

And having seemed as if they hated each other why was it that they were suddenly behaving as if they loved each other?

Could Mrs Bisset explain that?

She was sewing so calmly as she sat near the kitchen table, her needle flying along the seams of a dress she was letting out.

Why did it seem right for Chloë and George to be in love? George was quite old, quite grey. He was older than Fred Sprott, almost, Lacie would have thought, too old to be in love at all.

'Yet I don't mind it at all, for George,' thought Lacie, giving him her permission to be in love with Chloë as much as he liked.

Yet why did it somehow seem not right that Nora and Fred Sprott should love each other? Certainly it had been pleasanter when they were agreeing and not quarrelling, but . . . no, it did not seem right that they should be in love.

Could Mrs Bisset explain it?

And as for kisses. Rose and Dick had snatched kisses many times on the Lark Grange day. Rose's mother had smiled and said, 'Oh, those two! Just look at 'em,' and her father had said, yes, there'd be a wedding before long, and Gertie and Lacie had seen and smiled, whispering together about being grown-up and in love.

'I like people being in love,' thought Lacie. 'I LOVE love.'

So why her dismay at the kisses between Nora and Fred Sprott?

'Could you explain that, Mrs Bisset?'

The words were not spoken. Lacie went on with her silent struggle to sort out her muddled feelings. Something always seemed to stop her from asking Mrs Bisset about them . . . yet somehow this afternoon she could not forget them.

Fred Sprott was so difficult, so surly, always making threats of cutting folks in two and chucking 'em in the river. Sometimes he laughed, then his teeth gleamed and sparks shone in his eyes. At those times Lacie would begin to feel that she could almost like him, then he would go back to being rough and surly again.

And Nora? She was difficult to get on with. She was

like Fred Sprott in that if in nothing else. Apart from that they were like ill-fitting pieces of a puzzle. It seemed natural that they shouldn't agree ... not at all like Chloë and George who, moving against the same background of school and village, matched perfectly in every way, and in so doing made their pleasure in each other shine around them.

You could say 'Chloë and George' and it would be right.

You could say 'Rose and Dick' and it would be right. Better than right!

But you couldn't say 'Nora and Fred Sprott'. You couldn't! You couldn't!

'No, you can't!' Lacie cried out.

'Yes, I can.' Mrs Bisset was moving pieces of material about on the table, 'If I take this piece here – and sew it along here, then put it to this ... it'll do very well.' She jig-sawed some more material about, examined the effect then said, 'You needn't look so doubtful about it – it's going to be all right,' and she went on snipping and shaping.

But Nora and Fred Sprott ... no, that wasn't all right. The very thought of them together was of something dark and hidden, something that belonged to the underground room at Nettlewood, something that wasn't all right, never would be all right. Look how they had already given pain to Poor Tom.

Mrs Bisset held up the dress she was remaking and measured it against herself and Lacie assured her that it would look very smart when it was finished. Mrs Bisset replied that it would have to do whatever it looked like, then added that some folks wouldn't put it on to wash a floor. Some folks? Like – like Nora, for instance? Mrs Bisset nodded, bit off a piece of thread, then suddenly burst out that she hoped nobody was going to throw herself away on somebody she looked down on, for that wouldn't do either of 'em any good.

Lacie knew who was meant by that 'nobody' and 'somebody' and thought of Nora throwing herself away into the dark, ramshackle river-smelly Sprott house. Would she wear an old coat and a red knitted cap instead of a red bandeau, and help with the boats and haul people over the ferry. And what about Gertie?

Mrs Bisset looked up.

Lacie was embarrassed. Her thoughts had run away with her. She hesitated then said that Gertie wished she could live at Celery Cottage.

'Oh does she? Well, she used to.'

'Both of them. She and her dad.' Lacie laughed. 'It would be awful for you at Celery Cottage with him there, wouldn't it?'

Mrs Bisset made no answer to that, but after a moment remarked that every girl in Owsterley had been in love with Fred Sprott when he was young.

Lacie was astonished. With Fred Sprott! All the girls?

Mrs Bisset was quite sure about it. All the girls — except one, the only one he cared about. She wouldn't have him, thought she was far above him. It was because of her that he had left Owsterley. He couldn't bear to go on seeing her, knowing that nothing would ever come of it. When he came back he was married. Then Gertie was born ... then his wife was killed in Hawksop, knocked down by a horse and cart. Jake Trudgitt's old horse, it was. It had taken fright and bolted.

243

Lacie was full of pity. Mrs Bisset threaded her needle.

'That left Fred on his own, except for the baby, poor little Gertie. I took her in when the war started, and Fred joined up. Albert had died – that's Mr Bisset as was – and Bertie was a little lad.'

The clock ticked.

'He's a fool to himself is Fred Sprott. That's his trouble. He's clever and could get on. He just needs a helping hand – but he can't see it, no, not even when it's under his nose.'

She broke off, then put all the sewing together and cleared the table.

The session was over.

Chloë and George came in from a walk and Lacie helped to get tea ready. She was glad that she hadn't told Mrs Bisset about Nora and Fred Sprott, sensing in some way that it would give her pain.

Lacie sighed.

Another secret!

And secrets take a lot of bearing on your own.

Lacie and Bertie got on well together. Sometimes they carried a simple meal into the garden and talked. Bertie hoped that Lacie wouldn't be gone before Pear Day, for even though he had left Owsterley school he always managed to be present on the occasion. In fact, he told her modestly, he was superintendent of it.

Gertie Sprott still had not been seen. The Sprott house was silent. Every night as she drew the curtains in Lacie's bedroom Mrs Bisset said, 'Dear me, still no light. Out again. They must be keeping him busy in Nettlewood.'

The word sent a dark shiver through Lacie's being and she tried not to think of that secret she had, with Fred Sprott and Nora in the middle of it.

Time went on pleasantly.

In the mornings Lacie helped Mrs Bisset about the house or ran errands.

In the afternoons there was usually a stroll into the fields, George and Chloë walking slowly together while Lacie and Mrs Bisset looked for blackberries.

The evenings were drawing in. Each night the curtains were drawn a little earlier. After tea the fire was livened up with twigs and a big log put on. Mrs Bisset sat sewing in the chimney corner as Lacie and Bertie played Snap under the lamp on the table, and from the next room, like a hum of friendly bees, came the murmur of Chloë and George planning their life together.

23

Cloudburst

LACIE had been back at School Cottage for almost a week when she was awakened in the middle of the night by a sound which she had almost forgotten about. She sat up in bed.

Mrs Bisset, with a shawl over her shoulders and looking like the walking ghost of a feather bolster, padded across the bedroom floor to close the window.

She apologised for her intrusion and explained that rain was 'siling' down.

There was no blackberry picking on the next day, nor on the next nor the next. Having begun, the rain apparently was unable to stop.

Lacie didn't mind wet days. School Cottage was cheerful whatever the weather. She helped Mrs Bisset with the baking – and there was that large filled-to-overflowing bookcase still unexplored. Soon after breakfast George splashed in, leather motor-coat glistening as he peeled it off to drip itself dry until after supper when he put it on and splashed away again.

It rained and rained, not stopping for the church-goers on Sunday.

Some people might have squelched through the fields, and Mr Bindle must have had a very damp ride on his bicycle, but the inhabitants of School Cottage stayed snugly at home. Bertie Bisset came to tea, though. A drop of rain didn't worry him.

'It's the same everywhere,' he said . . . 'the men on the boats coming from up river say it's not stopped raining for four days an' nights. Fred Sprott's just told me.'

'Fred Sprott had better look out then,' replied Mrs Bisset, then added, 'and so had all of us.'

The next day George was to take Chloë to see his mother and he was loth to give up the idea in spite of the weather.

On Monday morning the rain had stopped, though the air was very damp, and the clouds were very heavy. Chloë looked dubiously at the state of things outside, but urged on by George, went upstairs to finish packing her clothes.

Mrs Bisset, too, was concerned about the dark clouds moving across the sky. There was a long walk home ahead of her to Celery Cottage and various agricultural matters there were pressing on her mind. She looked abstracted as she went about from room to room with freshly laundered clothes.

Lacie made herself busy in various small ways and tried to change her mood. There was no reason why she should be depressed. There had been reassuring letters from abroad. All danger was over and she would soon be going home . . . But before that there was Nettlewood.

If only she needn't go !

She had a sudden idea. Her face brightened. Why

couldn't she stay at Celery Cottage with Mrs Bisset and Bertie? She hurried on as a look of refusal dawned on Chloë's face. Mrs Bisset wouldn't mind. She was so kind. Surely she wouldn't say no?

'That's just it. She wouldn't,' Chloë replied. 'She wouldn't like to refuse. For that very reason we must be careful not to put too much on her.'

Lacie's face fell again.

'It was good of her to come here at all,' Chloë was going on. 'She's had to neglect lots of things at home. There'll be no end to catch up with when she goes back.'

There was a busy time coming on now with the celery. How that poor woman worked!

'But I'd help her,' Lacie cried, unwilling to abandon her one chance of evading Nettlewood. 'I can scrub floors now. I could feed the fowls and collect the eggs – and if somebody told me what to do for the celery I'd do that too.'

Chloë smiled and shook her head. She and George would be back in a few days. School began next week.

'A week today.' Lacie had a long face. A week would be a long time at Nettlewood.

Chloë promised that as soon as she was back in School Cottage Lacie should know.

Lacie asked how.

'I'll stand on the bank and wave a flag,' Chloë was smiling, 'so remember to look out for it.'

'I'll be looking all the time,' said Lacie.

George appeared at the bedroom door, seized a couple of suitcases, asked Chloë if she thought she were going to Paris, then staggered downstairs. Lacie was just about to follow him when Chloë stopped her.

There was still one small matter – Lacie's five-pound note. She had better take it. Suppose Chloë were delayed or something – suppose Lacie had to go home earlier than anybody expected? But she must give it to Nora for safe keeping. A five-pound note was a big responsibility.

'Chloë!' called George and she flew downstairs.

Lacie folded the note into her purse.

At last the motor bicycle was out of sight. Lacie gave it a last wave then followed Mrs Bisset to the back of the house.

Before she went inside Mrs Bisset again looked at the sky, then added a big black umbrella to her possessions which were already assembled at the back door.

She took a last look around the house.

Everything was tidy. Nothing could set on fire. The lamps were trimmed, the sticks were in, the coal-bucket full, the fire was laid – and she'd set the table for a meal. There was nothing more she could do so she locked the back door and put the key under a flowerpot in the coal-shed. Then she took up her umbrella and was ready to go.

'Come down to the boat with me,' Lacie pleaded, 'just to wave goodbye and so that – ' She stopped. She had nearly said, 'So that I won't have to meet Mr Sprott by myself.'

Mrs Bisset hesitated – then said it was getting late and she ought to be going. All right then, just for one minute but she really mustn't wait longer.

They went to the Sprott steps. The boats were at the bottom but there was no Fred Sprott.

After a minute or two Mrs Bisset began to move away.

Where had the man got to? Rather irritably she told Lacie to give him a shout.

Lacie didn't want to give Fred Sprott a shout. She wished she could take a boat and row herself across the river as Gertie could.

The water was well up the steps. Mrs Bisset's feet were moving about as if they were twitching to be on their way. With resolute strides she went to the Sprott house and rapped at the door with the umbrella handle.

Fred Sprott came out.

He was eating a corned beef sandwich and had grown a black moustache. When he saw Mrs Bisset he looked surprised, then pleased.

'If it isn't Missy Bissy,' he said, a smile gleaming under the moustache, 'this is a surprise. I was just having me dinner.'

'You're a bit late with it,' remarked Mrs Bisset.

'Or p'raps it's me tea. I'm on me own, you know and things are a bit anyhow.'

'Poor thing!' said Mrs Bisset. His smile gleamed again and she pulled herself up straight and looked formal as she said, 'I've only called to see if you're ready to take the child across. By the look of the water it's time you got started.'

He glanced at Lacie, and made some remark which she could not hear.

Mrs Bisset looked annoyed and replied in a low voice – but Lacie heard what she said – that the poor child couldn't help it if she was bandied about from one place to the other.

Heavy drops of rain began to fall.

'Drat it!' cried Mrs Bisset, 'we're all going to get caught in it.'

'Come in for a minute, then,' suggested Fred Sprott but Mrs Bisset refused, saying that once the rain had begun it wouldn't stop in a hurry and that there was Bertie to think of.

'Oh, Bertie,' said Fred Sprott, then moved after her as she was going away. He put his hand on her arm.

'I've been wanting to tell you, that is meaning to tell you –' he moved his hand away – 'trying to tell you . . .' he stopped.

'Well?' said Mrs Bisset.

He looked awkward.

'I don't think I'll be able to help in the fields wi' the celery – as – as usual.' ·

Mrs Bisset said nothing.

'I'm a bit . . . a bit on the busy side, these days. What with one thing and another I've a lot on. Something I didn't reckon on has cropped up, if you see what I mean and –'

'I see what you mean,' she interrupted him.

'I don't see how I can manage it – you know I always help out when I can – ' Fred Sprott was getting himself tied up, and stopped talking.

'It's quite all right.' Mrs Bisset was very dignified. 'Don't concern yourself about me. Ebenezer Bonem is giving a hand already. He's over seventy-one but he can still put in a good day's work – better than many a one who's young but not so willing – and of course there's Bertie.' She finished with a gleam of triumph as if she had now said everything.

'Oh, aye.' He hesitated. 'Will you manage then, d'you think?'

'Think? I know I'll manage, or we'll manage,

Bertie, Eb'nezer and me. We'll get on all right. We won't need any help. As a matter of fact,' she added as she turned away from him, 'I'd rather do without it – under the circumstances.'

She hurried up to Lacie and gave her a quick hug as if to put an end to the session as quickly as possible.

Lacie gave her a hug. There hadn't been many hugs since she came to Owsterley.

'You'll be all right,' said Mrs Bisset. 'It's not as if you're going to strangers.'

'Yes, it is,' said Lacie.

Mrs Bisset looked troubled. 'What with one thing and another,' she said under her breath then added firmly, 'Never mind, love, you'll soon be back here again.'

She sounded kind but made it clear that she meant to get away. More heavy drops of rain began to fall. They made splashes as big as pancakes – well, small pancakes.

As she was hurrying away Fred Sprott called after her. 'Come into the house till the rain stops. Don't be a fool.'

She turned round to answer him.

'P'raps I am a fool,' she said, 'and thanks for telling me ... but I'm meeting Bertie and I've got to get back to see Mr Bonem before he leaves work,' then, putting up the umbrella, she hurried down the street.

Fred Sprott muttered under his breath and threw the remains of the sandwich into the river.

'Eb'nezer Bonem !' he said. 'It's a good name for him. He's all bones.'

He looked at Lacie who flicked a smile across her face.

252

'Get into t'boat then.' He sounded exasperated. 'Or are we goin' to tek all day?'

Black river. Black sky – and he was surly black.

'It's surly.' Fred Sprott echoed the very word Lacie had thought of so that she was startled and wondered if she had said it aloud.

'The river,' he explained, 'it's in a bad mood.'

'So are you,' she thought.

'So are you,' he said. 'Aren't you on speaking terms nowadays?'

As usual she found it difficult to know what to say to him. Her brain rolled about to discover some small talk. She stared at the speeding river and asked, 'Will – will the Aegir be coming, do you think?'

'Aegir? You've heard about that, have you?'

'Yes. I can't think what it's really like though, except that it's weird and frightening.'

Like a monster. Like an ogre.

'Oh, is it?'

'I'd like to know more, of course.' She stopped.

'I'll write a book about it' – he said bo-oo-ok – 'and then you can read it. You've got plenty of time to waste.'

A streak of lightning flared across the sky and she screamed. Thunder followed.

'Haven't you seen lightning before? Don't it thunder where you've come from?'

She thought how contemptuous he sounded and wondered what she had done to deserve it.

After a moment he said, 'All right. Don't be scared. Put that oilskin o'er thy head.'

Rain was coming down heavily. She didn't want the oilskin.

'Please thisen.' His speech was becoming more broad as his irritation increased. 'It's goin' to come down heaven's hard in a minute. Get soaked if thou'd rather.'

He said no more for he was having to pull with all his strength against the current. Lacie could feel the power of the river beneath them. It was trying to tear them away, out of course. It *would* tear them away.

She gripped the edge of her seat with both hands.

Black river. Black sky. Black surly Fred Sprott. He seemed made of blackness.

The only brightness was the glitter of raindrops caught in his black moustache and amongst the black stubble on his cheeks.

She turned her head away.

When she looked at him again he had put on his red cap. A pirate's cap. A devil's cap.

She suddenly seemed to hear George saying, '*Courage, mon amie, le diable est mort.*'

But the devil was not dead. He was alive.

She looked at Fred Sprott.

'It's him,' she thought, 'Fred Sprott is a devil.'

She stared at his face. It was stern and hard. It looked as if it never smiled.

'I hate him.'

Her eye caught his.

'There's nothing to be scared of,' he said. 'I'll draw in to the bank a bit further down.'

Now she noticed that the boat had been pulled far past the landing stage.

At last in lightning, thunder and lashing rain they were over the river.

She was out of the boat before it touched the bank.

'Watch out!' he cried, annoyed. 'You'll have us both in t'river and I don't fancy a swim even if you do.'

She forgot to thank him for the ferry but turned her back on him without speaking and began to climb up the slippery bank. Suddenly, with a scream, she recoiled and stood as if rooted to the ground.

'What's up now?' He was irritated. Her scream had startled him.

Shuddering she pointed at black slugs, black slugs everywhere all over the grass.

'Oh, them! They're nowt. For god's sake don't be so soft. I've never seen such a milk-sop as thee in all my life.'

He bent back to the boat.

She turned her face to him, blazing with fury.

'I hate you!' she screamed, 'I hate you! You're rough and horrible and vile. You shouldn't even be allowed to speak to people let alone kiss them ... and I do believe in the monster, that ogre that comes up the river! It's you! It's you! You're the ogre! You're the monster of Nettlewood!'

She was aware of his astonished face gleaming with rain as he lifted his head. She took two steps away then turned back, her rage still bursting out.

'And I pity Gertie,' she shouted, 'I pity her. I'd rather be dead than have you for a father!'

Then she stumbled up the bank over the slimy slugs on the slimy grass and ran all the way through blinding rain into the house.

24

Granny Betts

IT WAS a good thing, perhaps, that Lacie was beside herself with rage against Fred Sprott. As she ran through the front door of the house the darkness in the hall was so profound that, had she been calmer, she would have shuddered to enter it, but now she rushed straight through it into the kitchen and stood sobbing with her back against the door. For a long time she was unable to stop.

A voice said, 'Whativer's the matter? Anybody'd think there was a pack o' wolves after thee.'

Somebody was shaking her, but not roughly. It was Granny Betts who was saying, 'There! there! Don't tek on so. Summat's scared the bairn. Whativer it is it's nowt to break thy heart over.'

It was Granny Betts who was leading her to the fire and putting her into a chair and taking off her wet shoes. It was Granny Betts who shuffled away and brought back a dressing-gown and slippers.

Soon Lacie was sitting in a small chair near the fire with only an occasional gulp as the aftermath of her storm of sobbing.

Granny Betts lifted the kettle from the hob and

made tea. Lacie, as she wiped away the rest of her tears, said that she didn't want any tea, th-th-thank you, but Granny Betts took no notice and poured some for her. It was dark and strong and slightly smoked but Lacie drank it.

'That's better.' Granny Betts sat down in the rocking chair on the opposite side of the fire. 'Now, what's it all about?'

Lacie didn't want to say, couldn't say.

'It's better if it's told, whativer it is,' – and Granny Betts looked very wise. 'It's allus better to tell it to somebody, 'specially to somebody like me who knows how to keep her mouth shut. So tek thy time, I can wait.'

And she waited, looking into the fire.

At last Lacie said, 'I – I was rude to Mr Sprott.'

'Rude to Fred Sprott?' Granny Betts gave a cackle. 'Rude to Fred Sprott? Is that all thou's cryin' about? That's nowt. He'd been rude to plenty of folk in his time.' She laughed again. 'It won't do him any harm to have a taste of his own medicine.'

Lacie was only slightly reassured, and answered,

'I – I said awful things.'

'Awful things? Nay, I can't believe it. What awful things dost tha know about Fred Sprott?'

But Lacie could not tell her.

'I wasn't polite,' was all she could say, 'and I shouted at him. He must be dreadfully angry. I – I wasn't at all polite.'

'Not polite?' echoed Granny Betts. 'Folks can't allus be polite, little lass. They have to let go sometimes, or they bust. It's natur'. Like cloudbursts. Thou's just seen one o' them tonight.'

'Was it a cloudburst?' Lacie showed a gleam of interest.

'Be sure it was — and we'll have some more of 'em yet. The weather's broke. Rude to Fred Sprott, eh?' and Granny Betts cackled again. She had several bouts of chuckling during the evening.

She must have noticed Lacie's involuntary glances at the door for she said, 'She won't be coming in yet awhile if that's who you're lookin' for. She's had a busy day with her.'

'Is Mrs Mountsorrel worse?'

'She's not better, that's a fact. Frettin' an' worryin' don't help anybody.' Granny Betts poked the fire with a stick and watched the end of it blaze, then smoke.

'Is she very sad?' asked Lacie.

'Sad?' repeated Granny Betts. 'I've never asked her.' She thrust the end of the stick into the fire and watched it catch alight. After a time she went on, 'Countin' the cost, that's what she's doin! Countin' the cost and don't know how to face the reckoning.'

'Is she — is she so very poor now?' Lacie had heard plenty about the diminished Mountsorrel resources and could see for herself the broken down house and ill-kept grounds.

'Aye . . . and she's just finding out how poor she's allus been, even when she was rich. I've niver been as poor as she for all I've been so skimped.'

Lacie's eyes were heavy. The heat of the fire was making her drowsy but she made an effort to keep awake. Secrets were in the air again. Nettlewood secrets.

'Frettin' and regrettin'.' Granny Betts rocked in her chair. 'Dreamin' an' schemin' there she lies . . . an' not a bit of good can come of it now. It's all too late. If she'd had her plans an' good ideas a time ago things that are wrong now could 'a been right . . . or at least better.'

Lacie's head nodded and drooped.

Granny Betts jabbed at the fire and Lacie jerked her head up again.

'But she left folks alone to struggle on as best they could.' Granny Betts held up another smoking stick for so long that Lacie began to cough.

The stick was thrust into the flames.

'I know one thing though,' said Granny Betts, 'I know one thing if I know nowt else.'

There was a pause.

'I'll die of old age,' cried Granny Betts, 'an' p'raps it won't be long before I do — but it's not old age that she's dying of. It's conscience that's killing her.'

Lacie thought, 'She isn't talking to me, she's talking to herself . . . or to somebody else she's thinking of who isn't here . . . but not to me.'

Granny Betts, her lips moving, was rocking to and fro and staring into the fire.

Suddenly she got up and soon Lacie was drinking cocoa and eating burned toast.

There was a silence. Granny Betts seemed to have gone to sleep. Her eyes had closed but after a time she moved in her chair and began rocking again, saying 'Poor misfortunit boy!' several times.

'Isn't he home yet?' Lacie asked.

Granny Betts shook her head.

'Some folks allus get t'dirty end o' t'stick,' she said, 'there's no rhyme nor reasin in who gets t'best end.'

'It wasn't fair about that room,' Lacie burst out, 'it wasn't fair, the way they took – the way it was taken away from him and everything spoiled.'

'A lot o' things isn't fair,' said Granny Betts. 'Most things han't been fair to Tom . . . nor folks neither. Even me.'

'You!' exclaimed Lacie.

'Aye me. Old fool that I am. It wasn't fair o' me to badger him to go and see her even if she did beg for his company.'

'That wasn't very wrong, surely?' said Lacie.

'Wrong?' repeated Granny Betts. 'I don't know. I thought it was right but now – . She upset him with all her daft talk about – about things that'd been better left alone. Her whims an' fancies scared him though I kept telling him to tek no notice of 'em. But she's got a way of talkin' so that folks pay attention.'

'Yes. I suppose Mrs Mountsorrel is used to getting her own way,' Lacie remarked. 'It certainly sounds as if she is.'

'Aye, she's used to that,' said Granny Betts. 'But she can't force things round to her way this time. They've gone too strong against her now.'

She rocked so vigorously that the chair creaked in protest.

'Once – she could ha' helped us an' we could ha' done wi' a bit of attention . . . but now . . . too late.'

Too late. Too late, creaked the chair.

'We're used to our own ways, Tom an' me. Folks buzzin' around us only bring us mix-ups and upsets . . . eh dear, dear, dear!' and she rocked and rocked in the rocking chair that was older than she was, while

Lacie sat and pondered about mix-ups and upsets — how one mix-up seemed to lead to another, and how one upset seemed to come from another . . .

Nora and Fred Sprott had made the bonfire and stolen Tom's secret room . . . that had certainly upset Tom . . . but Nora wouldn't have been at Nettlewood at all if it hadn't been for Mrs Mountsorrel. If Mrs Mountsorrel hadn't come to Nettlewood Tom wouldn't have been so mixed-up — perhaps — .

'Now he's run off like a sceered rabbit,' said Granny Betts, opening her eyes and looking at Lacie, 'an' not been home since goodness knows when.'

'I'll go and look for him tomorrow.'

'Thank ye kindly, lass.' Granny Betts was rocking more gently. 'But he's all right somewhere. I've no cause to sit and whittle about the lad . . . not about where he is anyway. He knows plenty o' places to keep warm in an' he's not feared o' woods an' fields. It's only folks that baffle him. He'll not be found till he wants to be found. I'll just have to let him be.'

She looked more cheerful as she added, 'He's not goin' hungry though. That's one good thing. If I leave a bit o' supper out it's gone by mornin'.' She smiled. 'An' it's not our Gertie that's tekken it!'

Lacie had forgotten about Gertie.

'Aye, she's here,' said Granny Betts, 'and not turning out so bad considering that she's part Sprott . . . though she's more Betts than Sprott as anybody can tell — anybody who knows Bettses an' Sprottses, that is.' She paused to get a breath, then said, 'She sees him. Though she don't tell me I reckon she does. She's a sharp un' — an' that's more Betts than Sprott, that is.'

261

The reiteration of the name Sprott brought a shadow to Lacie's mind and she remembered the earlier events of the evening.

Granny Betts understood the expression on Lacie's face. 'Fred Sprott won't harm thee . . . nor anybody else . . . not by calkilation anyhow. But he don't think long enough to count the cost o' what he does sometimes, and often as not it's him who's loser . . .'

She got up from the rocking chair, her bones cracking.

'I've set too long,' she grumbled, 'I should ha' been at home by now for Gertie's on her own unless our Tom's back.'

Lacie got up and began to go quietly away, but Granny Betts called her back and gave her a hot brick wrapped up in a bit of blanket to keep her warm in bed.

'Lay-a-bed in t'morning,' Granny Betts said graciously, 'there's no call for thee to earn thy keep tomorrow.'

At the door Lacie stopped and asked if Rose had come back.

'Nay, she's not, more's the pity. That other object still comes. She'll have to do for a bit longer, I expect.' Granny Betts looked glum but resigned. 'Be off now, bairn, an' get to sleep or we'll have to prop thi eyelids open wi' match sticks.'

The brick fell out of bed with a thump. Lacie opened her eyes. There were sounds in the house. People seemed to be rushing about.

She shivered as she dressed. The morning was dark and gloomy. Through a cataract of water which was falling from a broken gutter above her window she saw that it was still raining. The lawns were wet and heavy, half-covered with sodden leaves. The croquet hoops were still there.

So much had happened since the night of the croquet game. Had people really been so happy? Had this garden, now so mournful, ever been the scene of such entrancing pleasure?

She had meant to go for a long walk to look for Poor Tom but this was out of the question now. She would be drenched in no time.

Going into the kitchen she steeled herself to face Nora and wondered if Fred Sprott had already been in with his story of the outburst on the river-bank the night before. Lacie wanted to give her version first but she still was not sorry so she wouldn't apologise. She didn't like him and nothing, nothing would make her say she did.

Nora was not in the kitchen. Neither was Granny Betts but the new helper was there.

Lacie said good morning then added in a friendly way that she didn't know her name yet, only that it used to be Trudgitt.

The woman cut her short and said, 'Well, it's not Trudgitt now. What d'you think that is?' and stuck out her hand with a wedding ring on. Then with a brief, 'T'tea's in t'pot,' she went out, clanking a bucket.

Nora flashed in and out again, leaving Lacie with a bumpy heart and a mouth opened to say the first words of an explanation which was never begun.

Granny Betts crossed the kitchen with a quicker step than usual, hardly noticing Lacie and muttering to herself, 'Conscience, that's what the trouble is wi' her. It's conscience that's killing her.'

Having said a good thing once Granny Betts wanted to say it again.

'Has something happened?' Lacie asked the former Trudgitt who looked right through her and would have tried to walk through her if Lacie hadn't nipped out of the way.

This morning the grown-ups had certainly sealed themselves into their own world.

The kitchen fire was choked with ashes. There wasn't a bit of red in it. The kettle wouldn't boil on it and it was impossible to toast bread in front of it. Lacie had to be content with a breakfast of bread and butter and cold tea.

Granny Betts came in and said, 'That cock'rel was crowing in t'night, the nuisance. I've a good mind to go out and wring its neck.'

'I'll go an' do it,' said the woman who had been a Trudgitt, and put down her bucket.

'That'll do, that'll do,' Granny Betts was annoyed. 'Don't be in such a hurry. It's nowt to do with thee if it crows all night.'

The woman clattered her bucket and walked out.

'The impudence!' said Granny Betts.

'I don't know her name yet,' Lacie told her, 'so I don't know what to call her.'

'I know what I call her,' muttered Granny Betts. 'Her an' her mucky apron.'

'She must be Mrs Somebody,' Lacie said.

'Aye, an' I'm sorry for the somebody she's missis of,' retorted Granny Betts and went out of the kitchen in the direction of the sick-room.

Lacie went outside. The rain had stopped at last but the sky was low with dark clouds, and the sun, when it did struggle out, had a watery gleam.

A motor car had stopped at the bottom of the front steps and Lacie was surprised to see old Doctor Plumtree walking away from it. Then she saw that a younger man had been driving. The two of them hurried into the house without noticing Lacie. Evidently there was no time this morning for the usual chat about how tall she was growing.

Kicking a stone she walked slowly about on the terrace wondering what she could do to pass the time.

Drops of rain began to fall.

She had a brainwave – she would go and collect the eggs. She made haste to the fowl-house. It would be warm and dry in there.

The Mrs Somebody was just coming out of it with eggs in a bucket.

'None left,' she shouted as she strode past. 'Tha should look sharp in t'morning instead o' lying abed.'

It was raining heavily again and, disliking the prospect of going back into the house, Lacie made her way to the barn thinking that she would try to make friends with the baby owl.

It was not owls she heard as she stood in the dimness beneath the rafters.

More like howls.

Somebody was sobbing noisily in the loft.

Lacie found the ladder which led to the barn's top storey, then groped her way upwards and poked her head through the trapdoor. It took some time for her eyes to become accustomed to the dusty twilight up there.

Yes. There was somebody.

Somebody was sprawling upon a pile of hay in a corner and sobbing bitterly.

It was Gertie Sprott.

25

Plotting

LACIE poked her head further up into the loft.

Yes. It was Gertie.

She was making so much noise that although the floorboards creaked at every step Lacie crossed the floor without being heard.

'Gertie!' she said softly. 'Gertie, it's me.'

Gertie lifted up her head. Even in that poor light it was possible to see the marks of grief upon her blurred and swollen face. Her hair had bits of hay sticking all over it. Lacie was astounded to discover that Gertie could cry like that.

What was the matter?

'It – it's him,' Gertie managed to gulp out at last.

Lacie wondered with a feeling of panic if some dreadful thing had happened to Poor Tom.

'Medad.' Gertie burst into another storm of sobs.

Now Lacie thought that something terrible had happened to Fred Sprott, and felt a throb of guilt as if her hatred of him might have concentrated itself into some awful blow against him.

She could feel the blood draining from her face and her heart was giving great slow thumps.

'He hit me,' wailed Gertie, 'right across me face.'

Lacie did not speak. She had to give her heart time to right itself.

'Right across me face,' wept Gertie. 'Medad hit me,' and she went on crying but not so loudly.

'But I thought – ' Lacie's voice sounded quite strained with the relief of finding that Mr Sprott had not been demolished after all – 'I thought,' she said in a firmer tone, 'that he was always hitting you.'

'No, he's not!' Gertie sat up, shaking her head indignantly. 'He's never hit me before – well, hardly ever.'

'But he's always talking about cutting you in two or knocking your head off.'

'Oh, that!' Gertie was impatient. 'I take no notice o' that. But now he's really gone an' hit me – HARD. He smacked my face and called me a "noxshus little monkey", an' it's all because of that Nora. I HATE her.'

Lacie's heart gave another jerk at the sound of Nora's name.

'I hate her.' Gertie's wet eyes glittered in the dim light. 'An' I hate him.'

'Wh – what's it about?' Lacie asked.

'It's about her an' medad. Both of 'em together.' Gertie sobbed again.

After a pause Lacie asked, 'What about them?' Gertie let out another howl.

'They've tekken up wi' each other, him an' her – an' I can't bear it, I can't.'

Lacie's mind was whirling round. Gertie must have discovered the secret meeting place.

'Poor Tom found out,' she was going on, 'he telled me. He's seen 'em together all lovin' an' kissin'. She's

268

no right to kiss medad an' if she marries him – ' sobs broke out again – 'she'll be my mam.'

'Stepmother,' Lacie said. Gertie gave another howl.

'I'll die if he gets married to her,' she cried, 'you know I can't stand her. If he marries her I'll run away. I'll have to. I can't abide being near her. I told medad I'd run away only I didn't say where to. I told him I hate her, an' I do, an' I told him I hate HIM an' I do. I H-H-HATE him,' and she put a particularly forceful 'h' on that hate.

'So do I.'

The words were ready to jump out of Lacie's mouth but they never left her tongue. Suddenly she realised that they were no longer true. Her feelings now were a curious mixture of surprise and relief. She no longer hated Fred Sprott. The hatred had gone.

'I used to hate him,' she heard herself saying.

'You! Medad! What for? He's never done you no harm.' Gertie sounded astonished, then annoyed.

'Well, I don't hate him now,' Lacie replied slowly, 'I thought I did but I don't. I don't know how it's happened but it's the truth now. And you don't hate him really. You know you don't.'

But Gertie was determined to stick to her hatred.

'If he marries that Nora I'll hate him. I'll never forgive him, never.'

She began to dry her face on her sleeve, then cried again, 'I'd have to have her for a mam. Her! Me! But I won't! I won't! I won't!'

And she banged on the floor with her heels.

There was silence, then the slightest of sounds in the rafters, a velvety stirring of the air and the sensation of a flight nearby.

It was Iboo. They had forgotten him.

'Sss'h,' whispered Gertie. 'Somebody's down there!'

There was a rustling on the floor below, then the sound of feet moving stealthily.

The girls held their breath.

A head appeared at the top of the ladder. A shock of hair gleamed in the dull light.

'It's our Tom,' said Gertie.

'Poor Tom,' he said, coming up another rung of the ladder so that a little more of him appeared.

'He's mis'rable too,' said Gertie. 'Aren't you, our Tom?'

'Aye,' he replied, 'I am.'

'Nobody knows where he is except me.' Gertie sounded boastful. She had swallowed some more sobs and mixed some of her sniffs with a sneeze.

'You don't know, neether,' said Poor Tom, 'except for this very minute while I'm here. I'm not telling you where I'll be when I've gone – an' I'm goin'.'

He took a step downward.

'Don't go!' cried Gertie. 'Come in here. It's nicer –' she gave a sob – 'it's better when you're here too.'

Poor Tom drew himself further up the ladder then he stepped into the loft and stretched his legs.

A pair of wings shook. The owl was sitting on his shoulder.

'Don't thee fidget, Iboo,' he said.

He sat down in the hay, hunched his knees under his chin, and asked how his granny was.

'All right. She wants you to come home.'

'Aye,' was all he replied.

The owl moved, then settled, and moved and settled again.

'He hates 'em as well, don't thee, Tom?' Gertie sat closer to him, 'that Nora and medad?'

Tom said slowly, 'They took everything from me, all the things I liked best an' never even told me. They waited till I was gone then they took 'em away and threw 'em on a fire. They didn't even want 'em, just burnt 'em all alive.'

'An' you hate 'em for it, eh, Tom?' said Gertie. Tom rubbed the middle of his chest, and said it ached him there. Was that hatin' 'em?

Gertie was doubtful. To her, hating was more of a spitting, stabbing, scorching kind of feeling.

'His room was a secret,' she said into Lacie's ear, 'but I never told it, though I knew it all the time.'

Lacie was just going to say 'and so did I' but she lost the chance for Gertie was rushing on, 'You know the bonfire we saw that night wi' birds an' animals all burning, an' that stuffed cow – '

'Don't,' said Tom, 'and it wasn't a cow.'

'It was all that hijeous Nora's fault,' cried Gertie, 'she did it just for spite.'

The bird shook his wings.

'Sssshh! Thou's scaring Iboo,' Tom reproved her. 'His little heart is beating like a kettledrum.'

He got up and stretched his legs. He looked like a bundle of old clothes.

Gertie peered up at him through the gloom, and told him so.

'No wonder she didn't look at thee,' she burst out.

'Who?' asked Lacie, thinking that surely Granny Betts would look at Tom whatever the state of his dress. 'She'd disapprove though, of course, at his untidiness, I mean.' Lacie finished her thought aloud.

'She wasn't there,' said Tom, 'that's why she didn't look.'

'But – she's always there . . . or here . . .' Lacie was puzzled, 'if she's not in the cottage, she's here at Nettlewood.'

Gertie whispered, 'He means Rose, not me granny.'

There was a silence. Tom had Iboo in his hands and was gently stroking him.

'I couldn't find her,' he said, 'although I went looking. I never set eyes on her.'

'You went to Lark Grange?' Lacie was surprised.

Not in it – Gertie was eager to tell what she knew – near it.

'I was round about,' said Tom, 'for days an' days . . . but she wasn't there.'

'Perhaps she's gone away,' Lacie said.

'She said she'd be there and I could go an' talk to her if things started goin' wrong.'

Lacie remembered. Yes. It was true.

'I could go an' tell her and she'd be there and tell me what to do.' Tom was speaking slowly as if saying aloud words which he had said to himself many times.

'An' things did go wrong . . . so I went looking for her – but she wasn't there.'

'Perhaps she couldn't help it,' Lacie said, 'perhaps she had to go away. Perhaps she's gone to Dick's place.'

'Aye, p'raps she has.'

Gertie pulled at his coat and he hunched down into the hay again, sighing deeply as he stroked his face along the owl's feathers.

'He likes Rose.' Gertie sounded as if she were telling a secret.

Lacie was not surprised. Everybody liked Rose.

'I mean, he likes Rose...better than anybody—nearly better than he likes me granny. Don't thee, Tom?'

'Aye.' He gave another sigh. 'But Granny's always where she says she is . . . and Rose wasn't there, though she said she would be. Rose wasn't there.'

His face went down to the owl again. Lacie stared at him.

'But, Rose – ' she began.

'Nobody can stop him liking her if he wants to.' Gertie sounded ready to quarrel about it. 'He can like her if he wants to, just the same as anybody else can.'

Lacie said nothing aloud – only, 'Poor Tom, poor, poor Tom,' to herself and that seemed to express everything.

He stood up suddenly.

'I'm off! Go back now, Iboo. Get away with thee.'

But Iboo stayed where he was. Again Tom tried to send him away.

The bird moved his wings but did not fly.

'I've got to be hiding or she'll get me,' said Tom. 'She'd just like to know where I am.'

'He means the old Missus,' Gertie put her mouth close to Lacie's ear, then suddenly sneezed into it. When they had both recovered from the effect and from a fit of giggles as well, Gertie said that she meant Mrs Mountwhatsername. She was trying to catch him and get him made different.

'Improved,' Tom said.

Lacie remembered her conversation with Granny Betts.

'But Mrs Mountsorrel is ill. She can't do anything now.'

Tom shook his head, 'As soon as she's better she'll be on at me again. I wish she'd never set eyes on me, I do. I wanted to keep out of her way right from the start but me granny said I must be nice an' polite so as to show she hadn't brung me up like a savage. Me granny thought it'd do us a bit o' good if t'other 'un liked me, but it hasn't done us good, only bad.'

He sounded so unhappy that neither Lacie nor Gertie could say a word. He rubbed his cheek against the owl on his shoulder and went on, 'There's folks coming an' goin' all the time now. It's gettin' like a market place round here. I don't know who's after me and who's not an' I'm tired o' dodging 'em.'

'I'm sure you're all wrong,' Lacie began.

'That's just what they all say,' he cried. 'Poor Tom's all wrong. You're the same as all the others.'

'No, I'm not.' Lacie was indignant.

'I'm not goin' to stop here to be collared and shut up behind doors an' improved. I've had enough of 'em all except me granny – an' Rose if she was there but she wasn't. I'm off!'

'So am I,' said Gertie, 'we both are.' Then put her hand over her mouth.

The owl stared and blinked.

For a time nobody spoke, but Gertie sneezed.

'I suppose you mean,' and Lacie was not quite sure of it, 'that you're running away?'

'I just hope he's mis'rable when I've gone, that's all,' said Gertie.

'If you mean your dad,' Lacie told her, 'he's more likely to be furious.'

'I don't care if he is,' replied Gertie, 'I s'pose you'll run and tell now.'

Lacie treated this remark with contempt. She put her head in the air and turned to go away.

But now Gertie wanted to tell everything. She and Tom were going to Bridgeover first. From there Tom would make for Bird Hill Farm – because Dick had offered Tom a job with the horses, hadn't he?

'An' Rose might be there,' Tom sounded more hopeful, 'an' I want to see Warrior again and Dick doesn't think I'm daft like some folks do ... and Rose doesn't neether.'

'P'raps medad'll be sorry when I've gone,' Gertie said, 'but it'll be too late.'

Lacie had been thinking. Now she asked how far it was to Bridgeover and if they were going by bus.

Both Tom and Gertie burst out laughing. Bus! Gertie's laughter got mixed up with sneezes and she had to take time to recover her breath. They knew there wasn't even a proper road. It was all across fields and dykes. But that didn't matter.

'There isn't even a proper road from here, not this side o' river,' she said. 'It's all across fields and dykes. But we're not going that way.'

She paused and glanced at Tom. He must have agreed to the disclosure for she went on, 'We're takin' a boat. I've been before with medad. I can leave t'boat at Bimble's boatyard like he does when he goes to Brijjuver on t'river.'

The plan was so daring that it dazzled Lacie.

Whew! She had a lightning image of a furious Fred Sprott.

Gertie intended to present herself to an aunt in Bridgeover, a relation on her mother's side.

'She doesn't like medad,' Gertie explained, ''cos she

wanted to bring me up and he wouldn't let her. She'll let me stay with her, just to spite him – if she don't I'll run off somewhere else.'

'I hope you've got her address,' said Lacie. This annoyed Gertie for some reason and she flashed out that it was all that Cousin Nora's fault. If it hadn't been for her Gertie wouldn't be going – nor Tom neither.

'It's old Missus's fault mostly,' said Tom. 'She's at t'bottom of it all. If she hadn't come – ' He lost himself.

'If she hadn't come,' Lacie picked up his train of thought, 'Nora wouldn't have come here, and I wouldn't be at Nettlewood.'

Suddenly she burst out, 'You needn't think you are the only ones who – who are miserable. What about me? I don't like being here. I want to go home.'

She stopped, then asked if there were a station in Bridgeover.

'That's it,' shouted Gertie. 'That's where me a'ntie lives. Near the railway station. I remember now. Smoke comes through the window when a train goes past.'

Lacie was thinking of her five-pound note. That would take her home. Perhaps her parents would be there already. If not, they soon would be. How nice it would be if she were there first to welcome them.

Suddenly it seemed to her that she too must get away from Nettlewood.

'Let me come too,' she cried, 'I want to run away as well.'

26

Flight!

Tom and Gertie looked at each other.

'If she comes,' Gertie said after some thought, 'it's sure she won't split.'

'I wouldn't split in any case,' retorted Lacie, confident that she could claim a good record where keeping secrets was concerned.

Tom looked at Gertie. If they got sick of each other Lacie would be good company and *she* didn't rattle on and give folks sore ears.

Lacie smiled gratefully at him while Gertie considered her as a candidate for the running away partnership.

'All right then,' Gertie said at last, 'as long as she don't start being clever and picking fault wi' everything we've got planned.' Before she could say any more she had another attack of sneezing.

Shouldn't she wait until her cold was better? Lacie suggested, but Gertie indignantly denied that she had a cold. Her 'froat' tickled but that was because a bit of hay was sticking in it, and anyway the running away was going to be done that afternoon whether she had a cold or not.

So soon! Lacie's heart gave a jump. Wouldn't

tomorrow do? Tomorrow? Gertie must go today. She'd go now, this very minute – Tom nodded his head in agreement – if she could be sure her dad was safely out of the way. She didn't want him spoiling everything – Tom shook his head in sympathy – by setting off after her, at least not until she'd got a good start. Then he could do as he liked and she just hoped he'd be miserable.

Tom said that he would keep watch on Fred Sprott who was sawing logs in the old pig sty.

'What about her?' The hostile tone of Gertie's voice meant that she was thinking of Nora.

'She's busy in the sick-room,' Lacie said, 'I think Mrs Mountsorrel is worse.'

Gertie looked interested. 'Was she screamin'?'

'No, she wasn't. I only said I think she's worse. Nora seems to be with her all the time now and there's a sort of feeling . . .' Lacie stopped, and, remembering the mysterious atmosphere in the house, felt a surge of relief that she was about to leave Nettlewood.

They arranged to meet later in the afternoon with whatever they had collected for the journey.

'C'llect? What shall us c'llect?' asked Tom.

'Food,' said Gertie.

'I can't get much o' that.' Tom looked worried.

'Neither can I.' Gertie looked at Lacie. 'So she'll have to get it.'

'Me?' cried Lacie. 'Where from?'

'Out o' t'pantry o' course.' Gertie was scornful. 'Don't you know where food's kept? You get it, then we'll hide it in the hay till we can start.'

'You'd better keep out of that hay,' Lacie advised as Gertie began sneezing again.

278

The gong boomed.

'That's your dinner, lucky thing. I wish I was coming for it but I've got to go to me granny's to scrape 'taters.' Gertie began to shake hay from her clothes.

As the gong boomed again Lacie said, 'I won't get anything if I don't go now. Mrs Um, I don't know her name, doesn't seem very good tempered.'

'Neither is me granny,' replied Gertie with a sigh, 'especially since our Tom's been away. I expect she'll be worse when he's gone for good but I can't help that. She won't let it out on me though, 'cos I won't be there.'

Tom was looking mournful so she dug him in the ribs and said she'd have to be going and would see him later, he knew where. He followed the two girls down the ladder and they all looked cautiously out of the barn door. Rain was still streaming down.

It wasn't very nice weather for running away.

Gertie tossed her head, and said that Lacie needn't go if she didn't want to. Lacie did want to but . . .

Gertie tossed her head again.

Tom stood behind the barn door not wishing to be seen. Iboo, still upon his shoulder, was blinking at the rain.

Now that there was more light the girls could see how crumpled and stained Tom was, and that there were marks of earth on his face and hands.

'No wonder Rose didn't look at thee!' said Gertie. 'What a sight!'

Lacie, seeing Tom's look of pain as he thought of Rose, trod on Gertie's toe.

'Ow!' cried Gertie. 'But it's true. Just look at him. I

279

don't know what me granny'd say if she could see him.'

'She'd say, "get a wash".' Tom gave a little smile. 'An' that's what I will do if I can get near to t'pump.' He stepped back amongst the shadows in the barn.

Gertie ran off to Granny Betts' cottage to boil a pan of potatoes and Lacie, trying to dodge the rain, made her way into the house.

'She was thinking over the new dilemma which had come into her life – how to take food from somebody's larder without somebody knowing, food which belonged to somebody but not to her.

Some of it was intended for her, she worked out for the sake of her conscience. As she was a guest she was entitled to eat. But whose guest was she? Not Mrs Mountsorrel's, surely. She probably didn't even know Lacie was in the house.

It was an uncomfortable problem and she began to think that if she delved any deeper into it she would probably discover that she had no right to be in Nettlewood at all.

She supposed that it would be all right if she just took a fair share of whatever there was, then she sighed over the complexity of her present affairs.

The doctors had gone. The house was quiet. She went into the kitchen. The woman whose name she did not know was kneeling on the hearth-rug and kneading dough in a panchion as big as a dug-out. A fire was roaring in the range and the woman's face was red. Hairpins were falling out of her hair.

That bread would be dangerous – but of course Lacie wouldn't be there to eat any.

She stood and watched the woman who went on

kneading the dough and took no notice of her. There was no mention of dinner and no sign of it either except a smell of boiled cabbage, so Lacie went out of the kitchen.

There seemed to be a coming and going about Mrs Mountsorrel's room. The door was open and the sound of voices came out. Other sounds, too, came out, sounds which Lacie could not define, whispers, breaths, murmurs. She kept far away but the atmosphere of that room seeped through the air and disturbed the house.

In her own room she packed a few things. As she was intending to travel by train from Bridgeover she decided to take her best coat. She changed her shoes for better ones and put on her second best frock. Somehow she had never found the opportunity for giving Nora the five-pound note. It was still in her purse which she put into her case. She hadn't a raincoat but she put ready a woollen jacket and a scarf.

Perhaps there would be one of Fred Sprott's oilskins in the boat. Boat? Her heart gave a jump. Was she really going?

Hunger made her feel aggressive. With a firm stride she went back to the kitchen intending to demand her dinner.

The dough had been put in baking tins for a second rising on top of the range.

Granny Betts was looking at it with a cynical expression.

She turned to Lacie and said, 'Hey, you, little 'un, what's your name now, I allus forget it. This here little round 'un is for thee.' She pointed to the only round loaf amongst all the oblong ones. 'I told her – ' she jerked her head at the woman – 'to prick thy name on it wi' a fork but she didn't know it either. Not that she'd know owt. So do it thiself.'

As she put the fork into Lacie's hand she whispered, 'That dough isn't riz enough. I ne'er saw bread made i' that fashion. It'll be same as her puddens for sure, as heavy as lead.'

Lacie pressed her name into the dough. 'But I won't be here to eat it,' she had almost said.

Granny Betts hurried back to the sick-room. She looked very spry and conscious of her own importance.

'She's in 'er element,' remarked the woman. Lacie looked at her without understanding.

'Er, the old 'un. It's egg-an' milk to her, being so busy.'

As Lacie still looked blank the woman rolled her eyes upward and said, 'Is she thick-headed or summat?' as if asking somebody on the ceiling.

'Who, me?' asked Lacie.

'Ne'er mind,' said the woman, 'get on wi' thi dinner. It's about time.'

She took a plate from the oven and banged it on to the table.

'If thou wants owt different,' she said, 'thou'll 'ave to go and get it somewheer else. That's all there is 'ere.'

'If I weren't so hungry I wouldn't eat it,' was Lacie's mental reaction to such ungracious behaviour, but she was hungry and she did eat it — and she hoped that she taught Mrs er-Um a lesson by thanking her very politely for it.

'Don't thank me,' said Mrs Um, 'it's nowt to do wi' me. I on'y warmed it up ... and don't choke thiself on it. Anybody'd think thou'd got a train to catch.' Which remark made Lacie stare at her with such startled eyes that Mrs Um said, 'I reckon everybody in this place is barmy, or next door to it.'

As Lacie ate she considered the long and probably arduous journey she was about to make and thought that at least she'd got some food in her belly. That would stand her in good stead. This was one of Granny Betts' expressions and Lacie smiled.

'Don't know what there is to grin about,' said Mrs Um. 'I've not seen much to laff at round here.'

'I'll be glad to get away from you, anyway,' thought Lacie.

'Don't say much, does she?' said Mrs Um, still talking to the ceiling, 'I don't reckon she's said one word to me yet. 'Appen she thinks I'm not worth speakin' to. Well, I'm off out to feed t'fowls. She can say owt or nowt for all I care.'

She stood with her hands on her hips and for a moment considered life.

'There's nowt but work 'ere,' she said — the word sounded like 'wock' — 'It's all wock an' never stop. I don't think I'll be 'ere tomorrow.'

Something on the fire caught her attention.

A pudding was boiling in a big iron saucepan. Mrs Um took off the lid and, with a fork and in a cloud of steam, lifted out a sopping bundle wrapped in a cloth and tied up with string.

She dumped it in a soup plate, saying, 'There's your pudden. Help thisen.'

Then she went out.

Poor Mrs Um! She was not very amiable. Was she remembering her five bairns left at home? Was she wondering if they had fallen into the copper or pulled the kettle off the hob and scalded themselves, or set the place on fire? What would she find when she returned to her untidy home? (it must be untidy with five bairns left to themselves in it all day). No wonder she wasn't happy. But who was happy in Nettlewood? Not Mrs Mountsorrel, not Poor Tom nor Granny Betts . . . Gertie was miserable, bursting with misery about Nora and Fred Sprott . . . and what about them? Were they happy? But Lacie's thoughts quickly shifted away from them and returned to the pudding. It was still steaming furiously.

She got up and approached it.

Perhaps the wet cloth ought to come off? She picked at the string and at last the pudding was revealed.

There were currants in it. She supposed that it was a Spotted Dick — Mrs Um's version of a Spotted Dick, anyway.

Having been told to help herself Lacie did. She cut at least half of it and somehow slithered it into a paper bag which she had found in a drawer in the table, then went away quickly as she heard Mrs Um coming in.

'Well, if that don't beat all I ever set my eyes on!' exclaimed Mrs Um at the sight of the ravaged pudding. 'It's a wonder she's not etten t'cloth as well. And 'er such a skinny thing too, I can't think where she's put it all.'

She would have been surprised if she had seen where Lacie *was* putting it — at the bottom of her suitcase.

Now to keep watch for the signal. There was to be a special sign from the barn door which could be seen from the kitchen window, so she lurked about all the afternoon in the back part of the house, effacing herself as well as she could if a grown-up appeared, and keeping constant watch across the courtyard.

The house began to fill with the aroma of baking bread.

Still there was no signal.

What was the trouble? Wouldn't Fred Sprott disappear from the scene?

She saw him crossing the courtyard with a basket full of logs, and dashed out of the kitchen just in time to escape him.

She heard him splashing about under the rainwater pump in the scullery, his labours over for the day.

He was in the kitchen having his dinner. Would he eat the rest of the Spotted Dick?

'Nay, I'm not one for pudden,' she heard him say, 'you take it home for the kids.'

Mrs Um sounded pleased as she said, well, all right then, if he didn't want it she'd got plenty of them as did, and she hurriedly put the pudding into a basin and that into a basket as if fearful that he would change his mind.

Lacie wished they would stop talking and go. But no, Fred Sprott was not in a hurry. He was dipping his black moustache into a mug of his own herb-beer.

'Good stuff!' he remarked to Mrs Um. 'You should try a drop.'

'Ah shall if ah get a chance,' she said, and of course he told her to fetch a mug for herself.

'Oh lor,' sighed Lacie. 'They'll be hours and hours!' And she crept away. She was worried about missing the signal, then decided that both Gertie and Tom would know better than to give it while Fred Sprott was in the kitchen, and they would certainly know he was there.

At last he was safely out of the way. Lacie dodged about from kitchen to scullery, and in and out of the back passages, always trying to keep the barn door in view.

'What's up wi' the bairn?' exclaimed the exasperated Mrs Um after they had bumped into each other for the third time. 'She's worse nor an ill-sitting hen. In an' out till me head's goin' round.'

Lacie said that she was waiting for the rain to stop.

'Then, tha'll wait a long time by t'look on it,' retorted Mrs Um. 'But it's nowt to do wi' me. Old woman told me to tell thee thy bread's baked.'

'I suppose you mean Granny Betts.' Lacie had not liked the disrespectful reference. For the sake of accuracy, as Mrs Um was a stranger, she added, 'She's not my granny, though.'

'I don't care whose granny she is,' snapped Mrs Um, 'as long as she's not mine, the old nuisance.' And she tramped back to the kitchen where the loaves were all out of their tins and propped up against each other on the oven top so that the air could get out of them.

Full of delight Lacie put out her hand to take the round loaf which was hers, then she dropped it.

'Ah could a telled thee it's hot,' said Mrs Um, 'but ah thowt tha'd have enough sense to know it thisen.'

She went away in scorn to fill the kettle at the pump.

In contrast to the inky afternoon outside the kitchen had a cosy look in the glow of the fire.

It almost seemed a pity to be leaving it. Almost? It *did* seem a pity –

But –

Lacie looked through the window and saw Poor Tom's head peeping round the barn door.

He waved three times, then disappeared.

Quick as thought Lacie grabbed her bread then, flipping it from hand to hand, ran into her bedroom.

She put on her woollen jacket, put her coat and scarf over her arm, somehow concealing the loaf, then picked up her case and waited for the opportunity to run across the yard without being seen.

It was much easier than she expected it to be.

Mrs Um went to the front door to sweep dead leaves from the top steps.

Lacie cautiously looked into the kitchen.

Nobody was there.

She stared at the array of loaves. Should she help herself? There was nothing to stop her but her conscience. She had only to put out an arm – and she longed to do it – but her arm would not stretch forth.

She sighed with a sense of regret for a lost opportunity, but left without taking any more bread.

'I shan't tell Gertie,' she decided, 'she'd call me a fool.'

The rain had almost stopped.

Silently she ran across the yard.

Tom and Gertie were waiting in the barn.

'Thought you was never coming,' said Gertie.

Tom was shivering, though he was wearing a thick overcoat, an old one, much too big.

'It's medad's.' Gertie gave a mournful sniff. 'That's where his pipe burned a hole in t'pocket.' She stood looking at it until Lacie gave her a push and suggested that they make a move.

Suddenly there was a movement in the rafters. Something swooped down.

'Oh, it's thee!' cried Poor Tom as the baby owl settled on his shoulder. 'I thought I'd given thee thy marching orders.' He looked upset as he fondled it. 'Go away now. I've got to leave thee.' He put it on his hand and threw it into the air, but the owl flew back to him again and again.

'Drat thee, Iboo!' cried Tom at last. 'Be gone withee!'

He began to push a heap of hay aside and revealed a trapdoor. As he lifted it up Lacie saw steps going down.

She shrank back.

'It's not very dark,' said Tom, 'and it's not very far. Gert'll go first.'

So Gertie went down first, Lacie followed and Tom went third, having at last got rid of Iboo who was shaking feathers down from the rafters.

'People will see the trapdoor . . . ' Lacie said.

'Much good it'll do 'em,' replied Tom, 'they'll be too late to stop us.'

They were in one of Nettlewood's famous tunnels.

'They're all over the place,' Tom said, 'it's just like a rabbit warren. A lot of 'em have fallen in now, 'cos water gets in.'

Lacie thought that it was a pity that all the tunnels hadn't fallen in for ever.

This one smelled of earth and was slippery underfoot and slimy at the sides. She hated it and closed her eyes.

'In some parts you can see bones,' Tom's voice was solemn, 'where they say folks were buried long times ago.'

Lacie hardly dared to breathe the stagnant air which

288

belonged to the dead. Just as she felt she could not bear to be down there for another moment a wave of fresher air flowed in.

The tunnel opened out where the ground at the east side of the house fell steeply to the moat. There were many bushes and a tangle of tall nettles. The entrance was covered by loose boards that had been sewn together by brambles and the winding stems of creeping plants.

It was still raining.

Somebody once had put a tree-trunk across the moat.

'Not me,' said Tom, 'it's allus been there.'

Now it was black and slippery. Somehow they got over it without falling off.

They had to run across the water-meadow. The ground was sodden, and sucked at their feet.

Up the river-bank.

'Sluggies is out,' said Tom and Lacie saw with a thrill of horror the black things on the grass.

Tom said, 'Mind where you put your feet. Don't tread on 'em.'

As if anybody would want to !

Lacie's heart sank as she saw the full-flowing river.

Already there had been so many hazards, the tunnel, the tree-trunk, the squelchy, slippery flight across the meadow – now she had the full realization of danger.

The landing stage was under water. The two boats were pulling at the ends of their ropes as the river raced past.

Gertie was busy, putting things into *Wobbler*.

She looked at Lacie. 'Well, get in,' she cried, 'or we'll be half-way there before you've started.'

'Wouldn't it be better – ' Lacie heard her voice

saying faintly – 'to wait till tomorrow – or another day when it isn't so wet and so dark?'

Tom was in *Wobbler*. His teeth were chattering.

Gertie was ready to let go the rope. 'Get in if you're going,' she said.

Lacie was considering whether or not it would be better for her to withdraw from the expedition when she discovered that one of her feet had got into the boat and that the other was following it.

'Hold on!' shouted Gertie.

They were away.

As the river raced past it grabbed the boat, whisked it into midstream as if it were a toy, then tossed it about as if contemptuous of it.

'We'll be all right in a minute. Just let me get me breath back,' Gertie gasped out.

This wasn't running away. It was racing away.

Racing away, racing away. They were going at the maddest pace on the current, borne upon a power so great it seemed as if it could at any moment lift itself from its earthly moorings and rush upwards and onwards for ever through all the universe.

Racing away!

27

'Is This the Aegir, Gertie?'

CLOUD. Rain. River.

'I wish we'd started off earlier.'

Lacie almost had to shout the words to make herself heard above the rushing noise of the river. She looked at the lowering sky. It was so dark, not like daytime at all.

Gertie cast a careless glance upwards, and said that when the clouds had gone over it would be lighter.

'It'll be teatime at me granny's.' Poor Tom sounded homesick already. 'It was nice when we was together, just the two of us, in front o' the fire.'

'Well, she's not in front o' the fire now,' said Gertie, ' 'cos she's busy with Mrs Mounthingummy.'

But Tom didn't want to talk about Mrs Mountsorrel. He clutched the old overcoat around him and shivered inside it.

Lacie looked at the dark water and wet sky and thought of a kettle singing on the fire . . . There would be no cosy teatime for her today. She turned round in her seat, as if to give a goodbye thought to the comforts of School Cottage whose chimneys she could still see if she stared hard through the rain.

'That's funny,' she cried. 'There's smoke coming out of the chimneys – but nobody's there.'

Neither Gertie nor Tom could see smoke and soon the chimneys vanished from sight as the boat sped down the river.

Gertie was in her element, making magnificent strokes with the oars and not caring how much water she flung over her companions.

'You may like being wet through,' said Lacie, 'but I don't.'

'Nor me, neether,' said Tom.

Gertie became annoyed and told them that they must be daft if they didn't like being on the river better than anything else in the world.

'I am daft, then,' said Poor Tom, 'and most folks'd agree about that.'

In the old overcoat and a cloth cap which he was wearing back to front he looked like a sad-faced clown got up to do a turn in a circus. Gertie was almost buried in one of her father's jerseys. Lacie, not warm enough in her woolly cardigan, began to put on her best coat.

Gertie shrieked with laughter.

'What did you bring that for? She looks like a stuffed monkey in it, don't she Tom?'

But Poor Tom hid himself underneath the cap.

Lacie said that as she was going on by train when the boat ride was over she didn't want to look like a scarecrow, then she noticed her feet in their second-best shoes which were covered with mud.

'I'll never get them clean,' she cried, 'I forgot to bring a shoe-brush.'

Gertie went into another fit of laughter at that, but after a time she grew mournful, and said that nobody was following them yet.

'They won't have found out we've gone,' Lacie told

her. 'Nobody takes much notice of us in the daytime, not of me anyway, not at Nettlewood.'

'Nor of me, neether,' said Tom. 'Granny'll just be thinking I'm where I always go when I've gone.'

'Where's that?' asked Gertie.

'That'd be telling, wouldn't it?' said Tom, 'an' I'm not daft enough to tell thee.'

He was sitting in the prow of the boat, and looked like a figurehead of dejection. He turned to glance down river.

'I don't like t'look o' where we're goin',' he said, then looking up river he added, 'an' I don't like t'look o' where we've been, neether.' So he closed his eyes and dived into his coat again.

Gertie rested the oars. The boat sped onwards.

'Look! it goes by itself,' she cried. 'It's as easy as falling off bikes.'

'Do you mean motor bikes?' Tom asked. 'I'm sorry when folks fall off them.'

'What's he jabberin' about now?' said Gertie. Lacie made no remark at all, thinking that silence was safer.

The boat rushed over the water – or rather the water rushed along with the boat. Soon, even Lacie and Tom began to give themselves up to the excitement of its motion.

As they were borne along their heads were almost at the level of the top of the banks. The flat countryside seemed so much below the river that Lacie wondered what would happen if the water spilled over.

'What d'you think'd happen?' asked Gertie.

'Folks 'd have to swim,' said Tom and she laughed so much that he was gratified and tried to think of

293

something else just as funny, but she got bored with his attempts and told him to shut up.

Suddenly the boat bumped, lurched, bumped again and recovered.

'Whoops !'

They were all laughing now. Lacie said it was like being on a switchback, only wetter, and that she was almost enjoying the ride. 'But the water's certainly much higher than it was. Look how near to the top of the banks it is now.' Gertie, the river expert, didn't seem worried, however, and said carelessly, as she tossed her damp hair from her eyes, 'It's all this rain, you daft thing. It's got to go somewhere, ha'n't it?'

'I thought it was all goin' down my neck,' Tom said and was pleased when the girls were amused at him again.

After a time Lacie said, 'It hasn't got lighter. If anything, it's darker,' and she shivered.

Gertie told her not to be such a whittle-stick but to look in the hold for some pieces of canvas which would 'keep t'cold out'. The canvas was found and soon gave the three of them a feeling of warmth, almost of cosiness, and made them more cheerful and good tempered with each other. They were friendly and made jokes.

Gertie, looking up river to see if her dad were following, cried out suddenly as she saw a shape in the water. It was her dad coming after them. No, it wasn't. Yes it was. No, it was a log – but she pushed at it with an oar and told it to get away and mind its own business.

They were convulsed with laughing over that.

Other debris was floating down the river, planks, logs, branches of trees, a wicker hamper, some broken crates. Gertie kept pushing things away from the boat.

The *Wobbler was* wobbling.

'What's a matter wi' it?' cried Tom, gripping the seat. 'I don't like it dancin' about.'

Gertie manœuvred out of the way of a barge which was coming up. It was well lighted and she should have moved earlier but had been fooling about. A man leaned overboard and shouted something, but she pretended not to hear.

He shouted again and waved his arms.

'I got out o' the way in plenty of time,' she grumbled, 'what's he goin' on about?'

'He says what the 'ell are us doin',' Poor Tom said, 'and that we'd better clear off home – and pr'aps we should,' he added in a low voice.

The girls made no reply.

Gertie stopped rowing, saying she was hungry. Lacie produced the loaf. Honesty compelled her to mention the Spotted Dick – she saw Gertie's eyes gleam – 'But I think we'd better save that for a rainy day.'

The others did not see the joke, not even when she pointed it out to them.

Gertie's contribution was some of the potatoes she had boiled at dinnertime. She had put them into a clean rag but unfortunately had sat on them so that now they looked like a poultice. She had also brought a few sticks of rhubarb. Tom dug his hand into his pocket and brought out some green apples and pears.

'That's all I could get hold of,' he apologized.

The picnic looked rather meagre when it was spread out on a piece of canvas, but, Gertie supposed, it was better than nowt.

The loaf was eaten first. Lacie gave a warning about concealed hairpins and described the cross Mrs Um and her untidy hair.

Tom clutched his throat, pretending to choke. The girls pleased him by appreciating his pantomime and he went on being cheerful for some time afterwards.

Nobody found a hairpin in the bread, only a grey doughy mass in the middle of it. Granny Betts had been right about it not having 'riz' enough. In disgust Gertie threw a lump in the river. 'It's not a bit like the bread Missy Bissy bakes. I wonder if she'll miss me, her and Bertie.'

Lacie, too, was remembering Bertie Bisset. She was eating a pear which made her think of Pear Day, and remarked that she wouldn't be there to see him give out the pears.

'I shall.' Gertie must have forgotten that she was running away. 'He'll give me more than he gives anybody else 'cos he knows me the best.'

'He won't give you any at all,' said Lacie. Gertie was annoyed. 'Of course he will,' she cried, ' 'cos he likes me the best, as well.' And she glared at Lacie who smiled and said, 'But you won't be there. You've run away, remember.'

Gertie did remember and looked glum.

Poor Tom was staring around.

'It's got a lot wider,' he said, 'it's like being in t'middle o' nowhere.'

He went on saying 'wider and wider' and 't'middle o' nowhere', until Gertie snapped at him and told him to be quiet.

More barges loomed out of the dark and sailed past – some up, some down river.

Men on board shouted.

'I should a brought a lantern, then pr'aps they'd stop shouting,' said Gertie. 'I'm sick o' everybody goin' on at me.'

Suddenly there was another sharp reminder of the power beneath the boat, which bumped and struggled and was tossed up and down. Gertie tried to calm it.

The easy ride was over.

A cold breeze got up. The river rose to meet it. The boat lifted and plunged.

'It's like being on wild horses,' Lacie gasped.

'Not hosses.' Tom, though frightened, could still defend them. 'Tigers, more like.' When he had got more breath he went on, 'Nobody'll ever get me on this here river again – chucking us up an' down till I feel sick.'

'Oh, don't be seasick,' cried Lacie. It was the wrong word to use to Tom. He was more worried than ever.

'It's not t'sea, is it?' He was horror-struck. 'I can't abide t'sea. Yes, it looks like t'sea. Eh dear, eh dear!'

Once more Gertie told him to shut up. She had put on her father's red cap. To Lacie it seemed like an ill-omen.

'Why did you bring that?' she cried. 'It's not yours.'

'Yes it is. It was me who gave it medad.'

'It's his then.'

'No, it isn't. I've given it meself back again 'cos he don't deserve it.'

A new mood crept over them.

'Nobody can say it isn't dark now,' Poor Tom said, but Gertie still said it would brighten up.

'Not it,' retorted Tom sounding as if he thought nothing would ever be bright again. 'When are we

297

goin' to get anywhere? When are we goin' to get off this river?'

Here and there in the distance lights showed. People with homes and fires were settling down for the evening.

'Is anybody follering?' Gertie asked again.

'He'll not follow thee,' said Tom. 'He's too busy.'

Nobody spoke for a time then Tom said, 'Where is it we're goin'? I've forgot.'

'You'd forget your head,' snapped Gertie.

Tom put up his hand and touched the crown of his cap as if to make sure that his head wasn't missing. 'No, I wouldn't,' he replied, 'I'd forgot that thy dad's cap was on it, though.'

Lacie reminded Tom – and herself at the same time – that they were all bound for Bridgeover, then he was going to Dick's farm, to ask for a job with the horses.

'Aye, an' to see Rose if she's there. I've got it now. It was the river that drove it out o' me.'

'And I shall catch a train,' Lacie continued as if to reassure herself that there was a sensible programme ahead. Did Gertie still intend to go to her aunts?

Gertie nodded, and said that she was going to Bimble's boatyard first to leave *Wobbler* for her dad.

'How will he know it's there?'

Gertie was indifferent to the problems her father was going to have.

'If he han't enough sense to think of it for himself,' she said, 'pr'aps Bimble's 'll have enough sense to tell him.'

'They could telephone, I suppose,' Lacie liked to have things in order, 'then they could let Miss Throssel know and she could give a message.'

Gertie cut her short.

'Yon's Bridgeover,' she cried. 'Look! Them lights yonder.'

Lacie felt a surge of relief.

'There you are, Tom,' she called out cheerfully to the other end of the boat, 'we're not so far from somewhere after all.'

She broke off. The wind was blowing so strongly and the river heaving so roughly that Gertie was in trouble. They all were in trouble. As the boat pitched up and down a string of Sprott words was let loose on the air.

'I thought I'd bust an oar,' cried Gertie. Her efforts were now so great that Lacie ached with her in sympathy.

'What's wrong wi' *Wobbler*?' asked Tom then – 'it wants to turn round and go home, I reckon.'

Wobbler was certainly behaving in an erratic fashion, not going straight forward over the waves as a well-rowed, well-behaved boat should do, but half-turning ... then going forward again as Gertie wrenched it around. Up and down ... sideways, forwards, rocking, shaking.

'We're not getting anywhere,' shouted Tom. 'Look! Stop us, somebody! We're goin' back'ards.'

It was true. A feeling of panic went through Lacie.

'We're gettin' further away from the lights,' cried Tom, 'further an' further.' Nobody spoke. When he asked, 'Are we goin' back home, Gertie?' nobody took any notice of him so he answered himself, 'Aye, that's it. We must be goin' back home.'

Lacie had been staring so hard into the deepening

gloom down river that she had almost convinced herself that she could see the Aegir gathering itself up into a great billow to come and overwhelm them. They would be lifted up, tossed into the air — thrown backwards and then . . .

She gripped the side of the boat. No. It was only a mass of cloud lying there, hardly moving. Or was it moving? Was it a wave, the great wave of the Aegir? Here was a wave, and another, and another, quite big enough to make the boat seem very small. It was heaving and rolling in waves.

'Is — is this the Aegir, Gertie? Is — it here?'

But Gertie was fighting the river and had no breath to answer silly questions. All she wanted to know was, 'Can anybody see medad?' and told Lacie to stop bothering about the Aegir and look out for the sight of the *Wavey*.

'There isn't any Aegir,' said Gertie. 'Not till me-dad says so. I keep telling you.'

There was no Aegir.

There was no Fred Sprott, either.

The two were already associated with each other in Lacie's mind, and ever after this night she never thought of the Aegir without seeing Fred Sprott's face in it.

Water splashed overboard.

'If — if it isn't the Aegir,' said Lacie, moving her wet feet, 'wh — what is it? Wh — what's happening?'

'It's t'tide.' Gertie stopped for a long breath and took it in as if it hurt her. 'It's t'tide, an' it's takin' us back an' I can't fight it no more. I'm beat.' And she let the boat turn round and drift. She rested the oars and bent her head.

Poor Tom looked at her defeat in horror.

'Hey – ey!' he cried. 'Young Gertie Sprott! Hold thy head up or what shall us do? Us two don't know how to go on wi' boats.'

Lacie agreed in a dismal voice.

Gertie lifted up her head.

'I s'pose I can breathe for a minute, can't I?' she snapped.

'That's right,' said Poor Tom. 'Let her breathe, poor thing.'

'I'm not stopping her, am I?' Lacie was also feeling irritable. If only she could row!

'You should ha' learned,' said Gertie.

'I never had the chance, did I?' retorted Lacie. 'I'd have liked to learn, but I couldn't learn without a boat, could I?'

'Stop row-ing,' groaned Tom, 'and start rowin' – somebody, I don't care who.'

Lacie was too excited to congratulate him upon the pun.

'I'll row,' she cried, 'at least I'll have a shot at it.'

So she sat by Gertie's side, took an oar, and promptly lost it, letting it go as if an unseen power had wrenched it from her hand.

Gertie let out a long wail, crying that her dad would kill her and it was all Lacie's fault.

Lacie replied that she had no objection to taking all the blame, and mentally added that as Fred Sprott disliked her so much already it wouldn't matter if he disliked her a bit more.

'We're miles away from the lights,' said Poor Tom, again. 'We're miles away from anywhere.'

He put his head in his hands.

'What about Bimble's boatyard?' Lacie asked. Gertie replied that Bimble could do what he liked with his boatyard and that it wasn't likely that it would walk away, but would still be there at whatever time they got to it.

Lacie asked another question.

'Well, what about my train?'

TRAIN?

In the dimness she could see the white blurs of their faces. She went on, as if the waste of water around them did not exist, 'I'm supposed to be catching a train, you know.'

'Run and catch it then,' said Gertie, then they all laughed.

They felt better after that and Gertie worked with a will – and one oar – to get to the bank.

'Where is the flippin' bank?' she kept saying.

'It can't have disappeared,' said Lacie. But it had.

Tom was craning his neck. 'I don't reckon there is a bank,' he said at last. 'We've got into t'sea somehow an' we'll all be shipwrecked.'

He drew his neck into his coat and a wave splashed overboard. He stuck out his neck again and said, 'What did I tell you? This is no river. Not it. It's t'sea that's got round us somehow.'

How long they drifted Lacie could not tell. Gertie kept on trying to get to the bank which none of them could see. But the waves were not so rough.

Lacie suggested that it was a good time to eat the Spotted Dick and said that Gertie must certainly have the largest share of it as she had done the most work.

The thought of the pudding cheered them and Lacie began to grope around for her case. Suddenly the boat bumped, rocked and bumped again.

It had touched land.

'We're there!' cried Gertie, for once in her life forgetting a pudding.

They jumped out, splashing up to their shins, then began to drag *Wobbler* out of the water. Gertie and Tom were stronger than Lacie but she put such a great amount of mental effort into gripping the side of the boat and willing it to move that she felt she could claim at least an honourable influence over the exertions. Tom's cap fell off and was lost and one of Gertie's legs got stuck in the mud – 'Oo! me leg, me leg!' she yelled, convinced that it was never going to be got out – but at last *Wobbler* was high and dry. Well, not exactly dry but 'it's out o' that wet river,' said Tom.

Poor battered old *Wobbler*!

'We'll have to leave it,' Gertie said when they had exhausted themselves with pulling it. 'We'll come back for it tomorrow – or at least I will – and take it to Bimble's.'

They were squelching in ooze and their one thought was to get out of it. Gertie soon forgot about Bimble's and Lacie forgot about her train. They floundered about, stumbling over rounded leafy things which Lacie was vaguely aware of as being cabbages, then got to some drier ground, and, at last, to a cart-track.

They set off along it towards the lights of Bridgeover which gleamed in the distance.

'Where's Dick's farm?' asked Tom, waiting for the girls to catch up with him, 'or am I goin' somewhere different now?'

303

'It isn't far from Bridgeover,' Lacie told him, 'when we get there we'll ask somebody where it is.'

The wind was cold and blowing a thin, sharp rain before it.

'Listen !' Tom stood still. 'Hosses !'

A horse came galloping out of the gloom.

'Dick ! It's Dick – and Warrior !' Tom ran forward so that the horse reared and its rider swore as he was pitched forward.

He was not Dick. The horse was not Warrior.

Tom stood back in the shadows, dumb with disappointment.

'Who are you?' demanded the man. 'How many o' you are there?'

Lacie stepped up and told him, adding that they were looking for Bird Hill farm.

'What ! Stilbush's place?'

Lacie explained that they – or rather – one of them, had urgent business there. It *was* urgent to Tom so she was telling the truth.

'Well, you've got a long walk,' said the man, 'so I hope you like stretching your legs.' He asked them if they were reckoning on seeing Dick that night, by any chance.

'Certainly,' said Lacie, 'it's very important.'

'Oh, is it?' said the man. 'Well, however important you think it is you won't see Dick Stilbush tonight.'

'Why not?' Lacie's voice had a tremble in it.

'Because he's not there, young miss. And you'll not see him tomorrow neither. Why not? I'll tell you. He and old man Stilbush have gone down south to buy some hosses Dick fancies, and they'll be gone the best part of the week. Still, you know your own business best I suppose, and it must be important for you to be traipsin' about here on a night like this. If you want to know the way I'll tell you, then you'd better get moving as sharp as you can. There's a deal too much water around, and likely to be more so don't waste any time.'

He told them the way to Bird Hill farm, then told them all over again before he touched up his horse and rode away.

Lacie was annoyed with herself. She should have asked him the way to the station. Perhaps he might even have known the times of the trains – then the sky opened and rain streamed down in cataracts.

'Run !' yelled Gertie and set off as fast as she could go.

'Aye, run,' cried Tom, taking Lacie's hand, and they ran after the flying Gertie.

They were all so blinded by rain and confused by their misfortunes as they splashed and stumbled through the puddles lying on the track, that they nearly missed the shed.

28

Acknowledged

THE door was broken so they easily got inside. A farm
cart was taking up most of the room and Tom disappeared round the back of it. He was much more at
home in barns than in boats. He rustled straw about
and said cheerfully that it was champion, just the stuff
to get 'em dry and keep 'em warm – and so were some
sacks which he discovered in the cart.

Soon all the wet outer clothes were hanging on a
nail which Tom had found by the simple process of
getting scratched by it. He pushed the door back into
place to keep out the draught and kept on saying,
'We'll soon be as right as rain,' until Lacie begged him
not to say the word any more.

She had some dry clothes in her case and thought it
would be sensible to put them on, then with a shock
she remembered.

The case was in the boat.

She gave a wail of dismay but the other two remained
unconcerned. They had already settled into their
separate mounds of straw.

'But all my money's in it,' Lacie said.

'It'll still be there tomorrow,' and Gertie sank

deeper into her straw and sacks, murmuring drowsily that nobody was daft enough to be roaming about that place where *Wobbler* was, not robbers, nor burglars nor anybody with any sense.

Lacie, not wishing to disturb the peace, refrained from mentioning that the Spotted Dick was also in the case, and let Gertie ramble on about getting up early and taking *Wobbler* to Bimble's. The others could come too, she was saying, if they wanted a ride on the river as far as Bridgeover, it'd be nice on the river in the morning.

Tom stopped her. No fear! No more boats for him. All he was going to think of now was sleep. They settled down.

After a time a strange sound came from Gertie's mound of straw. When questioned about it all she could say was, 'I – it's m-my t-teeth. I c-c-can't stop 'em rattling.'

'Something's rattling,' Tom agreed. 'I was beginning to think t'place was full o' rats.'

Lacie hurriedly curled up her feet beneath her – she had taken off her shoes and socks – and smiled in the dark. It was rather a weak smile and nobody saw it but a pun has to be noticed.

'I'm cold,' moaned Gertie. Tom threw some more straw over her but, 'I'm hot!' she cried and threw it all off again.

Tom had placed himself near the door saying that if anybody came whoever it was would have to fall over him first.

'Nobody'll come.' Gertie's voice was mournful. 'Me-dad don't care about me any more, only about that cross-tempered nurse called Nora.'

Presently Tom said, 'I'm not goin' to Dick's place now he isn't there, am I?' Before Lacie could answer, Gertie had a violent attack of sneezing and he did not repeat the question.

A draught was coming through a hole in the roof. Something else was coming in too. Light. Straight through the hole the full moon shone. Now they could see each other. Tom said that they all looked like straw dolls and Gertie replied that she didn't care what she looked like, if she didn't get something to eat she would die – then she remembered the pudding and bitterly blamed Lacie for not allowing it to be eaten before. While the two girls were arguing about it Tom rustled himself out of his straw and offered to go outside and look around to see what he could find.

When he came back he had something in his hands. Gertie was the first to see what it was.

'Only a mucky old turnip!' she cried.

'Was you expectin' me to bring you a hot dinner?' asked Tom.

He was the sort of person who always had a clasp knife, so peeling and cutting up the 'tonnip' as Gertie called it, did not present them with a problem. Eating it did, though. They were so thirsty and its flavour was so strong and harsh.

They all said in the morning that they hadn't slept a wink, but Lacie was certain that she had heard Gertie snoring, Gertie said she had twice spoken to Lacie without being answered and both of them had heard Tom babbling about the old Missus spoiling everything and being to blame for everything that had gone wrong, even for him being called 'Misfortune' and

'Bad Luck' and not having his 'proper' name, the name he should have had a right to.

'That's 'cos his dad never married his mam,' whispered Gertie. 'His dad wanted to marry her but old Mrs Mounthingummyjig stopped him. Some folks call our Tom a bastard 'cos o' that – but I haven't got to talk about it. My froat's sore, anyway, an' me head aches.'

Lacie never forgot that night. She never forgot the taste of that turnip nor the harsh touch of the straw – nor the sound of it as Gertie, coughing and groaning, tossed about in it all the time.

It was no good trying to sleep. The moon had disappeared. The wind roared and whistled, rain drummed on the shed and fell through the hole in the roof.

'It's nearly as bad as being in that boat,' Tom said, then sat up with a great upheaval of straw and in a soft voice as if he were confiding a secret said he was sorry about the school teacher, the nice one, who had got hurt when the motor bike went wrong. 'I'd like her to know I'm sorry,' he said.

Lacie pulled her wits together. 'So it was you who meddled with it.' She kept her voice very quiet, 'But why?'

'I thought it might a come to take me away,' replied Tom, 'so I tried to make it so as it couldn't go. But it did go. I was mis'rable when she got hurt.'

Lacie tried to clear up another mystery, the one about the corn which had been found in the petrol tank of Nora's car, but he was vague about that.

'It might a been me. I misremember.'

When Lacie asked him what he had got against motor cars all he could say was that he mistrusted folks who came in 'ingines'. Hosses were all right, but not 'ingines'. The old Missus had come in an 'ingine' – a big shiny motor car *that* was – and nothing had been right since. If she were to take him away it would be in a motor car, wouldn't it? So naturally he was suspicious if he saw one at Nettlewood.

'Mrs Mountsorrel won't take you away – ever.' Lacie suddenly felt quite sure about it and decided to be firm in putting down Tom's fears. 'Perhaps she might have meant to once, but she won't now – and she won't send you away, either, with anybody else or to anybody else.' She quickly added, 'You won't have to leave Granny Betts. I'm sure of it. Everybody is . . . but you won't understand.'

He was silent, sitting hunched up in the straw. After a time he asked, 'What am I running away for then? Whatever got into me?'

Lacie hesitated, not wishing to reopen old wounds. There had been the matter of the bonfire and his hurt feelings over losing the secret room.

'I've got over that!' cried Tom. 'They did burn all them things but I know where there's lots more, and t'place is full o' secret rooms if I want 'em.'

He was quiet again then asked, 'Where will Rose be now?'

'I should think she's at home,' Lacie said.

'Back at Lark Grange?'

'I suppose so.'

He went deep into thought.

'I don't think I'll run any more,' he said at last, 'if Dick's not there an' Rose has gone back, I think I'll go back to Granny.'

'Good,' said Lacie.

'She'll be there, Granny will, like she always is, and maybe Rose . . .' he stopped to think, 'maybe Rose'll be there like she said she would be, once, but she wasn't.'

Lacie couldn't help yawning, then Tom yawned too. He nested himself in the straw and said they'd better get some sleep, somebody was sure to come early in the morning to fetch the cart and it was best for them not to be caught in the shed.

'Why not?' Lacie was indignant. 'We're not doing any harm.'

'Lots o' things are doing no harm,' said Tom, 'but they get caught just the same.'

It was late when they woke up. So much for their resolution to get up early.

Lacie yawned and blinked and ached as she pulled herself out of the straw. Tom had opened the shed door and she saw that another dark day lay outside.

'We'd better make haste,' he said.

She went up to a heap of straw and shook a shoulder which was sticking out of it. The shoulder shrugged her off.

'Stop it, our dad!' muttered Gertie. 'I'm not gettin' up an' I'm not goin' to school.'

'Oh, come on!' Lacie gave her another shake. 'Of course you're not going to school. There's no chance of that.'

The sky growled. She left Gertie and went to the door where Tom was standing.

'Was that thunder?' She gave an anxious look outside. He nodded.

'Aye, and by t'look o'things, I'll be walking straight into it on my way home.' But he sounded cheerful.

Gertie gave a hacking cough.

'Go an' make her get up,' Tom told Lacie, so she went back into the shed.

Gertie was sitting up and rubbing her eyes which were swollen and watery. Her face was a mottled red and she sneezed again.

'It must be the straw.' Lacie stared at her.

'Straw?' said Tom. 'That's nowt to do wi' straw. That's measles.'

'Measles?' Lacie was horrified. 'But she can't, she CAN'T have measles. We're running away.'

'I'm not.' Gertie's voice was hoarse but firm. 'I'm goin' home to medad.'

'And I'm goin' back to Granny,' said Tom, 'so we'd best get movin'.'

Lacie hesitated. Did she look as wretched as they did with their tousled hair all over bits of straw, and muddy crumpled clothes?

'And it's worse for me,' she thought. 'I'm the one who's going on a train.'

As she began to straighten out her damp and dirty coat she noticed some pieces of broken wood in a corner.

'If only we'd got some matches!' She looked at Tom, half expecting him to produce some – he usually had a collection of useful odds and ends in his pockets – 'We could make a fire, and dry our clothes and – '

But Tom was shocked.

'Matches!' he cried. 'There's no lighting fires, me lass, not where there's straw about. This place'd be a bonfire in no time.'

Now he could say 'bonfire', Lacie noticed, without the least shadow of concern. Good. But a bonfire — just a little safe one — would be nice, all the same.

'We're losin' time,' Tom said. 'Look sharp, you two.'

He had folded up all the sacks and put them back in the cart, and had tidied up most of the straw. Going over to Gertie he tried to pull her on to her feet but she stuck where she was like a lump of iron.

'Let me be,' she groaned, 'let go o' me, our Tom,' for he was holding on to her wrist, determined to yank her out of the straw.

'She's burning hot,' said Lacie.

'Like a furnace,' Tom agreed. 'I'll grab one arm and you grab t'other. Upsa daisy!' and Gertie was on her feet.

She drooped and snuffled as Tom and Lacie struggled to put her into Fred Sprott's still-wet jersey and pulled his damp red cap over her head.

'I don't know how she's going to row that boat today,' said Lacie. 'It's going to be a dreadful problem.'

But as it turned out that wasn't a problem at all.

They had not taken more than a few steps from the shed — it was on the edge of a turnip field and Lacie immediately spotted where their supper had come from — when Tom plonked down his feet. Lacie also stopped. Gertie was sagging between them and didn't care whether she stopped or not.

'What is it? What's happened?' Lacie was looking around in amazement.

The way they had come the night before was covered with water. Miles and miles of water.

The boat had gone.

After a pause Tom said, 'Fred Sprott won't be pleased.' Gertie said nothing.

'She doesn't seem to understand anything this morning,' said Lacie.

'Good job too,' Tom replied, 'what she don't know about she won't grieve over.'

Lacie was just wondering why it was that he was not generally regarded as being sensible when she remembered her case and her money. 'It's gone!' she cried. 'Everything's gone!'

So that settled the question of what she should do.

'Come on,' said Tom, beginning to move. 'Back home.' He sounded cheerful. 'I'd much rayther walk it than boat it.' He hoisted Gertie further up on to her legs and, with a sure instinct for home, turned his face in the direction of Nettlewood.

The cold wind had dropped and now the air was warm. Too warm. A heavy sky pressed down on them, the heavy earth dragged at their feet as Tom and Lacie, and Gertie stumbling between them, began the homeward trudge.

They looked a doleful trio, yet flowing between them was a feeling of relief. Even though Gertie didn't understand what was happening she wasn't grumbling, Tom was humming under his breath — the tune wasn't remarkable in any way but it was cheerful — and Lacie had given in to Fate. Everything had been decided for them.

'We'll get a telling-off I expect.' She was imagining Nora's cross looks and Fred Sprott's fury over the misuse of *Wobbler*. 'Still, it won't be me who'll get the worst of that.' She counterbalanced the gloomy picture of reproach and recrimination with a pleasanter one of a tin bath in front of a fire and lots and lots of soap.

'And soup,' she cried, 'hot, hot soup.'

'Stew,' said Tom, 'with dumplin's an' gravy. Buckets full o'gravy.'

He emphasized his words by squelching his boots into the black ooze on the track.

'I always thought soil was brown,' said Lacie, 'but this is so black.'

'It's good stuff for growing celery,' replied Tom.

At the word 'celery' Gertie looked up. 'I wouldn't 'a run away if it'd been Missy Bissy he was set on. I'd 've liked that. I thought he wanted Missy Bissy – ' her voice was tearful – 'an' I reckoned she liked him – but he boxed me ears just for talkin' about it an' he told me to mind my own business an' not be such an interferin' little nuisance. That's why I jumped on his gram'phone record though it was his fav'rit an' mine an' all.'

'You jumped on the record?' Lacie was shocked, 'surely not on *Lay my head on your shoulder* ...' She broke off for Gertie had begun to sing in a croaky voice the first verse of Fred Sprott's 'fav'rit' song.

'She says it's his favourite,' Lacie muttered to Tom, 'but she's the one who's always playing it – or singing it.'

'Well, she needn't sing it now,' said Tom as Gertie gave forth her raucous notes.

> *Lay my head on your shoulder, Daddy,*
> *Turn your face to the West ...*
> *This is the hour the sun ... goes ... down.*

'Hey – ey !' cried Tom. 'Tha's mekkin' it rain again, our Gert.'

315

Lacie was wondering if the benefit of tying her wet scarf over her damp hair would be worth the trouble of doing it, when . . .

'Look behind,' said Tom. 'Something's coming.'

They heard the rumble of wheels and the plod-plod of a horse, and stood aside as a farm cart came lumbering up.

It was the cart from the shed.

The carter peered from underneath a sack which he was using as a hood, then stopped the horse which splodged down its massive hooves so that four fountains of black chocolate flew upwards.

'Hey up!' said the carter, 'wheer ye from?'

'Owsterley,' replied Lacie.

'Ows'tley? Y're on t'wrong side o' t'river, then.'

'We're going to Nettlewood.' Again it was Lacie who spoke. Poor Tom seemed to be shrinking back into himself.

'Nettle-ud, eh?' said the carter. 'Nettle-ud, aye.' He looked at them thoughtfully, then said again, 'Nettle-ud, um.' After another look he said, 'Well, ah did think ye was three walkin' scarcraws but now I can see ye're yooman beans. Get in if ye want a ride.'

Tom was looking at the horse in a shy but friendly way and made a move towards it.

'Into t'cart, lad,' said the carter, 'not on t'hoss. Well, wek oop a bit then, ah've not got all day.'

Tom hesitated. Lacie sensed that he was unwilling to add to the horse's load and whispered that the cart was empty and not very heavy to pull and that the horse looked strong and that there was Gertie to think of.

'What y' clacking about?' asked the carter. 'If ye want a ride get in, if ye don't, I'm off.'

So Tom helped Gertie, then Lacie, into the cart and climbed in himself.

'It's a wet day for a walk,' said the carter, 'though there's some folks as likes it, seemingly. Gee up, ged on wi' thee.'

The horse shook its mane and moved off.

The carter was silent for a time, then said that he could give them a lift for a mile or so down the road. 'That little 'un sounds in a bad way,' he added as Gertie gave another groan. 'Cover thisens up wi' them sacks. They'll keep a drop o' rain off.'

The same sacks! There they were in the neat pile which Tom had made. There were a few turnips, too, in a corner of the cart. Lacie hoped that she would not be invited to partake of them.

Plod. Plod. Plod.

Gertie. Lacie. Tom. They huddled together under the sacks. The carter was wearing, as well as his sack hood, a cloak of sacks across his shoulders, and some sacks were laid across his knees and sacks were gathered about his legs.

He looked round suddenly, giving his head a jerk towards Gertie.

'She's got a funny look. Ah reckon she's got maisles.'

It took Lacie a little time to realize what he meant.

'Well, she'll not gi'e 'em to me,' he said, 'so I'm not bothered. 'Oss won't catch 'em neether.'

Lacie, thinking that perhaps he was a family man, asked him if he had much experience of measles.

Aye, he had. Plenty – and of fevers and mumps, and chicken-pox and croup and whooping-cough. His lot had been down with 'em all . . . Sometimes all five of 'em at the same time. Five? Aye, five bairns.

317

Thus assured as to the extent of his familiarity with infectious ailments Lacie was glad to confide in him about Gertie, and said, 'She keeps saying she's going to die.'

'Well, she moan't dee in my cart.' His back heaved. 'Tell 'er to wait till she gets home,' and he chuckled for half a mile of slow-bumping road. After a time he asked, 'Is it Fred Sprott's lass?'

'Yes.'

'Ah thowt it wor.' He chuckled again. 'He'll a summat to say when he sees 'er. Traipsin' about in this weather an 'er wi' maisles.' He gave another look over his shoulder. 'An' isn't that the young feller from Nettle-ud, the one they say is a bit weak in the –.' He touched his head with the end of his whip-handle. Lacie quickly stopped him from saying any more by thanking him for the lift. 'We were going somewhere,' she told him, 'but we had to change our plans, then we got caught in the rain.'

'Aye,' he said, 'ye look as if summat's caught ye.'

He stopped the cart at a gate.

'Yon's my road.' He pointed to a path that led to a cottage crouching in the distance. 'Theer's five on 'em o'er theer,' he said. 'Six, wi' t'Missus.'

Thoughts were turning over at the back of Lacie's mind. She mentioned his missus.

'Does she stay at home every day?' she ventured to ask.

'Nay,' said the carter, 'she's mostly out,' and he changed the subject.

A wide ditch brimming with water was running alongside the track.

'See this 'ere drain,' he said, 'there's a bridge o'er

318

it a bit further on. Get on t'other side and cut across them fields. There's a track that'll tek ye straight to Nettle-ud. It's a mucky walk but ye can do it if ye don't leave it too late.'

Lacie thought that by 'too late' he meant before nightfall. It had been growing much darker and she asked him the time.

'It's on'y three or four o' t'clock, or thereabouts,' he replied, 'though it looks more like t'middle o' t'neeght.'

He pointed with his whip across the fields. 'Nettle-ud lies o'er yonder. Cross Black Dyke if ye still can, then go by t'Levels. But mek haste for t'watter's creepin' out. Bank's bust, they say, further down t'river. Oppen t'gate, young feller, an' save me gettin' down.'

Tom opened the gate and shut it again when the carter had driven through, and the cart rumbled away through the mist and the rain towards the distant cottage and the five bairns and the missus who hadn't gone out.

'So she didn't go to work today,' said Lacie. 'She said she wouldn't.'

'Eh? Who?' Tom was only half listening as he wiped rain from Gertie's face.

'I think it's Mr Um.' Lacie gazed after the disappearing cart. Tom looked puzzled but before Lacie could explain, Gertie whimpered pitifully. The carter turned round and flourished his whip as an admonition to them to be moving and in obedience to his gesture they at once turned themselves towards Nettlewood, soon came to the bridge across the drain, and set off across the fields.

'Telling me the road home!' muttered Tom, 'as if I don't know it for meself.' He was stepping out confidently now he was on home ground and said he knew the way like he knew the back of his hand and had known it so for many a mile already.

All the drains and ditches were full to the brim and some were overflowing.

The sky grew darker and seemed to press down. It was an inky purple. The air was heavy and warm. It was no longer raining but Tom said, 'There's a lot more coming. We'd better step lively.'

They walked on as fast as they could over the water-logged ground, Gertie dragging between Lacie and Tom.

A streak of lightning flashed across the sky in front of them.

'I thought as much,' said Tom. 'It'll break right over Nettlewood.'

More rain burst down.

'I'm so wet I don't care.' Lacie pulled off her scarf and shook her hair in the downpour. There was a sort of pleasure in it.

Thunder growled.

'Look yonder,' said Tom, 'I can see home.'

They plodded on. Suddenly he stopped and asked Lacie if she were quite sure that Mrs Mountsorrel wouldn't be taking him away. Again Lacie calmed his fears. He sighed with relief, then looked sorry. 'I wish I could a liked her more,' he said. 'I might a done if only she hadn't wanted to change me to her way o' livin'. I like Granny Betts' way best, you see.'

They went on again until he was struck by an even more disturbing thought.

'Granny Betts!' he cried out, and said as if he had never thought of it before. 'What if she isn't there?'

Lacie comforted him, assuring him that Granny Betts would be there as she always was, but he had meant something else, and went on, 'What shall I do when she's never there at all, when she gets old and dies?'

Lacie took a deep breath, then made her voice calm and firm. 'She's very strong and healthy. Everybody says so, and you — you must be a comfort to her so that she lives for a long time, and — and you mustn't run away again because she worries about it and that isn't good for her.'

'No, I won't.' Poor Tom began to hurry onward again. 'I'll never run off an' leave her, never no more. I'll look after her an' take care of her, just like she's taken care o' me, an' we'll be happy, as happy as skylarks.' Suddenly he called out at the top of his voice, 'I'm coming home, Granny Betts. How could I have ever gone an' left thee?'

He startled Gertie who looked dazed and asked what all the row was about.

'Are you sure that this is the way?' Lacie asked anxiously for they were now ankle deep in water.

'Just follow me.' Tom splashed forward then came back to help Gertie.

'Utch her up on my back,' he said.

Lacie had never seen him look so happy, not even on the Lark Grange day — but this look was different, somehow. She watched him and her heart was troubled but she didn't know why.

Somehow Gertie was hoisted on to his shoulders. He laughed as he strode on again, and her head in its red cap flopped up and down as if there were no sense in it.

'They've lighted up already.' Poor Tom stopped for breath and looked towards his home.

'No wonder,' said Lacie, 'it's like midnight.'

In the old days there had been no way into Nettlewood except by the bridge over the moat.

So it was now.

They could see the house and Granny Betts' cottage. They could see lights in the windows and smoke from the chimneys, but they could not, as they had meant to do, scramble down the side of the moat and up into the back gardens.

'It's an island,' cried Lacie. 'There's water everywhere.'

The moat was full and overflowing.

Tom bent his back to put Gertie down. She splashed into a foot of water. It seemed to bring her to her senses.

'Hey! That's wet,' she said.

Nobody answered her. She looked around.

'Floods,' she cried. 'T'floods are out. Oh, where's medad?'

All around the fields were under water.

'We'll still get through.' Tom was strong and calm. 'We must make for t' front o' the house and go over by the bridge. We'll be all right. It's been like this before.'

Putting their faith in him the two girls followed him through the rising water and the deepening gloom. When at last she saw the bridge Lacie could hardly believe her eyes. The world was transformed by water. The house rose out of the flood like an ark of stone.

'The river's everywhere,' she said, bewildered.

Water was rushing through the moat as if it were a

river in its own right, and spilling over in long surges that swirled around their feet, and all the time the sky groaned and flashed.

Poor Tom had nearly reached the bridge when he turned round and shouted, 'Keep back! Get to the tree.'

Lacie took Gertie's hand and together they struggled to the alder. Its flying leaves beat into their faces, its branches were flailing in the storm.

The swing's long ropes had been blown around the trunk. The two girls strained upwards and managed to grasp them.

With an ever-increasing sense of unreality Lacie looked towards the house and saw that a boat was moored at the bottom of the front steps.

Lights were shining in the windows. There was a lighted lantern beside the front door.

Suddenly Gertie yelled, 'Dad, oh Dad!'

Lacie shouted too. Whose name did she call? She never remembered. She and Gertie were close together, each holding a rope of the swing. A strong current swirled down and they were almost swept off their feet.

They pulled themselves up higher into the tree. Tom was standing at the end of the bridge holding the hand rail and bracing himself against the pressure of water which was rushing over the footboards.

He hesitated.

'Tom!' shouted Lacie. 'Come back!'

Somebody ran out of the house and screamed. It was Nora. Other figures appeared on top of the steps.

Lacie saw Fred Sprott seize the lantern and get into the boat. Another man was with him. They both yelled to Tom to stay where he was.

323

Tom was on the bridge and seemed to be testing its safety. Across at the house Granny Betts stood on the top step waving her arms. She was calling to him but the sound of her voice was lost.

He looked towards her, raised his hand, and in the lightning's gleam he smiled.

'She wants you to keep back,' screamed Lacie in the wild noise of the storm. 'Come to the tree,' and Gertie sobbed, 'Yes, come o'er here, our Tom. Come to t'tree.'

Fred Sprott was rowing over the lawn, bringing the boat to the bridge. Lacie still could not recognize the man who was with him.

As lightning flashed again another figure ran out on to the steps.

It was Mrs Mountsorrel.

Who else would appear in a shawl and a long white nightgown? She held out her arms when she saw Tom on the bridge and cried out but her words were lost as thunder crashed overhead.

Poor Tom looked towards the tree where the girls were clinging, then down at the water swirling over his feet, then across at the figures on the steps.

Mrs Mountsorrel called out again. The elements quietened and two words rang out,

'Tommy Mountsorrel! Tommy Mountsorrel!'

She broke free from Nora, and running forward, pushed Granny Betts aside, knocking her over.

Tom shouted and ran to the middle of the bridge. It crumpled and fell away beneath his feet, and he went down.

Lacie saw him fling up his arms, saw him in the water, then she gave herself up to nightmare. She heard herself screaming. She saw the white figure of Mrs Mountsorrel run down into the flood. She saw the flickering light of the lantern in the boat. She saw the lightning flash and heard the thunder roll. She heard Fred Sprott's voice, and Gertie's cry of, 'Dad, oh Dad!' She felt herself lifted down and rocking with the boat.

Somebody held her.

A name came into her mind, George Springles. But he wasn't here, he was somewhere else.

Courage, mon amie.

It was George Springles who carried her into the house and there was something in the clasp of his arms and the touch of his rough jacket that put her in mind of her father so that at last she was comforted, stopped crying, and, with her hand in his as he sat beside her bed, she fell asleep.

29

Mopping up

WHERE was she? Was this another part of the nightmare? It didn't seem like a nightmare. She felt so comfortable – and safe.

Lacie opened her eyes. She wasn't in Nettlewood. She was in School Cottage.

She stretched out an arm. The measles had gone; German measles, like Gertie's. Nothing much, but Dr Plumtree had said dear, dear, dear, dear, dear, that cough must be watched and there's been a certain amount of shock you know.

Shock.

Lacie's mind blocked. Over the river, over the trees – no, she wouldn't think of Nettlewood. School Cottage was so peaceful, so different – but there was something unpeaceful deep in her mind, something which was trying to get out.

Chloë came upstairs with a telegram. It said LACIE COME HOME. Chloë had known everything would be all right, hadn't she?

Although it was the first day of term she wasn't back at school, but on Dr Plumtree's orders was having another week's holiday. So was Gertie. Lucky Gertie.

The telegram was in a yellow envelope and in Miss Jessima Throssel's handwriting. Lacie kept looking at it. It would change everything. All these familiar things, her bed, the owl in the glass case, the furniture, the window that looked across to the Big School, would become mere items in her memory, seen only with an inward eye until, perhaps, forgotten and never seen at all.

Home which had once been so familiar and so real, now at this moment when she was buttoning her shoe, was not as real as here . . . and soon what was here and seemed so real would be like home seemed now, like a dream, a good dream which had turned a corner into Nettlewood and become a nightmare.

She clapped down a shutter in her mind and went downstairs.

Later in the morning Chloë went into the garden to snip at dead roseheads. Lacie could have snipped too, but, somehow, she only wanted to do nothing.

Little by little she let her mind return to the events of the past week. A makeshift bridge had been built over the moat as soon as the floods had gone down. George had driven her back to School Cottage.

Chloë was speaking in a bright but careful voice. Rain had caused the trouble. Heavy rain in the Midlands always meant that Owsterley had to look out. No, she and George hadn't gone to his mother's, but had turned back.

The river had swollen. Too much water going down had met a high tide coming up with a strong wind behind it. The west bank had burst in two places, near Bridgeover and at Nettlewood.

She paused, then went on. At first Lacie and Gertie had not been missed but in the morning Fred Sprott discovered that *Wobbler* had gone, and he was worried. The girls couldn't be found. He crossed the river in the *Wavey* hoping to find Gertie at home or at School Cottage with Lacie. Then grabbed a bicycle and raced to Mrs Bisset.

(Poor Fred! Gertie had wanted him to suffer.)

They were all in it by now, said Chloë, she, George, the Throssels, most of Owsterley. Police at Hawksop and Bridgeover and the men at Bimble's boatyard, were all on the alert.

Fred Sprott and George had got up a search party. They managed to cross the river to Nettlewood — but the storm held them up.

It had all been so dreadful. Lacie couldn't know how dreadful!

Then Lacie spoke. Chloë had promised to stand on the bank and wave when she got back to School Cottage. 'But you didn't,' said Lacie, 'I kept looking and I thought I saw smoke coming out of the chimneys. You were here all the time . . . but you never stood on the bank and waved.'

At the end of the afternoon George Springles came across from the Big School to have tea at School Cottage. He sat with Chloë and Lacie in front of a twig fire which they kept feeding with little branches. Sweet-scented sap ran out, hissing and bubbling.

Looking into the flames George told Lacie about Poor Tom. The flood had carried him away into the wood, and it was not until the waters had gone down that he had been found near the little ice-house.

Nobody could have saved him. He had been drawn under the racing torrent that swept through the moat, and swirled away and lost.

Fred Sprott had done all he could but the water was rising so quickly that Lacie and Gertie were in danger.

The twigs crackled and flared. In a faltering voice Lacie asked about Granny Betts.

Granny Betts had spoken little, had made no moan but had gone to Mrs Mountsorrel's bedside and stayed to the end.

Mrs Mountsorrel was dead.

There was silence. More and more twigs were consumed by the greedy fire.

'Poor Tom.' Lacie spoke his name at last. He was Mrs Mountsorrel's grandson. Granny Betts' daughter and Mrs Mountsorrel's son were his parents.

Poor Tom.

Molly Betts was pretty and refined, Granny Betts' darling and treasure, born late in her married life, long after her first child.

Poor Molly Betts.

Her ways had pleased Mrs Mountsorrel who had taken her as her maid to Italy where Tom Mountsorrel had seen her for the first time since they were children. They had fallen in love.

Lacie, remembering something Poor Tom had once said, was glad about the love. He had called himself a love-child but had said it was misfortune as well.

There was a moment's pause. Love-child, Chloë said, was an old name for a child whose parents weren't married. It was a beautiful name, and in Tom's case, a right one for there was a lot of love behind him.

Mrs Mountsorrel had been very angry about the love

affair and had soon sent Molly back to Nettlewood. When Tom Mountsorrel found out that she had been sent away he set out after her but caught a fever and died on the journey.

Lacie cried out in pity. It was a true story but not a happy one. Nevertheless she wanted to hear more and Chloë continued. Poor Tom was born some time after Molly got home. And then she died. Mrs Mountsorrel would have nothing to do with the baby and refused to acknowledge him as her grandson, though all Owsterley could see he was a Mountsorrel.

Lacie thought of the portrait in the picture room. Yes, Poor Tom had looked a Mountsorrel.

Granny Betts loved him and looked after him. She was allowed to stay on at Nettlewood as a sort of caretaker, and had scraped by somehow. She and Tom were happy enough in their own way, and so after all, Tom lived in the place he'd a right to live in . . . he knew and loved every inch of it just as if it were his.

'It was his,' cried Lacie, 'or it should have been.'

Everything had been all right till the other grand-mother came back that summer. She tried to make amends for her neglect of Tom, but her ideas only bewildered and frightened him.

'He called her Granny, though,' said Chloë, 'that pleased her.'

Lacie stared.

'As he stood on the bridge before it broke, he called her Granny,' said Chloë.

'He didn't.' Lacie's voice broke with passion. 'He was calling Granny Betts. I *know* he was. He was hurrying home to take care of her . . . He cared about her more than he cared about anybody, even Rose.'

Rose?

Chloë looked up.

'It was Granny Betts he called Granny,' said Lacie again.

It didn't matter. Granny Betts had said, 'Let her think it was her he called Granny. It's all she ever had from him. Let her be.'

After a time Lacie wanted to know why Mrs Mountsorrel had stopped her son from marrying Molly Betts if she'd been so pretty and nice.

The answer was pride.

Molly was a servant, the daughter of a servant and not good enough for the great Mountsorrels.

Great Mountsorrels! George said such rubbish made his blood boil.

'Well, they're not great now,' Chloë patted his hand. 'Poor Tom was the last of them and he's gone.'

The next day Lacie and Gertie went into the fields to pick wild flowers for Poor Tom and mixed them with red berries from the hedges. Gertie wanted to put in sprays of blackberries as well 'for he was awful fond on 'em'.

At night Fred Sprott rowed the two coffins over from Nettlewood.

It was twilight.

The sky, the air, the voices of the waiting people were tranquil. Even the sound the owls made came softly.

It was high water. The river flowed like dark silk. There was the splash of oars and the glimmer of lanterns as the boat bearing Poor Tom and Mrs Mountsorrel came over the water. The muffled boom of Lacie's heart was like the sound of a drum in her ears.

Mrs Bisset and Bertie were on the bank, waiting. Gertie was with them. Chloë and George were waiting. Lacie was with them. The Misses Throssel were there. The customers from the King of the River were there, all bareheaded and postponing their enjoyment of the first pint of the evening.

Mr Bindle was there, in a white surplice with a muffler under it.

A farm cart was waiting to receive the coffins and to carry them down that long village street to rest until morning in the church in the fields.

People followed in twos and threes.

'George will go and Fred Sprott will go, of course, but we'll go in and make some cocoa,' Chloe said with a shiver. 'Gertie can come in with us if she likes.'

'Bertie and me will follow,' said Mrs Bisset, 'and see the poor souls safely into church. Besides, we may as well go along with them, it'll be company for us on our way home.'

30

Sprott House

THE next afternoon almost everybody in Owsterley
went to the funeral. Rose Fennell and Dick Stilbush
drove in a smart new pony trap all the way from Lark
Grange. George Springles took the top class from the
Big School. Their high spirits at being let off classes
conflicted once or twice with the solemnity of the
occasion, but George had only to say, 'Now Standard 6
remember where you're going to,' and all was well.

The church was dressed for Autumn. Signs of the
coming harvest were everywhere. Vines trailed round
the pulpit and purple grapes glowed in the rich light
of stained-glass windows.

Mr Bindle spoke his words amidst sheaves of corn
for not all had been spoiled by the rain.

He spoke of Love and Pride, of the mistakes people
make and of the forgiveness they need. He spoke of
Pride brought low and of Humility raised up – then
Mrs Mountsorrel and Poor Tom, their mistakes and
their love, the pride, sorrow and secrets were all laid
together in the dark earth of the past.

Secrets? It surprised Lacie afterwards to hear how
much was known about Poor Tom and who he was.
People talked about him as they came out of the

churchyard and walked across the fields. Somehow, Lacie didn't feel sad – perhaps because the autumn day was so warm and bright. The pools still left in the hollows were bright, the sky, the leaves, the river, all were bright, and the children in school were singing 'All things bright and beautiful'.

At the Sprott house Mrs Bisset suddenly dived out of sight into the kitchen. At Fred's behest she had provided a comforting tea and Chloë, George, Lacie and Bertie – and the Throssels – were invited to eat it. Rose and Dick had regretfully declined the invitation as Dick had business to do in Bridgeover.

It was the first time Lacie had been in the Sprott home and she looked about it with interest, though she had to conquer a slight quiver as she stepped over the threshold, the place was so much connected with Fred Sprott, and so redolent of the river.

The house was high and narrow. You dived into the kitchen and climbed into the parlour where tea was temptingly spread upon a table in a window that hung over the boats rocking below. Yes, two boats. The *Wobbler*, minus Lacie's case and much the worse for wear, had been reclaimed.

Gertie was in raptures at having guests to tea and at seeing Mrs Bisset behind the teapot, an enormous one of a rich glossy brown. It looked the very symbol of comfort and long life and everybody turned gratefully to it as Mrs Bisset raised it above the teacups with an air both solemn and cheerful as she said, 'You'll all be ready for your tea, I'm sure. Gertie, are the kettles boiling down below?'

Gertie wanted to know why there wasn't an iced cake with candles on it.

334

Nora was not present, having excused herself from both church and tea-party on account of her imminent departure for London, and all the packing she had to do.

Granny Betts had refused to leave Nettlewood but Fred and Mrs Bisset were going over the river later on with a bit of something tempting to eat.

Fred Sprott was a genial host. He looked neat, almost well-dressed for once. The whiskers had gone from his face, the black moustache was no more. He made jokes and attended upon his guests, who, after church and solemn thoughts, were now enjoying the food and each others' company. Feelings of relief and pleasure were flowing round the table with the tea from that inexhaustible pot. Mrs Bisset, presiding over it, was like a High Priestess of comfort.

Suddenly, in the midst of all the laughter and conversation, Lacie remembered Poor Tom, and grew cold.

Everybody seemed to have forgotten him.

She looked round the table and felt separate and far away. Mrs Bisset, in her ample calm, was pouring tea for the Throssels. They held out their eager cups as if for life itself.

They were getting old. Some day they must die. Sunlight slanting in from the west over Nettlewood, showed up lines in Chloë's face, lines which Lacie had never seen before.

Some day, Chloë too, would grow old, would die.

Fred Sprott was laughing. The sun burnished his face, burned in his eyes. Surely he could never be extinguished. Lacie wanted to draw near to him as if to a fire from out of the cold.

She was sitting near George, poor old George, and

looked at him with tender pity. Even now that hateful piece of iron was making its implacable journey through his being. And one day, some day, he too would die.

She burst into tears and hid behind his shoulder. Everybody looked at her.

'Oh well, we can excuse a few tears at a funeral,' said Miss Throssel, looking as if any tears she might shed would fall with a clink of ice.

Presently Lacie dried her eyes. George consoled her with a piece of barm loaf and said in a low voice, 'We've all got to make the best of it whatever happens. Life goes on, you know, and it's all rather wonderful really.'

Wonderful life. She came from behind his shoulder.

Fred Sprott was speaking to her, being very friendly. She disliked him hardly at all now. Later, on an errand for another plate of scones she descended after him into the kitchen where Mrs Bisset was refilling the teapot.

'Nice tea,' he said, and Lacie was sure she heard him say, 'Kissy Bissy.' He was just going to say something else when he saw Lacie and exclaimed, 'Well, look who's here! If it isn't Miss See-all-and-say-nowt!' and laughed as he went upstairs with the teapot. Mrs Bisset, though flustered and flushed from being near the fire, nevertheless did not look displeased.

'Kissy Bissy!' Well! Well! But what about Nora? What would she say, what would she think if – ? As the problem knotted itself in Lacie's mind Fred Sprott called out for the scones. When he took the plate from her he winked.

The conversation around the table now was about other funerals, past and to come. Gertie, rather bored, pulled a face at Jessima Throssel, who was annoyed, so Gertie pulled another one, much uglier, whereupon Miss Epiphany sent a warning glance at her across the table, a glance that silently but with unmistakable meaning, said, 'Just you wait, Gertie Sprott. Wait till I've got you in my class!'

And Gertie, to everybody's horror, said a Sprott word straight into her face.

When the funeral tea came to an end and the mourners who had forgotten to mourn were ready to depart, they all said what a beautiful funeral it had been and gave thanks to Fred and Mrs Bisset for the delicious tea. Suddenly Gertie cried out, 'Don't go away, Missy Bissy, stay here. You and Bertie can both stay here, can't they, Dad?'

Fred Sprott looked at Mrs Bisset and she looked at him – then Chloë, George and Lacie left them and went back to School Cottage.

Lacie looked across the water and saw the dark outline of Nettlewood. It was darker than the darkness all around and its spell reached out and gripped her again. She thought of Poor Tom. He was the story, the history of Nettlewood. Some of its mystery and pain had touched her and would always be a part of her, sinking within her as a leaf sinks into the mould.

Chloë called. The door of School Cottage was open and Lacie went in.

31

'Don't Shoot the Bluebird, Fred!'

ON CHLOE'S birthday Nora left Owsterley. George came out of school for a few minutes to put her luggage in the car then, after the briefest of goodbyes, she drove off like a rocket, almost knocking over Fred Sprott who happened to be crossing the road. He looked at the cloud of dust which was following the car and remarked that soon it would be too dangerous for folks to walk about.

He was wearing the red cap but took it off as he approached Chloë. He was just going to do a bit of work in his garden which had been neglected lately. George dashed into school where faces were pressing at the windows and a lot of noise going on, and Chloë invited Fred Sprott to see her garden which hadn't been neglected at all.

It was glowing with the colours of September. After a pause he said, 'It's a picture, a little paradise.' He looked at Chloë, then said again, 'a little paradise.' He strolled about in a pleasant fashion, stopped under the pear tree and helped himself to a pear. He'd been up that tree many a time on Pear Days long gone by.

'When your dad was headmaster,' he said to Chloë, 'he'd usually got it in for me, but on Pear Days he knew I was best for the job. I could climb and lug heavy baskets about and make other lads behave. Me – the worst in school.'

'No you weren't, I didn't think so anyway,' said Chloë, then told Lacie, 'when the other kids got on to me for being the headmaster's child I knew I'd got Fred to rely on. Somehow he'd always be there, just as if he'd shot up out of the ground.'

He laughed and said that he'd been a bit older and bigger than she was, that's all, then he twiddled the red cap in his hands and took a step nearer to Chloë.

'Happy Birthday !' he said.

She was surprised. How on earth had he remembered that?

'It's the asters for one thing.' He looked at Lacie. 'I remember being asked to her tea-party once, here at School Cottage. She wasn't more than seven or eight. I was a rough little tyke in them days and I don't blame folks for not wanting me in the house. But I was asked – once – so I went an' I reckon I behaved as well as any.'

He had been too polite to eat anything, Chloë said, and she'd been sorry.

'Not half as sorry as I was, after, when it was too late,' he replied, then went on to Lacie, 'she wore a little wreath of them flowers – asters. Pink, purple, white. I even remember the colours.'

'That was a long time ago,' said Chloë, smiling and looking rather pink, she no longer wore aster-wreaths on her birthdays ; then, moving a step away from him, she asked what was going on at Nettlewood.

Lacie didn't want to hear about Nettlewood, the

339

sound of its name still gave her a troubled feeling. As she began to walk away she heard Fred Sprott say that he was sorry about all that rubbish and stuff that was burnt over yonder. Sorry, sorry. She kept hearing the word – then . . .

'I didn't know the lad set so much store by it . . . never thought he'd take it so hard or I swear I'd never have touched it.' Chloë murmured something and he burst out,

'I don't trample on folks's feelings, though nobody ever cared who trampled on mine.'

Chloë must have mentioned the secret room which he and Nora had taken for themselves because he said, as if trying to make light of it, that it had just been somewhere to go and get away from the rest o' the house, folks were nosey in Nettlewood, 'and anyway,' he hurried on, 'it was a good place for my wireless stuff an' all.'

He went on speaking in a low voice, bending his head towards Chloë and putting his hand on her arm as if he were trying to make her understand something. He looked humble, like a penitent, and with a flash of insight Lacie thought, 'he wants her to forgive him.'

Then she heard Poor Tom's name and Nora's, and again, Nora's.

Lacie began to pick asters, pink, purple, white. She sat on an overturned plant pot and began to thread them together. After a time, when she sensed a change of mood, she went back to Chloë and Fred Sprott.

'Won't Gertie be pleased?' Chloë was smiling. 'She thinks no end of Missy Bissy.'

Lacie, now clear as to what was being discussed,

agreed that yes, Gertie would be pleased and yes, everybody did like Mrs Bisset.

'That woman's as good as gold,' said Fred Sprott, 'I know it well enough.'

Chloë put out her hand and wished him happiness.

'Happiness?' He put both his hands around hers. 'I've taken a few shots at that in my time – and missed it every one.'

'That's not the way,' replied Chloë with a smile, 'that's not the way at all. Don't try shooting the blue-bird, Fred.' And she pulled her hand from his.

'Hey, you!' He looked at Lacie. 'What's that you've got there?' and, taking the wreath of asters she had made, he suddenly put it on Chloë's head.

Lacie stared. Chloë was astounded and blushed.

'Well, little owl-eyes,' he said to Lacie, 'you're seeing something this time.' He put on his red cap and turned to go, then hesitated.

'She reminds me of you in a way – ' his eyes were on Chloë – 'like you used to be. Not in her looks exactly, but in her ways. Aye, she reminds me of you.'

He turned and walked away. Chloë did not move but stood looking after him, the aster-wreath dangling from her fingers.

He was gone.

'It was you!' breathed Lacie. Chloë was still flushed. The asters fell to the grass.

'You were the one,' said Lacie. 'He loved somebody once, very much. Just one, more than any other, when he . . . when you were young. It was you!'

Chloë cried out that she'd never heard such non-sense, it was years ago, it was nothing! They'd been kids, just kids – then she told Lacie to pick up the

341

asters and put them in water and to stop bothering about things she didn't understand.

But after tea – a birthday one with a cake from Mrs Bisset – when George had gone back to school for an hour to coach some prospective pupils for Hawksop Grammar School, the conversation somehow again got around to Fred Sprott.

It wasn't fair. He had brains. He could have been so different. He ought to have gone to school in Hawksop as Chloë and Nora had gone ... he could easily have got a scholarship, he was clever enough but nobody bothered about him.

Chloë sounded angry. Once, he had taken a book home from school to learn something which had interested him – and his father had thrown it on the fire.

'Sprotts were like that,' she said, 'but Fred could have been different.'

Yes, when they were children he was fond of her, and she of him, in a way, very fond. He always defended her in playground battles, was her champion. That rough Sprott boy! Well, he *was* rough, but not to her, never to her.

The trouble was, as they grew up, that he expected things to stay the same – as if Chloë could feel at seventeen what she had felt at seven. It was impossible, of course, and quite embarrassing. How could she? It simply wouldn't have done, would it?

Yet Fred Sprott couldn't see that ... or wouldn't see it. It wouldn't go into his head. A pity – because plenty of other girls liked him, quite nice girls. Yes, Nora had liked him – Chloë sounded impatient –

but he had never liked her which made it seem so incredible when they had taken up with each other, lately, at Nettlewood.

He left school at twelve, took jobs on farms, then went down river to work on the boats. Sprotts were always fond of water except for drinking and washing in. Water-sprotts, that's what they were.

He kept on disappearing, then coming back. When he went away Chloë was pleased, then wished he'd come back. When he came back she was pleased, then wished he'd go away. Yes, it was ridiculous.

Once, for her birthday, he gave her a baby owl which he had caught in the woods at Nettlewood. He had kept it secretly and tamed it, just for her.

Iboo.

Yes, *hibou*. She was learning French at the time and taught him the word for owl.

(And he in turn taught it to Poor Tom – Lacie thought of Iboo in the barn at Nettlewood.)

When the owl died Chloë had been upset and it had been stuffed and put in a glass case which she had kept to that very day. Time it was thrown away now.

One winter night when she was seventeen she was cycling home from school, laden with books and carrying a hockey stick. At the Biggills Fred Sprott stepped out of the dark. He had been away for such a long time that she had almost succeeded in forgetting him and certainly was not expecting him to loom suddenly out of nowhere. She was so startled that she fell into the road, books all over the place, then she flew into a terrible rage and said things to him which she was ashamed of even now. Never mind what things, unkind things, cruel things. He never answered, not a

343

word! But he took the hockey stick and broke it in two — then jumped over a hedge and vanished.

She got into a lot of trouble over that hockey stick, it wasn't hers. As for Fred Sprott, he disappeared from Owsterley, went up north or somewhere for a long time and Chloë left school and went to college. When he came back he was married. Soon there was Gertie, then his wife was killed in a street accident in Hawksop. When war broke out he joined up and Mrs Bisset looked after Gertie. In time Chloë became headmistress of the Little School. George arrived at the Big School after the war when a new headmaster was required.

'And now you love George,' Lacie summed up the story, and added, 'you couldn't marry him if you were Mrs Sprott!'

Mrs Sprott! Good Lord! What a name! But Chloë agreed with Lacie that Mrs Bisset would like it well enough. Then — 'Bother all Sprotts!' exclaimed Chloë, she was sick and tired of hearing the name. Yet five minutes had not gone by when, 'It's funny about Gertie,' she said, 'I simply can't be cross with her — not for long. Sometimes I really mean to tell her off — then she looks at me with those Sprott eyes of hers and, well, it's just as if I've gone back years and she is him looking at me.'

No more was said about Fred Sprott and when George came in Chloë was nicer to him than ever.

32

'– The Mighty Waters Rolling Evermore'

W.W.

WITH the two Sprotts and Mrs Bisset Lacie made her last visit to Nettlewood. They went to see Granny Betts who – it was said – had become just like a graven image with no interest in anything.

Outside her cottage door in a patch of sunlight she sat without moving. The pink sunbonnet drooped over her face and she made no sign of recognition when she was spoken to except that her chin quivered slightly. If a graven image could have been persuaded to take up its abode in a little cottage that smelled of musk and scented geranium, twig fires and paraffin lamps, it would have looked like she looked then.

On the doorstep was a half-empty cup with some tea and bread in it. 'Sops,' said Mrs Bisset, 'I expect that's all she's living on now,' and she tut-tutted to the kitchen to put away the eatables she had brought and to warm up a drop of beef tea.

Fred Sprott went to see to the fowls and attend to the garden. Gertie roamed through the cottage with an air of nonchalant freedom she had never shown before, but soon was bored and went to the barn to look for the baby owl.

There was something Lacie wanted to tell Granny Betts but she found it difficult to begin a conversation. It was not until she saw Gertie coming back with a jam-jar full of blackberries and pockets spilling out apples, that she ventured to tell the graven image what she wanted to say.

It was about Poor Tom.

'He was coming back to you.' Lacie spoke quickly as if trying to get it said all at once. 'He was hurrying home so that he could take care of you and make you live as long as possible.'

There was no response from beneath the sunbonnet.

'He was sorry he went away and left you,' said Lacie. 'It was all a mistake. He missed you all the time.'

Fred Sprott shouted that he was ready to go home. 'It was you,' said Lacie, close to the falling brim of the sunbonnet, 'it was you he called Granny, you and nobody else.' She could do no more and turned to leave. Just as she was turning away a hand caught at her dress. Granny Betts spoke at last. 'Don't go away empty-handed, lass,' she whispered, 'take that cup with thee and rinse it under t'pump.'

On the way to the scullery with the cup Lacie saw the aspidistra. It looked unloved. The soil around its roots was dry. 'It can't have had a drink of tea for ages,' she thought and emptied the cup over it.

It was time to go to the boat. The river was full. The oars lipped into the water as softly as kissing and Mrs Bisset smiled to herself. Fred Sprott's head was bare,

346

the red cap not to be seen. The wind sighed over the water and Nettlewood was left behind.

The next day was Pear Day and Bertie Bisset managed it perfectly. With the help of the big boys in Standard 6 the pear tree was stripped without a single mishap, not a branch was broken and there was absolutely no horseplay. Lacie helped to give out the fruit, first amongst the infants and then in the Big School and there, in the bottom class on the front row under Miss Throssel's eye and very much chastened – there was Gertie Sprott.

Before the end of the week Lacie was on a train going home. Amongst her belongings was a glass case with a stuffed owl in it, an owl which, when it was alive, had flown about the trees of Nettlewood until Fred Sprott had caught it and tamed it and given it to Chloë.

Lacie saw Owsterley again. Just before Christmas she went back for the wedding of Chloë and George.

The wedding reception was held at the King of the River in a room overlooking the water and had been prepared by the new landlord and his wife, Fred Sprott and Mrs Bisset – Mr and Mrs Sprott.

At each end of the room was a fire of blazing logs. Lamps hung from the ceiling amongst branches of laurel, holly and yew. Lighted candles seemed to be everywhere.

The wedding feast was spread on a long, white table. Not to be missed were quantities of celery hearts enticingly displayed in glass beer mugs.

Chloë and George Springles smiled upon their guests. Nora, unfortunately, was not with them. A wedding present of fabulous expensiveness had arrived with her love the week before and had been followed by a telegram explaining that she was on her way to New York on a nursing assignment.

After the feast Miss Jessima Throssel, although more at home on the Sunday School harmonium, was persuaded to preside at the pub piano. After all, people said, music is music whatever it is coming out of.

Rose Fennell and Dick Stilbush were dancing together and looking as if the next wedding would be theirs.

Bertie Bisset was there. He was wearing a white carnation which he gave to Lacie during the course of the evening. She dropped it when she was dancing and Gertie Sprott accidentally trod on it.

Mr Bindle was there, but did not dance. He moved about all over the place, smiling everywhere and saying what a lonely bachelor it made him feel to see such lucky chaps as George Springles and Fred Sprott.

Old Ebenezer Bonem was standing on the side-lines, his hands knotted together on the top of a stick he had cut from a hazel bush fifty years before.

He laughed as he heard Mr Bindle's words and said, 'Better be careful, Parson, who tha tells that tale to, or tha'll not be lonely much longer.'

Miss Throssel was near by and heard. She had managed to sit near Mr Bindle at table and Miss Jessima had sat within his reach – if he had wanted to reach – but now he was flitting about all over the place, like a butterfly dodging a net. Miss Jessima, frowning over the piano, looked at her sister frowning after Mr Bindle and thumped out a jangle of wrong notes – and Fred Sprott was amused and smiled at his wife as they danced together.

Lacie was amazed to discover how much she was liking Fred Sprott now that he was safely harnessed in Missy Bissy's reins of velvet. When, at a change in the music in a Paul Jones he appeared before her, and said 'Well, Miss Prim-and-Proper, how's things?' Lacie smiled and enjoyed a waltz with him. Even when he lifted her up at the end of it and whirled her around at shoulder height, she laughed and enjoyed it when they got a round of applause.

'I like to see him happy,' murmured Mrs Sprott and Fred was happy, surely. Surely? Suddenly he dashed from the party and came back with some left-over bags of confetti. Soon the wedding guests were throwing it over the bride and groom and over each other. Miss Throssel was covered in it. Miss Jessima, pounding on the piano, had half a bagful in her hair. Who had thrown it she didn't know. She seemed to think it was Mr Bindle, and gave him half a smile, which faded away when she saw that Sprott child hovering about with an empty paper bag in her hand. 'I'll tell my sister of you,' said Miss Jessima Throssel's eye to Gertie Sprott.

It was when the confetti-throwing was at its wildest and the music at its loudest, when everybody was laughing, it was then that a thought came to Lacie like a stab of ice – a thought of Granny Betts sitting alone in her silent cottage, without Poor Tom.

But Bertie Bisset came up and whirled Lacie away to join in a dance. Gertie Sprott was galloping up and down with a good-tempered little boy from the Top Infants and she certainly made him suffer for not being Bertie Bisset.

For the last waltz all the candles and lamps were

blown out and everybody watched as Chloë danced with George in the firelight, her head upon his shoulder. Then the music changed to a hunting tune and the floor was crowded with dancers in a glorious stampede from one end of the room to the other and back again.

So the happy evening came to an end. The bride and bridegroom went away but only just down the road to School Cottage which they were going to make their home.

And Lacie went to bed in a room at the King of the River and heard the water lapping through her sleep.

The next day she left Owsterley and she never returned. She went far away from the river and never saw the Aegir. To her it was always something she might have seen, part of a troubled dream of Nettlewood.

Goodbye, Lacie Lindrick.

One day in the time of high spring tides after a long spell of dry weather Gertie and her father went out in his new motor boat, *The Bluebird*, to meet the Aegir.

It was Saturday and many inhabitants of Owsterley were waiting on the river bank. After a time they became quiet and still, as if listening, and the river, too, was quiet and still.

There was a sound from far down river, faint at first but growing ever louder, then a cry went up from people on the bank, 'Aegir's coming!' and somebody called out, ' 'Ware Aegir!'

Aegir is coming, and the noise of its coming is heard like a warning; 'Ware Aegir!

'Ware Aegir! Beware of Aegir, this racing wall of

water! Sea-wave, salt wave, alien to the river yet familiar with it, ancient invader, ancient aggressor, surging from the sea as Nature wills it, to ride between the peaceful fields until, when Nature wills, its force is spent.

Aegir's coming!

The Bluebird went straight forward to meet it, lifted and soared above it, then safely rode the smaller following waves.

There was a great shout from the bank, then the crowd breathed, laughed, compared, criticised, broke up and went away. Last to leave was Ebenezer Bonem who stood alone and stared at the water. He would not see many more Aegirs but 'Aegirs come afore our time,' he said when he caught up with a few of his old cronies, 'and afore our feythers' time and long afore that, and Aegirs'll come when all on us is gone,' and, as if there were comfort in the thought, he rounded his back against the cold spring air and went away.

The river grew calm and full.

Nettlewood was deserted except for rooks and jackdaws, owls, magpies and other creatures of the wild which crept inside its walls or flew about its rafters. As years went by roofs fell in and chimneys rattled down in showers of bricks. Windows cracked in winter frosts, storms blew down doors. Birds flew in and out of the place as if they owned it.

One night people in the King of the River became conscious of a red glow on the water. They saw smoke curling into the sky and soon a tower of flames mounted high above what had once been Nettlewood.

The inhabitants of Owsterley who had run out of their homes did all that could be done.

They watched Nettlewood burn.

Fred Sprott, with one or two other men, went across the water to make sure that Granny Betts was safe but she was not to be found that night, nor seen until a day later.

Goodness knew where she had been.

Blackened stone and charred wood were all that remained of Nettlewood. Every summer covered them deeper with willow-herb and multitudes of nettles. Seeds of garden flowers mingled with those of the wild. Hollyhocks and lupins mixed with foxgloves where the stairs had been. Brambles roamed over the ruins of walls and little trees shot up.

It was all so long ago.

But, still, the wind sighs over the water. The Aegir leaps from the sea . . .

And the river, and time, flow on.